Provisionally Yours

Provisionally Yours

A novel

Antanas Sileika

A JOHN METCALF BOOK

BIBLIOASIS
WINDSOR, ONTARIO

Library and Archives Canada Cataloguing in Publication

Sileika, Antanas, 1953–, author
Provisionally yours / Antanas Sileika.

Issued in print and electronic formats.
ISBN 978-1-77196-285-8 (softcover).—ISBN 978-1-77196-286-5 (ebook)

I. Title.

PS8587.I2656P76   2019   C813'.54   C2018-904426-8
                            C2018-904427-6

Readied for the press by John Metcalf
Copy-edited by Chandra Wohleber
Cover design by Michel Vrana
Front inside cover: Interwar Map of Lithuania,
courtesy of Augustinas Žemaitis, http://www.truelithuania.com
Text design by Gordon Robertson

Canada Council
for the Arts

Conseil des Arts
du Canada

ONTARIO ARTS COUNCIL
CONSEIL DES ARTS DE L'ONTARIO
an Ontario government agency
un organisme du gouvernement de l'Ontario

Ontario

Ontario Media Development
Corporation

Canadä

Published with the generous assistance of the Canada Council for the Arts, which last year invested $153 million to bring the arts to Canadians throughout the country, and the financial support of the Government of Canada. Biblioasis also acknowledges the support of the Ontario Arts Council (OAC), an agency of the Government of Ontario, which last year funded 1,709 individual artists and 1,078 organizations in 204 communities across Ontario, for a total of $52.1 million, and the contribution of the Government of Ontario through the Ontario Book Publishing Tax Credit and the Ontario Media Development Corporation.

PRINTED AND BOUND IN CANADA

MIX
Paper from
responsible sources
FSC® C004071

For Feliksas

Only the person who has experienced light and darkness, war and peace, rise and fall, only that person has truly experienced life.

Stefan Zweig

1

THE BORDER GUARD studied the identity papers Adamonis had kept hidden through his escape out of shattered Russia, looking from his photo to his face, from his photo to his face. He told Adamonis to stay where he was on the train platform. Adamonis set down his suitcase and briefcase and pulled the collar of his woollen coat around his neck. The guard's superior came back without the passport and asked Adamonis to follow him.

He took Adamonis into a cold office in the corner of the train station where an unshaven man sat behind a desk in a room with a stove but without heat.

Adamonis could see his own breath and his interrogator kept on his coat and hat throughout the interview, taking many notes with a pencil that he stopped to sharpen with a penknife when the lead wore down. The man asked about Adamonis's career in great detail—called up for service in 1912, accepted into military school, moved to the Austrian front at the beginning of hostilities. Assigned to signals.

This last detail pricked the interest of the plainclothesman. Adamonis knew all about interrogation, and he listened to the questions with admiration as the interrogator followed the thread of Adamonis's military career in signals to his years in counterintelligence until the army collapsed and split into the red and white factions. This story could have got him shot a month ago back in Russia, but now he was in a place where he could tell the truth. At least he hoped that was so.

The interrogator asked him to wait outside among the exhausted families and ragged men in the waiting room.

"I'll miss my train," said Adamonis.

"Another one comes eventually. Maybe you'll get that one."

There was nothing to eat in the waiting room, a big hall in the Obeliai border station half-filled with cloth bundles upon which men, women, and children slept while they waited to clear customs and quarantine. Some never would. Adamonis sat on the end of a bench and took a piece of sausage out of his bag, and a boy was beside him as soon as he cut off his second slice. Soon there were two more children and his food was gone before he could taste another bite. He tried to go outside to smoke, but a guard stopped him at the door and directed him to a smoking room where he had to roll two cigarettes for others before lighting up his own.

His train departed.

Three hours later, the guard called him back into the room. Coal had found its way into the stove and a glass of tea and two biscuits as well as his passport were sitting on Adamonis's side of the desk. His interrogator came around from behind his desk, introduced himself as Lieutenant Oleka, and saluted.

"Welcome home, General," said Oleka. "I wonder if I could ask you a few more questions."

"No need to salute, Lieutenant. I'm not exactly in the army any longer. And I'd be happy to answer your questions."

The next morning, the whistle blew and the locomotive began to jerk forward, leaving behind the barn-like customs station with its hopeful or crestfallen men and women. One more hurdle overcome, and all in all, not the hardest one.

The window beside him had frost creeping out from the corners and the fields beyond were covered in snow. At least the carriage was warm, crowded as it was with Lithuanians fleeing Russia. There had been thousands of them scattered across the country, soldiers in the czar's army, bureaucrats and labourers, all going home now that the old czarist world had collapsed and the maw of the revolution was devouring so many. He was in a carriage with the lucky ones. He'd narrowly missed being shot along with all the officers on a ferry crossing the Prut River in Romania. On a flatbed train car he was denounced as bourgeois, so Adamonis had pushed the accuser and watched him fall under the severing wheels. The Soviets were especially bitter about having lost their war with Poland only months earlier. Anyone who chose to leave was a traitor to the cause.

The word *home* felt like the promise of a warm bed on a cold night. But what kind of a home would it be for Adamonis? His parents were dead and only his sister still lived in Kaunas, and when he'd last seen her, she'd been a teenager. As for the country, it had successfully fought off the Reds and the German Freikorps, but lost its southern part to the Poles. Technically, Lithuania was still at war with Poland, and that had made it all the more complicated to return from shattered Russia, forcing him to head north, skirting Poland to enter the country through Latvia.

Adamonis was tired and could let himself feel it for the first time in a long time now that he was safe. He craved a cigarette, but there was no smoking in his third-class compartment with its wooden benches, and it was far too cold to go out and stand between the cars. He could wait. He dozed and dreamed of places he had passed through in the months it had taken him to reach this country—the Polish *dvaras* where the spinster sisters had come to him because his fellow officers were stealing their silver. The sisters didn't mind the loss of the silver, but the thieves were wrapping the knives and forks in paper with notations written by a former guest, the composer Richard Strauss. The sisters wanted to save the music. They even offered him a page of the music after he'd saved it, but he'd turned them down. Now he regretted it because the women were probably dead anyway. He had narrowly missed being drowned when the Reds shelled the ice across which his unit was marching. He remembered the forest hung with clocks looted by rebel soldiers, but too heavy to carry all the way home.

After a long day's journey with stops at every country station, the train slowed as it entered a long tunnel and then pulled into Kaunas. Adamonis stepped off the train with only one bag and a briefcase, not much more than what he'd left with years earlier. As he walked along the platform toward the station he heard cries of delight and saw joyful reunions as men and women embraced and whole families charged into the arms of relatives. But he could see no sign of anyone who looked like his sister.

A young man with a long brown beard and eyeglasses came up to him in the hall.

"Mr. Justas Adamonis?"

He nodded.

"Michael Landa," and he put out his hand. "We've heard about you. I represent the Lithuanian government, and I wonder if we could have a chat."

Adamonis measured men quickly, as he had been taught. This one looked all right and he was alone, and that was good.

"Of course, but not just now. I've been away a long time and I think my sister is expecting me."

"We've spoken to your sister. She's agreed to let us take you over to her house a little later."

"Where is she now?"

"At home with her family. She's anxious to see you, but she's a patriot, and she understands. I hope you're a patriot too."

"It's a bit too soon to tell. I just stepped off the train."

"Then maybe you'll become a patriot. In the meantime, your sister lives here, and helping us will help her."

Adamonis wasn't sure if this was an appeal or a threat. He could be outraged or he could be agreeable, and he chose the second option. He didn't really know much about the government, but it couldn't be anything worse than what he'd left behind.

Landa led him out of the station and down the steps to a sled where a driver was waiting for them. Adamonis wore a felt fedora and a heavy wool coat, but the coat had become worn, as he had lived in it days and many nights for over a year. He was a solid man in ordinary times, but the last year of flight had thinned him out and he felt the cold as they drove along through light snow.

The city lay in a dim pool of woodsmoke and falling snowflakes, with men walking by as quickly as they could on the silent streets. A mother with a scarf over her mouth tugged along a child bundled in a knitted hat and felt boots. He saw only three cars in all.

Kaunas had been a czarist garrison town that now, after the war, had a capital thrust upon it. Vilnius was supposed to be the capital of Lithuania, but the Poles believed it belonged to them and had seized it three months earlier. With the occupation of Vilnius, the Lithuanians licked their wounds and set up in Kaunas, calling it their "provisional capital."

Seeing the city of his youth through the snow was like seeing it in a dream. He recognized Soboras, the massive Russian Orthodox church built for the garrison in the last century, but the low wooden houses and two-storey brick buildings seemed neither familiar nor unfamiliar, suspended between reality and memory.

2

MICHAEL LANDA lived in three rooms off the courtyard garden of an old wooden house with small herb and flower gardens on either side of the door and a picket fence to protect them. The plants were frozen now, in their winter sadness. A nimble old man in a dirty sheepskin coat was walking briskly back and forth in front of the gate when they arrived. The old man wore a peaked leather hat and had a weathered face, but the impression above all was olfactory; he stank of smoke.

"Ah, here you are, sir," he said, and he swung open the fence gate and held it for Adamonis and Landa as they passed, and then trotted up ahead and swung open the door. "Johnny-at-your-service," he said. "I'll put your bags inside the door and then I'll be outside in case you need me."

"Is that sheepskin creature your man?" Adamonis asked when he was inside.

"In a way. He's like a bird at a feeder. He works for tips and a bowl of soup and half a loaf of bread each day. He keeps track of everyone who comes and goes and he knows every porter and kitchen maid in the city."

The hall was full of boxes and two large trunks. Landa was either moving in or moving out. Everyone was in transition, finding a way to settle into the country they had recreated since the collapse of Germany and Russia and the rise of Poland. Lithuania was a precarious state, as vulnerable as a child on a tram bench crowded by heftier and unsympathetic travellers. The war had gone on here two years beyond the armistice in 1918, with enemies of one day transformed into temporary allies the next.

The combined dining-sitting room was lit by two oil lamps because the electricity had failed again, and the ceiling-high white ceramic stove radiated pleasant heat. The larger of two tables was set with white and black bread, white farmer's cheese, herring and onions and slices of smoked meat, butter, a bowl of honey, and blackcurrant jam, as well as a pot of tea and a bottle of *krupnikas*, the local honey liquor. Adamonis hadn't seen so much food laid out in quite some time. Landa poured a glass of tea and a glass of *krupnikas* and they sat down in a pair of facing armchairs with the low table between them. The wooden shutters were closed, and this along with the smell of the food and the warmth of the stove gave the room an agreeable sense of security.

"So you'll want to know who I am and why I brought you here," said Landa. "The answer is military intelligence, of which I am chief, and, recently, counterintelligence as well."

Adamonis had guessed something along those lines, but maybe not such a high position for such a young man.

Landa spoke freely about himself for a while. He was a farmer's son, the eldest of six; he'd intended to take over the farm and was in agricultural school in Riga when the war broke out. The topsy-turvy postwar world provided unusual opportunities, along with certain risks. Landa filled him in briefly about the recent wars against the German Freikorps, the Bolsheviks, and the Poles, and then invited Adamonis to fill his plate. They both did so and sat across from each other over the table, eating and talking. Adamonis did his best not to wolf the food.

For all his powerful position, Landa struck Adamonis as slightly green. And yet he wore his responsibilities comfortably and seemed to have no complexes about his lack of experience.

"So now that I know who you are, I'd like to know what's so important that you had to get me as soon as I stepped off the train."

"I'm coming to that. But first tell me a little about how you're acquainted with Feliks Dzerzhinsky."

Dzerzhinsky was a brutal and efficient man, the chief of the Soviet secret police, the Cheka, in Moscow.

"How do you know about this?" asked Adamonis.

"We received the report from the border and then it turns out other former officers back from Russia knew a fair bit about you. Flesh out the story for me."

"Dzerzhinsky was an underground Red living in the same courtyard as my parents in Kaunas in 1897. I was still a little boy and I'd fallen off a step and banged my knee and I bawled so long and hard that it was annoying him while he worked at a desk behind an open window facing the courtyard. He called me in and served me a glass of tea with sugar and a dollop of butter on top. I liked it so much that I'd look for him every day at his window. He took to me, and I became some kind of pet."

"So the monster has a heart?"

"Sometimes people with heart become monsters. He'd been kind to me, so when the police discovered who he was and imprisoned him, my grateful parents sent me there twice to bring him packages of bread and butter. I was so small, so insignificant, that the guards let me take the package directly to him. He was a lean and hungry man. The last time I saw him in Kaunas, he took my chin in his hands and said he'd never forget me."

"So your parents were sympathetic to revolutionaries?"

"Every normal person was sympathetic to political prisoners in those days."

"And that was the end of it?"

"Not quite. I was called up from military school in 1912, and a year later the Okhranka secret police started to cooperate with military intelligence, so I was trained on both sides, civilian and military. Then during the war, Dzerzhinsky was imprisoned in Oryol. I must have told this childhood story to someone who remembered it, so I was sent to see Dzerzhinsky in prison to feel him out about informing on subversives in the army."

"Did he remember you?"

"Not at first, but I reminded him. He looked much worse than I remembered him. He'd been beaten and his jaw was swollen. They kept him in chains. I tried to talk to him about his family, and he showed real flashes of humanity then, but it didn't last. I was still pretty green in my work and I must have smelled of military intelligence. When we parted, he looked me in the eye and said he'd never forget me."

"Did you ever meet again?"

"I wouldn't be here if we had."

"I understand you ended up with Denikin and his Whites after the revolution. Didn't you have any proletarian sympathies?"

"Not after what I'd seen as the revolution went through the army. People can be beasts—worse than beasts. Stupid. I saw a general clubbed to death when he tried to address the troops and they didn't like what he said. I saw a vote on the existence of God. I saw a radicalized army that refused to fight on May 1 even though the Austrians had launched an offensive against them. The Whites promised some kind of order. That appealed to me."

"What was the White Army like?" asked Landa.

"Not much better than the Red one in the end. We lost so many on the ice march that you'd think we'd have learned something about adversity. Then we were joined by the Cossacks and with our numbers up, we became the teachers of adversity. We were ordered not to take prisoners. It was more important for the fools to kill Jews and suspects rather than let me develop my sources. In the end, they were two murderous armies whose interests were beyond unravelling."

"How did you get away?"

"I was lucky."

He had the sabre wound on his shoulder and a bullet wound in his chest.

"Do you belong to any political party?" asked Landa.

"I barely know Lithuania at all. How could I belong to a party?"

"If you had to choose among the Christian Democrats, the Socialists, or others, which way would you lean?"

"The war cured me of politics."

Landa encouraged him to refill his plate, and Adamonis did so gratefully.

"So now that you find yourself here, what do you plan to do?" asked Landa between forkfuls of herring.

"Make a living, I guess."

"How?"

"I don't know. I could go back to one of the farms my cousins own, but I grew up in Kaunas and I'm not sure I have the knack for country living. Maybe I'll try my hand at business."

"What kind of business?"

"I have no idea, actually."

"It's a fragile place, Mr. Adamonis. The Reds nearly overran us and the German Freikorps almost did the same thing. The Poles outnumber us at ten to one and we're no match for them if they decide to invade. Instability here would be to the advantage of more than one great power.

But some of us are trying to build a nation. We could use someone with your experience to help us do that."

"To tell you the truth, my experience has left me weary of this kind of work."

"Please, Mr. Adamonis, you're talking like an old man and you still have a few years to go to forty. You're just tired now. Or do you find us too Lilliputian after your years among the giants?"

"Russia is a vast country suffering from madness. I grew up here. I'm happy to be back."

"So don't you want to help your country? It won't be much of a home if it belongs to someone else."

"What, exactly, are you proposing?"

"You could do something for us right now. Are you interested?"

Adamonis knew all too well that this was how it always began, with just a little favour, just a little job. Part of him was drained, but part of him was curious.

"I'm not uninterested."

Landa nodded. "I'll take that as a yes. Let's get started then. We have a very important international affair at risk at the moment and it's a problem we need to solve fast. Lithuania needs another German loan, badly. Germany keeps us afloat to undermine the Poles and we're grateful, thank God, because our soldiers don't have boots and the teachers get no pay. The German ministry of finance assigned a particular envoy to deal with this matter. The envoy has a very free hand."

Landa invited Adamonis to drink another shot of *krupnikas*.

"Our people met with the envoy in Berlin, where he was very agreeable. But now he's changed for the worse. He's been here for four days, and he's irritable and gets more impatient with every passing moment. That means the loan is at risk. It's possible the Poles or the French have turned him against us, or someone else is spreading rumours, or we've made a bad impression in some way. We've tried to amuse him at the opera and to sate him with good food and plenty of drink, but he scowls at us and complains about how uncivilized this country is. Imagine this kind of language from a diplomatic envoy! We need to find out what the problem is and convince him to approve the loan."

"Maybe he has personal problems back in Germany."

"He crossed the border in the best of moods."

"You know this?"

"Yes."

"Has he received any communication from Germany since he arrived?"

"Nothing we haven't seen ourselves."

"If the minister of finance and all his bureaucrats haven't been able to find the reason for his bad mood, and if your organization hasn't done any better, what makes you think I can do it?"

Landa shrugged. "We have some faith in your experience."

"This is a matter for diplomacy, not intelligence. Besides, I haven't lived in Lithuania for almost ten years," said Adamonis.

"I know that."

"I don't even know this German's name or where he's staying."

"Herman Steiner is his name and you can find him in room 214 at the Hotel Metropolis."

It was an impossible task, and they both knew it.

"And one more thing," said Landa. "I was hoping you could walk over there to take a look."

"Now?"

"Well, yes. You can leave your bags here for a while."

It was an outrageous request.

Adamonis agreed to it.

3

JOHNNY opened the door before Adamonis could turn the handle, and then he held it open and waved Adamonis onto the porch. Adamonis was enveloped by his stink of smoke and handed him a few coins.

"I'll walk with you a ways, Mr. Adamonis, and the smell of smoke will keep off the mosquitoes."

Interesting that Johnny knew his name. Johnny handled himself like an agent, but he looked like a peasant and had a peasant's sense of country humour, which Adamonis appreciated.

"It's too early in the year for mosquitoes."

"The fleas then," said Johnny. "I've never ever been bothered by them even though I've often lived in stables."

They turned onto Freedom Boulevard. The electricity had come back on but half of the storefronts were already dark, and the last of the shoppers were buying sausages or bacon for dinner. The night and the cold drove people inside when patches of ice lay like land mines across the city, ready to take down the unwary, particularly the drunkards trying to get home before curfew later in the evening.

Two- and three-storey brick buildings lined Freedom Boulevard, where horse-drawn streetcars ran up both sides of the treed central promenade. Since there was hardly anything else to do in the city, generals and ladies, criminals and barefoot peasants, vagrants and government functionaries, all strolled the promenade whenever the weather permitted it.

Kaunas lay between two rivers. The boulevard ran down past the presidential "palace" and then curved into a narrower road in the medieval part of the city before opening into a square with the cathedral and town hall. Beyond that lay the tip of the city where the Nemunas and Neris Rivers met.

"Where did you get this smell of smoke anyway?" Adamonis asked Johnny.

"By profession I'm a meat smoker. Before the war, when there were a lot more Polish estates, I'd hang the meat in the smokehouses and camp out there to watch over it to make sure it wasn't stolen, or foxes didn't get in."

"Right inside the chimney?"

"Of course. They were pretty big and anyway, the fire needs to burn low and long to preserve a piece of meat well. I travelled from estate to estate in the cool months and I worked as a hand during the warm ones."

They walked down the boulevard toward the Hotel Metropolis.

"How old are you, Johnny?"

"Hard to say. But I still have the welts on my back from the time when I was a boy serf, so that should give you some idea."

"And what do you think of this new country they're building here?" Adamonis asked.

"It couldn't be much worse than the old one. I say this: if you want to make a new country, go ahead, make a new country."

Johnny's indifference to the national project amused Adamonis, who had just signed on, in a manner of speaking, to help defend it.

"Before the war, in czarist times, didn't you want someone to speak in Lithuanian instead of Russian when you went to the post office?"

"I've never been to a post office."

"Well, when you spoke to a policeman then."

"I avoid policemen."

"You wouldn't have to if they spoke your language."

"I don't mind speaking a lot of languages. When the Russians were here, I spoke to them in Russian and I spoke to lords and ladies in Polish and I spoke to the Jews in Yiddish, or if they had enough Lithuanian, they spoke to me in my language. Kaunas was like a layer cake that way. Everyone added to the flavour."

"I think they're trying to build a sense of family here."

"Oh, I have family already, but not a traditional one, just country folk working in the city. Is this the place you're going to?" he asked.

They were standing outside the Hotel Metropolis on the corner of Freedom Boulevard and Daukanto Street. It was a two-storey building and had a windmill-like tower on the corner to make it seem more imposing. Stucco scrollwork played around the windows and the place looked altogether like what it was, a provincial hotel putting on airs. Still, it was the most brightly lit place in sight, a local hot spot.

Landa had said Herman Steiner was a tall, severe man with short greying hair and a heavy black raincoat, but no such man was passing in or out of the hotel at the moment. Adamonis decided to go in and look around.

"This is not exactly my kind of place," said Johnny-at-your-service. "I'll wait out here."

"No need to wait for me. It's very cold, and I can take care of myself."

"I don't mind the cold and I have no other business tonight." Johnny squatted down, took a pipe from his pocket, and settled in.

Adamonis entered the hotel without waking the uniformed doorman sleeping on a stool inside the lobby. The place must have been quite chic before the war, with white-and-black tile on the floors and herringbone-patterned wood panelling on the walls. A wide staircase led up from the lobby, and on the first landing there were four large stained-glass windows, backlit, with vaguely heraldic motifs. But everything had been let go. The floor tiles were cracked and the rug on the staircase was badly worn. The lighting was poor. The registration desk was to his right and a restaurant/bar through double doors to his left. The dour clerk was standing in the shadows, the only light coming from a small lamp on the counter. A piano was playing across the way in the restaurant.

"The bar's through the other door," the clerk said.

"How do you know I don't want a room?"

"You don't have any bags and you're alone."

Since the revolution, Adamonis was accustomed to the rudeness of service people, but he wondered how Herman Steiner would react to this place, the best that Kaunas had to offer.

The room contained two dozen tables, a small stage, a bar, and a billiards table in addition to the piano. But the piano fell silent just as Adamonis entered the room and he caught no more than the ghost of a white shirt fading into the shadows. The pianist had been playing "The Blue Danube," which had sounded eerie in the near-empty room.

One short bearded and mustachioed man was playing billiards by himself and the barman, like his hotel co-workers out in the lobby, stood frozen behind his counter. In addition to the *click* of the billiard balls, Adamonis also heard something from one of the dining tables and discerned through the shadows that it was someone eating alone. The man behind the bar was reedy, with a collar too big for his neck and an imperfectly aligned clip-on tie.

"I'll have a brandy and a cup of coffee."

"Regular or priestly?"

"I beg your pardon?"

"Regular or a big drink, like the kind the priests drink," It was a description Adamonis hadn't heard before.

"I suppose I'll have a priestly."

"We don't have any coffee. I can give you tea."

"That will do."

The barman poured a tumbler full of liquor, four fingers and part of a thumb.

"Priests seem to drink a lot in this country."

"They have that reputation."

Adamonis took a sip of the liquor. The man at the billiards table was portly. If they had been in the countryside, he might have been the local Polish lord, slumming among the Lithuanian villagers.

There was no sign of Herman Steiner, but Adamonis could see the lobby from the bar, so he intended to perch where he was and wait.

"Not many customers in the bar tonight," Adamonis said to the barman. The barman said nothing.

"It's early yet," said the billiards player, without looking up. "They'll rush in here later, around nine, and then the crowds will get dense until—*poof*—they'll disappear just before curfew." The man paused to concentrate on a complicated shot and then sank the ball in the pocket. "New in town, are you?" he asked.

"Yes and no. I grew up here as a boy, but I haven't lived here for years."

"Play billiards?"

"Badly."

"All the better. We'll play for small stakes, so you won't lose very much." He put out his hand. "Arturas Martynas. Former minister of finance, currently a businessman."

"Minister of finance? I'm impressed. How long did you serve?"

"A few months. The government here is like a cocktail party. Ministers come and go. Who did you say you were?"

"Justas Adamonis, former soldier, currently unemployed."

"You should come to work for me."

"You just met me."

Martynas handed him a cue and racked up the so-called Russian pyramid again. "It's a fast-breaking world we live in. We have to make judgments quickly."

He named a sum for each ball.

"What kind of business are you in?" Adamonis asked.

"I'm interested in banking and riverboats just now. The trick is to find the financing. There was a free market thousands of kilometres wide under the czar, but all that's been smashed to pieces."

"It sounds like you're nostalgic for old times," Adamonis said.

"Not really, but business is business. We don't have much to export except geese and pigs, and we can't afford to import much either, so we need to develop the internal market."

"But nobody has any money."

"That's it. You've hit the nail on the head."

"You need to make something out of nothing. That's why you're a banker too."

"Brilliant."

Adamonis won the first game by a single ball and Martynas won the second by the same. He was avuncular and talkative and disparaging of Kaunas, joking about its lack of sewers and barefoot country visitors, but he said it all with a light tone, to entertain Adamonis.

"Now listen," Martynas said as they went into the third game, "we could drag this all out. Or we can finish up this game and you can buy the champagne and we'll have a chat in my room."

"You live here?"

"Sometimes, when my wife is out of sorts. I'll be here for a few days."

"I prefer the spirit of competition," said Adamonis. "Why don't we just say that the loser buys the bottle of champagne?"

Martynas agreed reluctantly. Adamonis beat him by two balls. When they went to the bar, Martynas had some difficulty convincing the barman to let him have the bottle on credit. And as they were waiting, the woman who had been eating in the darkness turned to them.

"It's not real champagne, you know," she said in accented Russian.

"What was that all about?" Adamonis asked as they walked up the steps to the second floor with the cold bottle and a pair of glasses in hand.

"She's a French spy."

"How do you know that?"

"Anyone French in this town is a spy. They have no other reason to be here. They're transparent, though. They always give themselves away by their critiques."

The corridor on the second floor was very long, dark, and crooked, and the hardwood floor beneath their feet had buckled badly in some places. Martynas fished a massive key out of his pocket. The room had a very high ceiling, and a very tall window that reached just as high. There was also an armoire, a tiny table with a washbasin on it, a single padded leather chair, and a bed. The room looked lived-in, with a razor and brush by the basin, and what seemed to be a bundle of bedsheets on the floor by the armoire.

"Please take the chair," said Martynas.

Adamonis did as he asked and Martynas worked the cork of the champagne bottle, popped it, and poured them each a glass. They touched glasses and drank and Martynas plopped himself on the bed. Two boards under the mattress snapped beneath his weight so that the soft down mattress sank suddenly under his rump and he fell deep inside, folding upon himself with his arms and legs practically in the air. He looked like a crab that had been turned on its back. His champagne glass flew over to the other side of the bed and rattled onto the floor without breaking.

"Help me, Mr. Adamonis," he called. "It's as deep as a well in here."

Adamonis took him by the hands and pulled him up onto his feet where he stood puffing and agitated.

"That was a piece of bad luck," Adamonis said, not wanting to say anything about Martynas's weight.

"This hotel is a horrible mess," Martynas answered. They're very disorganized. Just look at that bundle of sheets. I put those there two days ago."

Luckily, they hadn't poured out much of the champagne, so Adamonis topped up Martynas's glass, offered him the chair, and leaned up against the windowsill, first looking outside to see that Johnny-at-your-service was still where Adamonis had left him, visible in the darkness due to his sheepskin coat.

It was clear that Martynas had invited Adamonis up to take his measure and to try to convince him to join one of his projects, but Adamonis was not really listening. He just waited until a decent amount of time had passed before excusing himself.

When Adamonis went downstairs, the bar was transformed, much as Martynas had predicted, full of people speaking in many languages and women laughing too loudly. Sitting alone at a table was the man who had to be Herman Steiner. He looked like a hungover drill sergeant faced with a particularly disappointing new band of recruits. He was pale and rigid and none of the looser girls in the bar dared to flirt with him. Adamonis took a drink at the bar and watched him, and when Steiner suddenly reached up to scratch behind his ear, Adamonis knew all he needed to know and finished his drink and went outside.

Johnny-at-your-service was still there.

"Do you think you could speak to the hotel laundry-woman?" Adamonis asked him.

"Like I told you before, those kind of people are my family. It should be no problem. But they don't work evenings. I'll have to check in the morning. What do you want to know?"

4

IN THE SNOWY WINTERS of Adamonis's parents' childhood, the police went up to the Green Hill forest that overlooked Kaunas to shoot the wolves that harried the town. Now his sister, Anele, lived with her family among the new houses springing up there. The sophisticated woman she had become astonished him. She was as lithe as an American, managed a house with two small children and a husband, and still found the time to run a dentistry office in a room dedicated to that purpose at the front of the house.

"I went all the way to St. Petersburg to study," she had said, "and I have no intention of wasting my education. Besides, it's pitiful how rarely they pay my husband, even if he is an officer. If it hadn't been for our relatives on the farm, when his pay was three and four months overdue and my patients unable to pay for the same reason, the children would have gone hungry."

For most of the war, Lithuania was behind German lines. His parents both died in the flu epidemic at that time, but he still had Anele and a vast clan of farm relatives out in the countryside.

Anele was warm and accommodating, but he didn't really know her. Adamonis had been away for so long that he felt a bit awkward imposing in this way. But he had nowhere else to go and the comfort of family was a welcome cloak after living without one for so many years. Her husband, Vilimas, had seen action at the front against the Reds, but Anele was the force that ran the house where Vilimas played a genial and supporting role. Anele welcomed Adamonis for what he was to her, the practically mythical older brother back from the war, scrawny now, and in need of care.

The children, a boy and a girl, stayed up late to meet their legendary uncle and they competed to sit on his lap and tell him about their dog, their toys, and the fine cook who baked them cakes if they were good. Vilimas plied him with Bénédictine and Anele looked him in the eye and assured him this was his home now. Then she put the children to bed, came back to tell him she wanted to hear his stories only after he'd recovered from what must have been a terrible trip. She sent him off to bed with a few unkind words about the government bureaucrats who had taken him away on his first day home.

There were dried flowers in a vase and a few Russian classics and a couple of Lithuanian poetry books on a shelf in the bedroom. So much had happened in one day, yet he couldn't sleep and sat up in bed with one of the poetry books, called *The Voices of Spring* by the national poet.

He was uneasy. The warm embraces of his sister and her family were welcome, but the contrast between the railway station that morning and the house he inhabited that evening made him anxious for his sister. She was so sure of herself and the family seemed so happy.

They didn't even know they were living on the edge of an abyss.

5

WHEN Adamonis got up late the following morning, Johnny was already waiting for him in the kitchen, drinking tea with the cook, Milda. He gave Adamonis the information he expected, and Adamonis instructed him to go to Landa's office and ask for an appointment in the afternoon.

Military intelligence was housed in a crumbling czarist office complex that was close to being the tallest building in town—fully four storeys high, practically a skyscraper in that city. A striking young secretary dressed in a grey business suit and with short brown hair came down to the porter's niche. She led him up two storeys and through a large room filled with a sea of clerks, some of them very old, men who had been in service since the time of the second-to-last czar, some typing and others working with pen and ink. Already the new country's machinery of government was full of cogs repurposed to the new reality.

"What's your name?" Adamonis asked. Her behaviour was cool, but he sensed some heat, to which he was attracted.

"Miss Pinigelis."

"Are you Mr. Landa's secretary?"

She didn't seem inclined to reply.

Landa sat behind a massive desk stacked with briefs. He pushed up his eyeglasses and came around to shake hands, smiling wryly at Adamonis, clearly not expecting much.

"Please sit down," Landa said. "Well, have you met with Steiner yet?" he asked when Adamonis had settled himself.

"I've seen him, but there's no need for me to meet with him. I know how to fix your problem."

"Really. I'm all ears."

"In the short run, get Steiner out of that hotel. It's critical. Have someone invite him to the spa in Birstonas for the weekend or take him to some country house. Above all, move him out of the Hotel Metropolis. I guarantee you that his mood will improve in two days. You can't afford to put up foreign dignitaries in that hotel."

"Why not? The Metropolis is the best hotel in town."

"But the best is not good enough. They may change the sheets from time to time, but there's a shortage of both coal and wood, so they haven't been boiling the linens. Some of the beds are infested with fleas. I saw Steiner pick one off his neck. Germans are fastidious and Steiner has probably spent the last five nights sleeping in his leather armchair. He sleeps poorly and he's groggy and irritable."

"I can hardly believe this. Some of our most prominent citizens stay in the same hotel."

"Yes, but those who do bring their own sheets."

"You're sure of this?"

"Very sure. Put the invitation in today and I guarantee he'll accept it. Make sure he's moved to another room on his return and I'll make sure the bed linens are clean for him from then on."

"You've only been here a day and you say you have contacts in the Hotel Metropolis?"

"I do now."

Landa leaned back and looked at Adamonis as if seeing him for the first time, or at least in a different light.

"You have no plans to leave your sister's house?"

"Not at present."

"Thank you. I may call on you again."

Adamonis had expected the meeting to go much as it had. Landa would be embarrassed for his country, and therefore unhappy about the news, unless it turned out to be right. He wasn't fool enough to swallow the theory just yet.

Miss Pinigelis was waiting outside for Adamonis. "You're smiling," she said. "I guess things worked out well?"

Adamonis was appalled at himself for showing his emotions so freely.

"I'm smiling because I'm happy to see you again."

"That may be true, but you were smiling before you saw me. Do you think you can find your own way out?" she asked.

He wasn't going to let her go so easily, not when she'd aroused his interest on first sight.

"I'm not sure," he said.

She walked with him to the porter's niche, waited until he had signed himself out, and then wished him goodbye.

Adamonis went back to his sister's house with the intention of reading a little poetry, but the howls of dental patients too cheap to pay for Novocaine drove him out and he spent the afternoon with a book of poetry in the Hotel Metropolis bar.

6

JUSTAS ADAMONIS's brother-in-law, Vilimas, glowed as he walked Adamonis through the displays in the War Museum, the new facility of which he was the proud director. Some of the museum's guns had been in the field not much more than six months before.

The Bolsheviks had tried their best in Lithuania, but were beaten back, yet they hovered ominously in underground cells. Remnants of the czarist forces had joined disgruntled German veterans in an effort to occupy Lithuania and make it a sort of client state to Germany, so they burned farms across the north for a while, and then withdrew. Poland had successfully fought off the Bolsheviks in the "Miracle of the Vistula" the previous summer, but the Poles had bitten off a corner of Lithuania and were considering another mouthful. All in all, Lithuania was a morsel to various ravenous states.

Adamonis had longed for home many times over the past several years. He had often been hungry and afraid. Even now, he thought about food all the time. But Vilimas's museum bored him. His soul itched for something more.

Adamonis was grateful when a civilian who introduced himself as Mr. Pranaitis was ushered into the museum.

Pranaitis carried a chauffeur's hat under his arm but wasn't wearing a chauffeur's uniform. He said that Mr. Landa urgently wanted to see Adamonis in a location in the Old Town.

Adamonis excused himself from his enthusiastic and disappointed brother-in-law and stepped out onto the street.

"The department car is under repair and the department bicycle is in use," said Mr. Pranaitis, and he asked Adamonis to follow him on foot. Pranaitis seemed proud of his hat, and he placed it carefully on his head before putting on his gloves. As he did so, Adamonis noticed that his fingernails were perfectly clean, which seemed a bit unusual for a driver who was probably expected to maintain his own engine.

Pranaitis gallantly offered to pay the fare on the horse-drawn streetcar that ran down the boulevard to the Old Town, but it was nowhere in sight.

Mr. Darius Pranaitis was talkative enough, a man from a farm near Siauliai, a city in the north.

"How long have you been in this job?" Adamonis asked.

"Eight days, sir, ever since the department got a car."

"And what did you do before you came here?"

"I was the principal of a high school in Rokiskis."

"And before that, what did you teach?"

"German language and literature. I translated for the occupying Germans during the war."

"So why is a high school principal now a chauffeur?"

Pranaitis blushed, a charming trait in a younger man, but he must have been in his early thirties. Actually rather young to have been a school principal.

"Woman trouble," he replied.

"One of the students?"

"No, no. A former girlfriend who made my life hell. I've tried to shake her off, but she follows me whenever

I manage to escape to some new town, and then tells the police that I'm a thief. Suddenly, I'm being investigated and my new employer gets nervous and lets me go. It's happened all too often. It's awkward."

"And why would she do that?"

"She claims I'm the father of her boy."

"Are you the father?"

"She can't prove that."

This was the excuse of every man in a paternity suit, but sometimes the excuse was true.

"There can't be more than five hundred automobiles in the country. How is it that a former high school principal knows how to drive a car?"

Pranaitis shrugged. "I came from a farm and all the boys had to learn to do everything. Machinery comes naturally to me."

He was being underutilized as a driver and Adamonis made a mental note of this.

They reached the end of the boulevard, where the presidential palace stood behind a tall iron fence and then the road ceased to be a boulevard, narrowed, and veered left into the old part of town, where the thick-walled buildings huddled tightly together. Pranaitis took him down an alley to a three-storey building and led Adamonis up two flights of stairs. He rapped smartly on a door, and let him in. Pranaitis stayed outside.

Adamonis stepped into a large, rather bare room. Mr. Landa and a knot of three other men stood in the middle of it. Two of them were smoking. The window was open and the room was cold and Adamonis could see that the men with Landa were bored and sullen. One of them stamped his feet to warm them.

Adamonis shook hands with Landa, but Landa didn't introduce any of the others.

"I want to ask you a question, Mr. Adamonis. Something in this apartment is suspicious, and I wonder if you can tell us what it might be."

"What do you mean by *suspicious?*"

"A communist operative works out of here. He's quite a dangerous one. We almost had him, but he disappeared from this building. Maybe he went out a back window or across a rooftop. He doesn't seem to have left any evidence behind. I wonder if you could look around in case you can find something my men missed."

"Not much chance of that," one of the men said, but when Adamonis looked to see which of them had spoken, none of them said anything more.

It was the most interesting thing that had happened to him since the last time they met. Adamonis was spurred, too, by the dismissive looks of the other men. Something was at stake here, both for Adamonis and for them. They had clearly failed at their job, and they would be happy to see him fail too. Adamonis hated sullen men, the kind who would rather have an operation collapse than lose face. The Russian army had been full of officers like that.

The apartment was big and clean and made up of two rooms. He had been trained for work like this in his early days in counterintelligence, and he knew it was important to take nothing for granted, to interrogate every item he saw. In the larger room there stood a double bed on a steel frame, and up on the wall a cheap picture of the Sacred Heart of Jesus as well as a decorative linen towel with the words of the national anthem. The floor was dirty, but Adamonis put that down to the shoes of the men standing there. It looked like the room of a religious patriot, and a neat one too because the room had been newly papered with a bright, floral pattern. A feminine touch? There was something wrong in that. An ascetic in a pristine room

would not have used flowered wallpaper, and someone
wanting a homey atmosphere would have added a small
table or two and a vase with dried flowers, or another picture of some kind.

One of the sullen men coughed. Adamonis went into
the smaller room, which had a table and two chairs, an
electric hot plate, and jars of tea and sugar, but no cups.
Nothing had been used. A ceramic stove was built into the
wall that separated the two rooms in order to heat them
both. The stove door was on the kitchen side, and Adamonis opened it and looked inside. It had been swept clean
since last use.

The flat consisted of rooms waiting for an occupant. It
might be a safe house that had never been used.

Adamonis returned to the larger room and looked at
the walls. He didn't want to start tapping them yet, first
trying to take in as much as he could. The others still stood
where they were, but one of them had turned on an overhead lamp. The rooms in old buildings were dark to begin
with, and winter light made them darker, and now the
men stood in the pool of light directly under the lamp. It
hung from a fixture on the ceiling and an electrical wire
ran along the ceiling to where it disappeared into the plaster of the exterior wall.

Adamonis let his eyes rest on the wire. Why should an
electrical wire attract the attention of his eyes? He would
have to find out.

The walls of the room were asymmetrical. Many of the
buildings in this part of town went back almost as far as
the Middle Ages, so asymmetry wasn't unusual. Adamonis
went to the window and put his head out to look at the
exterior wall. It was not asymmetrical at all. The outside
wall was straight, but the inside wall was not.

The window well was very deep and the windowsill
was very high and broad. Without knowing quite why he

was doing it, Adamonis gripped the sill. It wobbled. He grasped the windowsill with both hands and pulled, and the board came right out.

He could hear Landa saying something behind him but Adamonis moved quickly, focused on his discovery. One end of the shelf had rested against a wide board, virtually a door, and although he could now hear the men coming up behind him and speaking urgently, he pulled away the door and had begun to squeeze inside the secret chamber when he was struck once very hard across the back of the head. He fell to his knees, heard shuffling and a gunshot, and then lost consciousness.

7
_____

BY THE THIRD DAY, the ringing in his ears began to fade and his sensitivity to light diminished to the point where Milda could pull back the curtains and permit him to look out on the bare branches of the linden tree outside the window. As his head cleared, Adamonis began to reflect on the stupidity of his actions, his eagerness to get into the hidden room. He had let his enthusiasm for the hunt cloud his mind. But he hadn't been able to help himself. Even though he had claimed to Landa that he was weary of this sort of work, it was exactly this kind of work that brought him to life.

Later that day the doctor came by to order him to stay in bed for a week, and almost immediately after he left, Landa appeared, carrying his hat in his hand. It was odd that Anele or Milda hadn't taken it at the door.

"I think your family blames me for your injury," Landa said as he sat on a chair at the bedside.

"What did you tell them?"

"That you'd been assaulted by a thief, but I don't think they believed me. It makes them even more suspicious now that we have asked to have Johnny in the kitchen here every day and we put a man on the street out front. Not much gets by your sister."

"No."

"How are you?"

"Much better, thank you."

"I feel bad about what happened, but I want you to know I had no idea you'd be in danger."

"This kind of work is full of surprises," said Adamonis. "Who was that man in the room?"

"A communist agitator and printer. There was a Boston Press in there that needed 220 volts, which explains the thick wire you noticed. He was grooming a small circle of junior officers when one of them changed his mind and came to us. We had the circle under surveillance and were working our way up the food chain when the officer made some kind of slip and was killed by the printer before we could intervene."

"What did he hit me with?"

"A wooden mallet."

"I should be grateful he wasn't a blacksmith. Who fired the shot?"

"We did. It didn't hit him, but it convinced him to surrender."

"So that's that?"

Landa laughed ruefully. "No, not at all. That was just a day's work, and not entirely successful because we would have liked to find his superiors. There are other communist cells, and by the way, they'll know you now. Word gets out in a small place like this. It's a vengeful sort of town, but I'll make sure you're under our watchful eyes."

"Do you think that's necessary?"

"Oh yes. Listen, this place is complicated. The city is full of foreign agents and we no sooner expose one communist cell than another begins to operate. Then there is

the matter of corruption. To say nothing of internal differences so sharp that I swear some of our politicians would
sell us to a foreign power rather than see their opponents
win. And as for our department, we're short of experienced manpower. We could use a man like you."

"In what capacity?"

"I'm proposing you take over military counterintelligence and report to me. We're plainclothes, but you'd be
paid at a lieutenant colonel's rank. Quite a bit lower than
your last post in the army, but that's as high as it goes in
intelligence here. The salary is reasonable, but it doesn't
always get paid on time. You'd have a mixed bag of staff.
Adventurers come through like magpies to pick over this
place. The war shattered the world. Our job is to put it back
together in this country with whatever materials we have."

"I'll think about it."

Landa put his hand on his beard and paused before
speaking. "I'm taking a lot for granted with you," he said.

"Like what?"

"You haven't declared your love for this country, your
willingness to fight for it, your understanding that we're
finally free after centuries of being beaten down."

"Oh, I like this place well enough. It's my home now,
I guess. I just don't go in for big declarations. But I'll tell
you this. I'd do anything to keep this country from falling into the stupid chaos I saw in the last few years. I quit
the army when the Reds began to kill officers and I joined
the Whites only to see them be just as vicious and just as
stupid."

Landa nodded. "How long will you need to give me
your answer?"

"Give me a few days."

As Adamonis began to improve, to walk about the room
and sit by the window, Milda started to treat him in her

own country way, strong in the belief that as long as he ate well, he would heal. She fed him clear chicken broth, and soupy rice pudding with raisins. And then slowly she enriched his food to include crepes sweetened with birch syrup. Eventually she served him boiled chicken and buttered noodles. He began to feel the need to move around to avoid being stuffed like a goose.

On the fifth day following Landa's visit, after the bandage was off his head and he did not look quite so much like an invalid, Anele permitted the children to come into his room. Three-year-old Paul and five-year-old Margaret were shy at first but soon found him to be the least busy adult in the house and brought him books to read to them. When these were done, they asked him to make up stories.

"Are they giving you any peace?" Anele asked from the door when he was telling them folk tales that he remembered from his own childhood.

"I enjoy their company. I never realized I liked being around children."

"It's time you started to think about having some of your own."

"I'm not settled yet."

"But that man from the bureau of statistics offered you a job. He told me so himself. Could you bear to do something like that after all your adventures during the war?"

"I think I might take him up on it for the sake of the income."

"Anyway, I've got some news for you," Anele said, "to brighten your sick room. Now that things are settling down here, it's like everyone who ever disappeared is coming back to the nest. Do you remember your cousin Lily?"

"No."

Anele gave him an exasperated look and began a complicated series of explanations about the family tree that took Adamonis to his mother's cousin and her husband who had moved to America along with a child named Lily. He may or may not have remembered her from among the masses of children at one of the country weddings before the war.

"Your cousin Lily—" Anele began, but Adamonis didn't let her finish.

"She's not really a cousin, is she? I mean, she's more distant than that."

"Don't quibble. Cousin Lily married a former American diplomat, and now they're moving to Kaunas to live here."

"An American diplomat?" he asked. "What kind of diplomat?"

"I have no idea."

"And they're coming to Kaunas? How do you know this?"

"She wrote me a letter. Her Lithuanian language was atrocious. She left at an early age, so I guess she does better in English now."

"You mean they're coming for a visit?"

"No. To live for some time. Her husband is going to investigate business opportunities."

"So he's no longer a diplomat?"

"I'm not sure, exactly."

"Well, this is very interesting news indeed," he said.

8

"DOESN'T the new man have anything to add?" asked Novak, the minister of the interior.

The room was full of smoke and a particularly loud clock seemed to measure the time it took Adamonis to answer. Was it three ticks or four? It didn't matter. It was better to seem measured than glib. In sharp contrast to the chiefs of staff and their adjutants, who sat at the conference table in their uniforms and whiskers, Interior Minister Novak wore not only civilian clothes, but also a tie that was closer to a scarf, the sort of thing one expected to see at the opera.

"I'll do most of the talking," Landa had reminded him on the way to the meeting with the chiefs of staff. "Remember they have a lot of power because we're still under martial law. The minister of the interior, Peter Novak, will be there too. Say nothing to offend him but make no promises. He's competitive because of his own civilian counterintelligence service. Keep a polite distance and don't pass on any sensitive files to his department. The chiefs of staff don't like him, but they don't know you yet so nobody is on your side."

"Yet somebody permitted you to hire me."

"They give me a lot of leeway, and then they judge the result."

Minister Novak was now studying Adamonis with a look of mild concern and spoke again before Adamonis opened his mouth.

"Are you even aware of the threat from the Poles? You've been out of the country so long that you might not know about their networks here. Does the man who noticed a flea on the ear of the German envoy notice the conspiracies among the old Polish ruling class?"

Landa could not intervene. Adamonis was on his own.

"Not yet, no," said Adamonis.

"I could share some of my files with you, if you like. And of course I'd expect the same from you if you actually manage to come up with anything in the near future. It's all right. I understand. It takes time to get your bearings. Let's just hope nothing happens before you acclimatize yourself."

Silence hung in the air for a while.

"There is one lead I have," said Adamonis. He could feel Landa's eyes from beside him, but Adamonis looked back at the minister with the most genial expression he could manage. Adamonis explained that a certain émigré was returning to Lithuania with her husband, a former American diplomat. This man might still have ties with the United States government and they should make a good impression if they wanted formal recognition from the USA. After all, hardly anyone recognized Lithuania and endorsement from the Americans could pave the way for others to do the same.

"How do you know about this American? What are your sources?" Novak asked.

"I just know. An American former diplomat is coming to Kaunas with a wife who speaks Lithuanian."

Novak eased back in his chair and let it go. "In any case, everything you say must be speculation. You can't know the American's intentions for certain."

"Of course it's speculation. What else could it be?" asked Adamonis.

"Well, keep me informed for the sake of collegiality. And stop by to see me one of these days and I'll pass over something about the Poles."

"You'd better get something out of this for them," Landa said when they were out in the corridor after the meeting. "You can't just dangle treats in front of them without delivering."

"Do I have to prove something to them?"

"Of course you do."

"What about the German finances I helped secure?"

"That was a long time ago, in political terms. You're only as good as your most recent successes, and the more recent the better. Mistakes are more memorable than successes. Novak thinks it's more important to get ahead with the cabinet and the general staff than in the field."

"What do you think?"

"You need to do well in both. Otherwise your back is exposed."

"I thought you were covering my back."

"And so I am, within limits. I understand you fired the three men with me the day you found the secret room."

"That's right."

"One of them was Novak's nephew. You'll find it's a small town here."

"Are you saying I should hire him back?"

"Of course not. That would make you look indecisive. I've hired him back in my department, so you see, I'm looking out for you."

Landa walked partway to the office with him, and then went off to another meeting. Adamonis nodded to the porter at the door and climbed the stairs to his own department on the second floor. Miss Pinigelis looked at him quizzically from her desk outside his office, but he did not want to talk at the moment.

When he was in a better mood, he was glad he had asked for her as his secretary. She was fast with the paperwork and could parry the thrusts of intrusive men at his door—she also worked as a sieve, letting through only the essential files in order to keep his mind uncluttered. It didn't hurt that he was attracted to her, but he reined in his emotions. Mr. Pranaitis was his driver whenever the car was available—Adamonis could use a proficient German speaker who was also handy with cars—and Johnny-at-your-service was his assistant without portfolio. Johnny gathered intelligence on the streets and in the train yards by chatting to men and women of his class and developing a team of irregulars who would have been surprised to think of themselves in that way. They did favours for Johnny, and he did favours for them.

Kostas Chepas was a bland man in his late thirties, or forties, or fifties—it was hard to tell. He ran surveillance, a whole stable of followers who needed to be trained, used, and put into retirement quickly because Kaunas was such a small city and even the best of shadows was recognized eventually. Chepas was an invisible man, and as such he saw a great deal.

Adamonis had fifty office staff and as many operatives and a network twice as large spread out throughout the countryside, each of them writing reports of one kind or another that they wanted him to see. His desk was piled high with briefs and these were only the ones Pinigelis judged pressing.

He seated himself in his chair and swiveled around to get the briefs out of his sight and look out the window. Soon it would be spring and with any luck his hunch about the American would turn out to be true. As for the man's wife, his so-called "cousin" Lily, he had no memory of her at all.

9

THE HUMAN TELEGRAPH was sometimes more effective
than the real thing. Anele had planned a small welcome
luncheon for the long-lost American cousin, but word of
the couple's arrival seeped out to a burgeoning array of
family and friends. Anele managed to get the guest list
down to sixty people, far too many to fit inside her house,
and since the spring weather wasn't good enough yet to
hold a reception in the garden, she ended up taking a small
ballroom at the Hotel Metropolis.

But the battle over the guest list was just the first of
many struggles. The next conflict came with the hotel
chef, a dour Belgian who believed he was the most distinguished chef in the provisional capital, and thus in the
country. Anele's cook, Milda, reasoned that she should
be the captain of the table because the American cousin
"belonged" to her. Milda enlisted the farmer-cousins'
wives as allies, and these provided her with ammunition
of kegs of strong beer, a suckling pig, sides of smoked
bacon and pots of butter as well as slabs of black bread
half the size and weight of cemetery headstones. The Belgian didn't capitulate, but he was forced into an uneasy
alliance.

He laid out a pair of gigantic stuffed pike, one of them nipping at the tail of the other on the platter. They were glazed with aspic to make them shiny, as if they had just leaped out of the water. The Belgian had boned two geese and stuffed them with forcemeat and then cooked them so the skin was crispy but the filling moist and delicate. They had borscht and sorrel soups with dill-covered potatoes steaming on the side; boiled salmon in cream sauce and herring with onions as well as herring with mushrooms. They had sausages sliced as thin as paper to be eaten on white or black bread along with farm butter, pale now in the cold weather when the cows were eating hay. They had partridges and the suckling pig, whose skin had been carefully basted until it was brittle as spun sugar. For sweets they served compote of dried fruit, followed by hazelnut and chocolate tortes and a metre-tall tree cake that looked like a golden cone with branches and tasted like a very dense pound cake (a frequent fantasy during times of hunger in Adamonis's wandering across Russia). They had a feast suitable for a country wedding or a reception for an ambassador.

The hotel barman insisted that serious receptions included French wine and champagne at ruinously high prices. Adamonis paid for both, but in case wine wasn't enough, Vilimas ordered two cases of vodka, the country cousins brought homemade liqueurs, and of course they had to have *krupnikas*.

Outside the hotel, Johnny-at-your-service was in charge of traffic, which he imagined might include as many as four automobiles, and he held at bay a ragged company of street boys as well as a coven of barefoot peasant grandmothers in scarves and holding baskets on their arms, standing around to see what the excitement was all about.

The welcoming party was turning into a sensation.

The American who stepped out of the car, Robert Woolley, was slim and distinguished, with fine hair combed to one side and a tie knotted in the English fashion. His bearing was more English than American, charming, but with an air of restraint. He held out his hand for his wife, Lily, who stepped out of the car behind him wearing a feathered cloche hat, a long, loose drop-waist dress and a double string of pearls as well as a silver salamander broach above her left breast. Lily's eyes showed delight and mischief, and were expressive in the manner of a film actress. Adamonis thought that Robert Woolley was a very lucky man.

If Woolley was an undercover diplomat, he would have wanted to keep a low profile, but this was the sort of party that would make it into all the society pages of the newspapers published in Russian, Lithuanian, Polish, and Yiddish.

The couple's reactions to the assembled family, dignitaries, country peasants, and high society were a study in contrasts. Woolley merely pursed his lips. Lily, on the other hand, beamed at Johnny when he took off his hat to her, and then she turned that lovely emotional illumination first on Anele, and then on Vilimas, and finally on Adamonis, as the three stood at the hotel door to meet them. Adamonis felt as if she were looking only at him, and his heart leaped up at her smile. She cocked her head slightly, as if sharing a secret and then nodded at him, and Adamonis nodded back, even though he still couldn't remember her at all.

Two country girls in national costume stepped forward to give each of them flowers and then Anele presented them with the formal offering of a loaf of bread and a small glass of salt. Lily said something to her husband and they each broke off bits of bread, dipped them in the salt, and ate them. Vilimas, very fine in his museum director's officer uniform, offered them each a shot of vodka. Although alcohol was banned in America, each of them drank the liquor without hesitation. Lily whispered to her husband and he began to speak in English, which very few in the crowd understood, and when she nudged him, he switched to German, which almost everyone knew. It was not all that different from Yiddish. Woolley had a peculiar voice, very nasal, like that of someone with a head cold.

"Thank you very much for all of this, but you outdo yourselves. I am a simple man who has come to visit the native country of his wife."

"What do you think of our city?" called a peasant from the fringe of the crowd.

Woolley pushed his eyeglasses up his nose and looked around. "Providing things turn out well," he said, "I see a certain amount of unrealized potential here."

The small ballroom Anele had rented lay beyond the hotel restaurant bar, and as they passed by, the journalists from the yellow press gathered at the door, scribbling furiously on their notepads. The Jews, the Russians, and the Poles would have their own impressions of the event, all of which Adamonis would read in summary translations at his desk the next morning.

It was already hot inside the ballroom, whose recently dusted chandeliers made the room feel grander than Adamonis remembered it, and a series of people approached Woolley to speak to him either in Russian or Lithuanian, which his wife translated and then translated back his response. Woolley had German and English, but no other languages. These were mostly polite greetings, although Adamonis saw Martynas saying something earnestly to Woolley and shaking his hand repeatedly as if it were a water pump. The repeated toasts had loosened up Woolley, who smiled and nodded gamely.

Adamonis saw that he would not get much of a chance to speak to either of the guests, so he stepped out of the hotel to talk to Johnny on the street. Then, as a matter of habit, he walked around to the back of the hotel to make sure that Chepas's man was watching that door.

By the time Adamonis returned to the party, the volume in the room had risen in proportion to the alcohol consumed. The couple from America was always in the centre of a dense knot of men and women. Adamonis felt protective of his new-found cousin and her husband, but there wasn't much he could do to help them for the moment, so he tasted a few of the dishes on the table, in particular the stuffed pike, which smelled of fresh river water and parsley, and the crispy goose with cherry sauce, and he restricted himself to two shots of vodka because he was working.

The heat in the room became more intense, and when the noise began to rise even higher, Adamonis thought he'd better work his way more closely into the knot around the guests. It was hard work, elbowing aside others, when he saw one of the country cousins, a beefy farmer with hands the size of boxing gloves, leaning toward Woolley. Disaster was in the making because the farmer had a small covered pot that he was offering to the American. Lily should have been able to protect him but she was distracted and speaking to someone else.

This was what it must have been like to be in Sarajevo as Archduke Ferdinand's car came into view. Adamonis could predict the outcome of the farmer's action and was almost within reach of stopping it, but not quite.

Certain Lithuanians had only one joke that they played on foreigners from the West. Most Western visitors were not familiar with horseradish, and if they did know it, they thought of it as a tingle from the gravy on their roast beef. But Lithuanians liked their horseradish freshly grated in vinegar, and the aroma of this condiment was like the assault of the most violent of smelling salts. Woolley gamely plunged his nose deeply into the small pot and inhaled a lungful. The potency of the astringent mixture knocked his head back, and the avuncular farmer reached desperately forward to keep Woolley from falling, but only managed to push him, and the American fell to the floor. His head hit the boards with a *crack* and his eyes closed. There was a moment of stunned silence until one of the society ladies stepped forward to slap the face of the farmer.

Adamonis could see the fate of the new nation destroyed by a joke. The Americans would never recognize Lithuania now, never legitimize it, and the country might be wiped off the map by its enemies due to the coarse humour of a farmer.

Woolley had fallen with great composure, his carefully combed hair unruffled and his steel-rimmed glasses still square on his nose after his collapse. He looked like a man taking a quick nap in his study—either that or a man in his coffin as arranged by a skilled funeral director. All of this as one woman waved a handkerchief over his face and another wept at the shame of it all.

As Adamonis raised Woolley's head, he saw Lily on the other side of him.

"To the rescue yet again," she said to Adamonis in Lithuanian. He didn't know what she meant, but at that moment Woolley's eyes fluttered open.

"The liquor here gives quite a punch," he said.

A dozen heads bent over them and let loose a string of apologies in several different languages, but Woolley was still a little confused.

"What are they saying?" he asked Lily.

"They're sorry for you, dear."

"Sorry? What do they have to be sorry for? I feel wonderful. I'm breathing through my nose for the first time in weeks."

"Chronic sinusitis," said his wife. "It makes him miserable."

"But I don't feel miserable now." Half a dozen hands shot forward to help him up, but Woolley stood up on his own, and when someone offered him a shot of *krupnikas*, he accepted it, downed it, and looked around himself with an air of satisfaction. Like Lazarus, he had risen from the dead, and the resurrected man was nothing like the quiet undercover diplomat who had gone down a few moments before.

"Don't you people do anything but eat and drink?" he asked. "What about some music? If we cleared a little space, maybe we could have some dancing too."

The hotel pianist wheeled in his instrument from the bar and an accordionist came in from somewhere, and between the two of them, they played polkas and waltzes, much favoured by the country cousins, and then the modern dances: tango, foxtrot.

The transformation of Woolley was complete—he had turned into an American bohemian. He danced with energy and skill until his eyeglasses fogged up. He had no lack of competitors and companions on the dance floor. When it seemed impossible that he could go on, he went on.

Adamonis was leaning against the bar when the minister of the interior, Peter Novak, sidled up to him. Novak smiled mischievously, pleased with himself.

"This is your American spy?" he asked.

"I never called him a spy. He's a former diplomat."

"Not much for quiet diplomacy then, is he?"

"Maybe it's just a cover."

"Quite the cover." He paused and lit a French cigarette and then picked a piece of tobacco off his tongue before looking up at Adamonis pointedly. "And quite the intelligence coup you have here. I think you'd be better off with one of my Polish files. Remember to stop by." He straightened up and walked out the door without saying goodbye.

Adamonis had lived through many disasters in the army. He tried to console himself with the thought that in the bigger scale of things, this was not really a disaster. He should have known better than to be irritated by Novak, but he resolved to get something out of Woolley if his life depended on it.

Woolley carried the party until well after dark. By then, the kitchen help had found its way into the drink, and a maid and a waiter were kissing against a wall in the corridor and, most surprisingly of all, Milda and the hotel chef were sitting side by side, their arms around each other and a bottle of *krupnikas* on the bench beside them. In the ballroom itself, the same tunes were being played for the third and fourth times. A thick layer of tobacco smoke filled the top half of the place so they were practically in smog. The suckling pig had been demolished, the ears snapped off and the body not much more than a backbone with bits of flesh still on it, picked away at by passersby. The fish were altogether gone, even the heads, taken by a maid who intended to make soup.

Just when the energy in the room finally seemed to be flagging, someone called out, "Sauna," and this word seemed to catch Woolley's ear.

"Where is the best sauna in Kaunas?" he asked.

"The best one isn't here at all. It's in the spa town of Birstonas," someone said.

"How far is Birstonas?"

"A couple of hours' drive."

"Let's go!"

10

ADAMONIS had seen many sorts of comportment in his life, and in particular drunks in full alcoholic gaiety, but he had never seen anyone quite like Woolley in such a complete Jekyll/Hyde transformation. Birstonas was a popular sanatorium with parks along the Nemunas River, and to see the sun rise over the town would be an achievement for dedicated revellers.

By this point, half of the guests were gone and many of the others were barely able to stand on their feet, but Adamonis took charge of the expedition and organized a group of eight that would need two cars, which Johnny managed to hire from out front of the hotel. Anele had to go home to the children, but Vilimas and Adamonis shared one of the cars with Woolley and Lily, and four energetic young people were in the car behind them. A third government car with Pranaitis at its wheel and a pair of agents in the back seat.

It was dark and light rain began to fall, and they were bumping along and swaying on bad roads. Adamonis had hoped to pry some information out of Woolley, but Woolley just dropped his chin on his chest, braced his right arm against the window, and fell asleep.

Lily was between them, and Vilimas in front with the driver. Adamonis and Lily were sitting very close and they inevitably bumped up against each other. Adamonis was sensitive to her touch somehow, and he admonished himself for this sensitivity, thinking he shouldn't be reacting like a man much younger than he was. Mrs. Woolley looked over to her husband to make sure he was asleep and then reached over and put a hand on Adamonis's arm.

"This is the first chance I have to thank you, cousin."

"Are we really cousins, Mrs. Woolley?"

"Call me Lily, and I'll call you Justas."

"I appreciate it, but I'm not sure what you're thanking me for. Anele was the one who threw the party."

Lily had not removed her hand from his arm. They were wearing winter coats, but he could feel some warmth come through his sleeve.

"I don't mean the party. I mean for all those years ago at another party." They hit a sharp dip and she fastened her hand on his wrist to steady herself before finally letting go. Adamonis had lived as a soldier for a long time, and men without women soon fell in love easily, at the slightest look, at the slightest tenderness. "You don't remember what I'm talking about, do you?" she asked. "I'm the girl you pulled out of the well at our uncle's farm."

The incident came back vaguely to him. Wells in Lithuania used a bucket at the end of a rope on a long pole with a pivot and a counterweight on the other end. A little girl at a country wedding had ridden the bucket down, and none of her friends was strong enough to pull her back up again. Adamonis happened to be nearby and brought up the little girl in a white dress all wet from the waist down. He couldn't have been older than sixteen at the time and didn't think it was important. Children on farms fell out of trees, broke their arms, tripped into rivers, and set sheds on fire. What had happened to her wasn't much more than a little misadventure.

"Maybe so," said Lily, "but you weren't the one down the well. From where I was standing in the darkness on a bucket submerged in the water, things looked pretty bad. I was terrified."

It was hard for Adamonis to put the two pictures together, the one of the girl and the other of the woman beside him who spoke Lithuanian with an American accent. But he was glad she was grateful to him for something.

"What was it like to move to America?" he asked.

She laughed. "As frightening as the well at first. I remember a hotel bathroom in Königsberg, where we stayed before boarding the ship, and I saw the first bathroom sink in my life. I couldn't understand how the water was supposed to stay in the bowl if there was a hole in the bottom of it."

"Whatever made you decide to come back here?"

"Why, it's home for me. I've been longing for this place for years, just to see the house where I grew up and to pick raspberries from the canes in the yard."

"But your husband never picked raspberries in that yard."

"No. He's very kind. He indulges me."

"Has he found anything to do here?"

"Why, Justas, we've just arrived."

"And made quite an impression. I've never seen such an energetic diplomat."

"Former diplomat."

"Where did he serve?"

"He was a consul in Vienna before the war. That's where he picked up his German. He likes Europe and he hates what the war did to it. He has a little money and he's looking for opportunities to put it to work."

"This must be quite an out-of-the-way place for someone like him."

She chose not to follow his lead. "And what about you? Whatever became of the earnest student who was bound for glory in St. Petersburg?"

"I was tossed about the empire during the war. When I came back here at the beginning of the year, I found a position in the bureau of statistics."

"You can't be serious," said Lily.

"I most certainly am. I'm glad to have a government job."

"But when you were a young man, you wanted to be a pilot."

"Did I? I suppose so. I also wanted to be a circus acrobat. Are you disappointed in me?"

"I'm not disappointed at all. I'm glad I found you here again. Anyway, you must be very capable at whatever you do. And if you want to maintain your little fib, I won't mind and maybe I'll tell you a few fibs of my own."

"Fibs?"

"Everyone knows what you do, but you don't have to admit it. I won't force you. I watched you during the party. You were running things. You're the one who got these cars."

"Miserable specimens. We'll be lucky to make it to Birstonas. Tell me, is your husband always so high-spirited?"

"Not really. Actually, he's melancholy most of the time. He'll fly high while the alcohol is still in his blood, but then he'll pay for it later."

"Don't we all?"

"Some more than others. He's very law-abiding, so he hasn't had a drink in America since Prohibition, but he'll drink where it's permitted."

"And how is your life with him?"

She hesitated. "That's a very personal question."

"Well, you can fib if you want."

She laughed. "My husband gave me a whole new life. My parents were well off here, but that didn't translate into much in America. My father became a factory foreman and my mother was a visiting nurse while they were still alive. But the Woolleys were Worcester gentry. He helped me learn how to behave in the best houses in America. Actually, we made it to a few balls in Vienna too. Now that was something."

"What an impression our poor Hotel Metropolis must have made on him."

"He did have a good time."

"I'll say. The people in this country love high spirits. He'll be a success here. I only hope he finds the country to his liking. Just let him try to find a restaurant in the provinces, or an indoor toilet in the countryside. He'll be disappointed. I hope to be helpful to him, and to you too. Call on me. This place will seem strange to you after the way you've been living."

Lily thanked him with another squeeze of his arm.

A flat tire delayed the trip, but Adamonis sent the car with his agents on ahead, so when the partygoers finally arrived in Birstonas at three in the morning, two saunas were hot and ready and waiting for them, and a couple of rooms in the sanatorium cottages were at the ready in case energy flagged.

As soon as the car jolted to its final stop outside the sanatorium, Woolley sprang awake and asked for a drink of *krupnikas*. They stood around the cars drinking the liquor and coffee from thermoses, and Adamonis wondered if the mood would turn, but Woolley was on another tear, talking fast in English with Lily doing her best to translate for him. The others laughed at his jokes, but a little late, and it felt as if they were now at only the echo of a party. But Woolley was still game, so the men and the women separated and they had a couple more drinks before going into the saunas, and then a couple more before taking the mud bath, and more again as they were hosed down by sleepy-eyed attendants who couldn't quite understand why they had been called into work before dawn.

Woolley seemed to be the kind of man who could talk a great deal without saying very much. He was genial and told stories about American gangsters, student football, his impressions of Austria before the war and the details of his grandparents' farm in Massachusetts. And his energy was unflagging.

The rain had stopped during the night and a warm front moved in after it. The dawn over Birstonas was very beautiful. The town was the Baden-Baden of Lithuania, and like everything in Lithuania, it existed in miniature. The Tulip Sanatorium was a two-storey white stucco building with a lovely arch on the second floor and a glassed front like a train station. Directly behind the sanatorium lay a walkway along the banks of the Nemunas, a broad river that moved slowly with the sun just rising over the pine forest on its far side.

Aside from twenty minutes in the mud bath, Adamonis hadn't slept at all that night, but his years in the army and his job didn't permit him the luxury of sleep when he wanted it. The agents brought the remains of yesterday's food and set it on two riverside tables provided by the sanatorium, and there they still had enough leftover goose and sausages, bread and butter and cakes as well as liquor to feed a party twice their size. Although the morning was relatively warm for the early spring season, the sanatorium provided them with blankets to drape over their shoulders while they were drinking *krupnikas* and coffee, and soon Woolley's spirits began to rise yet again.

"How is your breathing?" Lily asked her husband.

"The best it's been in months. Honestly, that horse-radish has made me into a new man. I can smell the grass and the trees and the scent of honey in the liqueur. I can practically smell the fish in the river below us. Tell me, Mr. Adamonis, are there fish in the river?"

"Oh, yes. There are commercial river fisheries here and there."

"I think I would like to try my luck. Do you think you could get me a line?"

An important guest's desires knew no restrictions, so soon Adamonis's men had one of the local flat-bottomed boats ready for use, as well as a couple of imported bamboo poles with braided horsehair lines and a tin of worms.

For all his remarkable energy, Woolley's face was beginning to show some strain. There were creases around his red eyes and the wry smile on his face seemed to be frozen in place. He waved to the others, who watched them from the shore as Adamonis rowed out in the small boat. Woolley cast his line and let it sink to the bottom. Adamonis smoked and watched Woolley as the sun rose above them. Novak was probably right. It seemed increasingly unlikely that Woolley was on an undercover mission for the Americans. How could any organization trust a man as wild as this one?

The odds of catching a fish in unfamiliar waters were low, but within a few minutes Woolley had hooked something, clearly a heavy fish because it fought him and he had to let out line hand over hand and then pull it back in a couple of times when the fish tired. After several long minutes of fighting, he pulled the fish up toward the side of the boat. It was an enormous carp, a fish known for its strength and longevity, and when he leaned over the stern to take the fish by the lip to haul it into the boat, it tugged back, and Woolley slipped overboard.

"Damn!" he shouted as soon as his head came up from beneath the water. He had not even lost his eyeglasses.

"Can you swim?" Adamonis shouted.

"I can, but the water is freezing and my coat weighs a ton. Get me back in."

"Impossible," Adamonis said. Woolley held onto the stern as Adamonis rowed them back to shore. This took Adamonis a good three or four minutes, and by the time they reached the shallows, Woolley was blue and shaking. Attendants from the spa stripped off his clothes and covered him with blankets before rushing him inside to warm him in the sauna before putting him to bed in one of the rooms.

They returned to Kaunas later that day with a much-diminished Woolley sleeping under a blanket in the back with his wife at his side while Adamonis sat in front with the driver.

After a while, Lily tapped on the glass and Adamonis slid it back to hear what she had to say. "Now you've saved both my husband and me from drowning," said Lily when she was sure Woolley was asleep. "I'm doubly in your debt."

11

THE YIDDISH PRESS praised the new American investor, the Russian press implied he was a gangster fleeing American law, and the Lithuanian press commented on the positive effect of *krupnikas* on Woolley's dancing ability. The horseradish incident was described in great detail, as well as the potential for export of this product to America, where it could be used by epileptics suffering seizures.

Chastened but philosophical, Adamonis set the press summaries aside on his desk, stood, and looked down onto the early-morning street below him. A deliveryman was unloading crates from his wagon at a grocery store and a woman in a green headscarf was walking toward him along the sidewalk. Landa had advised against positioning his desk with a window so close at his back, but there were no tall buildings within sight and the angle required for a shot was too sharp to be successful unless he stood up close to the glass. The woman, as if sensing his eyes, looked up. Adamonis hurried downstairs.

"Hello," Adamonis said when he saw Lily, her head bent down at the porter's window. "What are you doing here?" This early on a Saturday there were few employees in the building.

She straightened up and gave him that magnificent smile of hers, the passport that gave her licence to go wherever she wanted. "Aren't you happy to see me?"

"Delighted," he said, and then thinking that sounded too formal added, "I'm very happy," and then felt he was being too earnest. The porter had come out of his vestibule and stood waiting in his rumpled grey suit and matching grey hair in cowlicks. Adamonis asked him to send up tea and led Lily inside. She removed her scarf as she walked beside him and shook out her hair. He took her coat at the office and asked her to sit with him at the low table he used for meetings.

"How did you know where to find me and how did you know I'd be here this early?"

"Anele told me to look here." Secrets were hard to keep in this miniature country. Lily looked very beautiful in the morning light. "I wanted to apologize to you for Robert's sake. I know his behaviour was terrible at the party and you were so understanding and helpful. I'm a little ashamed of him. I wanted you to know he's not usually like that."

"He has a commanding presence," said Adamonis.

"He comes from high society. He grew up with servants and he's used to getting his way. I had to get used to it too."

"Really? Yet he had a job working as a diplomat."

"He did, but Robert took orders from no one except the ambassador and he gave orders to everyone else. He had a secretary and aides in Vienna and he fit right in with the pomp of the place before the war, but those days are long gone now."

"You mean he has no ties to the government?"

"Not formal ones, but of course he still has friends. I told you, he's here for my sake and to look for business possibilities."

"I'd hoped he still might have some pull, actually. If the Americans recognized us, the Poles might be less bellicose."

Lily looked mildly irritated, but she sipped at her tea and softened her expression.

"I really don't understand this animosity. When I was a girl, everybody who was anybody spoke Polish. We're practically the same nation. The Americans love the Poles ever since Paderewski.

"Lily, they invaded us. They might do it again."

"In America they have a saying: If you can't beat them, join them."

"Why, Lily, I can't believe my ears."

She shook her head, annoyed with herself.

"All right. Sorry. I'm new here. Maybe I just don't understand yet. Did you think Robert could bring around the whole United States on his say-so?"

"I wasn't sure. I hoped he might."

"He's not exactly the master of American foreign policy and the Harding government isn't interested in Europe anymore, but Robert does know some people in Washington. Do you want me to see what I can do?"

"You'd be doing me a big favour," said Adamonis.

"I think I owe you something for saving my life all those years ago, and for saving Robert's life too. We can help each other."

"Oh?"

The Woolleys were having a hard time finding a suitable apartment and she wanted to get out to the countryside to see the cousins. Adamonis liked to listen to her, but at times he wasn't really listening to what she said so much as looking at her face and wondering how long he would have to wait until the warm smile flashed again. After a while, he heard a soft knock on the door and Miss Pinigelis came in.

"The porter told me he had brought you up some tea an hour ago," she said, "and I wanted to know if you'd like me to get some more hot water."

"Is it an hour already?"

Adamonis introduced them. Lily did not rise. Miss Pinigelis was very pretty, with her curls, but she was wearing a very sensible work suit while Lily was dressed in society clothing. He sensed them measuring each other and finding no mutual sympathy.

Adamonis did not look forward to the next meeting with the general staff. His reputation had suffered a reversal. Although Woolley might still provide a lead into the American government, Adamonis thought it best to leave this potential unmentioned and to play the penitent. Having no other option, he chose to smile good-naturedly as the others looked upon him ironically, but Minister Novak liked to insist on the point.

"Undercover diplomat indeed," Novak said, tapping his pencil on the edge of the oak boardroom table to underline his words. Through the clouds of smoke in the room Adamonis bore the lingering smiles of the chiefs of staff. Only his superior, Landa, did not smile, but Adamonis suspected Landa was holding himself back mostly out of loyalty.

"The newspapers named Woolley the best foreign dancer in the country. Now that's what I call keeping a low diplomatic profile. Tell me, was that carp still on the line when you rowed back to shore?"

"No, the carp got away."

"So, the fish escaped. You should have had it followed."

Novak's sarcasm carried an element of fondness to it, as if Adamonis were his younger brother, less experienced in the ways of the world. In a gesture of patronizing good fellowship, Novak reminded Adamonis that he had a lead about a new Polish conspiracy. Adamonis was keenly aware that any file Novak handed him would be either a problem case Novak's agents were unable to solve, or, more likely, a cul-de-sac. But it was important to demonstrate collegiality, and after the meeting Adamonis followed him back to his office for the file.

When Novak and Adamonis walked into the reception area in front of the minister's office, a middle-aged man in civilian clothing stood up and Novak hurried forward to shake his hand. "I hope you weren't waiting long," he said.

Konstantin Vasilyev was a White Russian general who had led the Lithuanian Army against the Reds the year before. He had been working with an untested volunteer army, but he was apparently a brilliant battlefield strategist and had succeeded beyond all expectations. He was briefly chief of staff, but his talents did not lie in the vipers' nest of military bureaucracy, and he retired with a handsome pension and full honours after the peace treaty was signed with the Soviets.

"I was passing through," said Vasilyev, "and I had a question or two and an anecdote I wanted to share. Did you hear about the problems Lenin was having with his rectum? He went to the doctor and dropped his pants, and the doctor pulled out Stalin."

The receptionist and four other men in the waiting room all laughed along and Novak chortled appreciatively.

Adamonis observed Vasilyev with great interest because of both his reputation and the circumstances of their meeting. A man of Vasilyev's stature who was willing to wait in the anteroom of a minister among other, lesser petitioners was a man who did not have enough to do with his day.

Novak introduced them, told the secretary to get the file for Adamonis, and then took the general into his office. The secretary, a punctilious young man in a wingtip collar of the kind worn mostly by prewar diplomats, changed his disposition as soon as the other two entered Novak's office. Government offices were full of men and women like this, civil servants straight out of Gogol. They were as annoying as flies and not much more important unless one was in their power.

The file on the rumoured conspiracy at the Lukiewicz estate was not exactly opaque, but so unsubstantiated that it was not worthy of mentioning at a meeting of the general staff. But Adamonis would not set his own agents on the case. He would go to the estate himself as one of the visits he was making throughout the country to familiarize himself with outlying offices.

The Lukiewicz estate was just north of the city of Kedainiai, and Adamonis requisitioned the car for a day and set out from the office with his driver, Mr. Pranaitis. Adamonis was removing some of the papers from his briefcase in the back seat when, just as they were entering the narrow streets of the old part of Kaunas, the car suddenly swerved and the window on his right shattered. Adamonis reflexively closed his eyes as glass shards flew across the seat and then opened them to see the stone that had done the damage bump against the opposite door and end up on the seat beside him. It was a heavy cobble that could have killed him if it had struck him in the head.

Pranaitis stopped, threw open the driver's door, and ran off after someone. Shaken, Adamonis stepped out of the car in time to see Pranaitis outdistanced by a young man tearing up the street. Adamonis retrieved his briefcase from the car, opened it, and reached in for his pistol but he did not remove it from the bag. He put his back to a wall and watched the street, which filled soon enough with people coming to see the accident. Once their numbers increased, he let go of the pistol, removed his hand, and closed the briefcase.

Pranaitis returned, red and breathless from the chase.

"Well?" asked Adamonis.

"He got away." Pranaitis wanted to say more, but Adamonis held up his hand.

"Later."

They returned to the office garage, where Pranaitis patched the window with a piece of greased canvas and Adamonis took the front seat beside his driver.

"Are you sure you want to go on with the trip?" Pranaitis asked before starting.

"Just go on," said Adamonis, and he fell silent. Pranaitis grew increasingly anxious as they drove out of the city, perplexed by his stern passenger.

"I don't know if the man was a vandal or an incompetent assassin," Adamonis finally said, "but we were probably observed by our enemies, and it's best not to show fear. We must be seen to shrug it off. And another thing. If the two of us ever come under attack, you stay by my side."

"I just wanted to catch the man."

"If we're under attack, we stick together."

Pranaitis nodded, but he looked hurt, like a man being blamed even though he had had the best of intentions.

Adamonis reflected on the incident as they drove on, the wind whistling through the imperfectly repaired window behind them. If the stone had been an assassination attempt, it was an inept one. On the other hand, he had heard of no incidents of vandals throwing stones at cars. There were still too few cars in Lithuania for them to be treated with anything but admiration—or even awe once one was in the countryside. It was more likely a message was being sent, but if so, by whom? The communists might have wanted to send a calling card. Could it have been the Poles?

The Poles and Lithuanians were like an estranged couple. They had been in a union together for a very long time until their empire collapsed and then the Russians ruled them both for over a century. When the czarist empire failed in turn in 1917, the two nations had different ideas about what independence meant. To the Poles in Poland and the Polish-speaking Lithuanian nobility, it meant a return to the old union. But the Lithuanian speakers wanted no part of this. To the Poles, it must have seemed like a wife who stands up one day and walks out, with many recriminations but without a proper explanation. To the Lithuanians, it was like escaping from an overbearing and controlling husband.

Another way to think of it was like the relationship between the Irish and the English. The Irish had gained their independence the same year, but they lost part of the North to those loyal to Britain, and they had many Anglo-Irish within the republic itself. Lithuania had gained its independence too, but lost Vilnius and its region and had many Polish-Lithuanians within the new country. Luckily for the Irish, they had a sea between themselves and Britain, but Poland was Lithuania's neighbour and the border could not be sealed thoroughly. No peace treaty had ever been signed and not many foreign countries were in a rush to recognize the new Lithuanian state because it might not last.

They made their way out onto the rutted country roads.

Pranaitis was still sulking. He worked mostly in the office now, but Adamonis also used him as a personal driver. Pranaitis was a good man, but his actions were intemperate.

"How are you adjusting to your new position in the office?" Adamonis asked him.

"Pretty well. The job suits me and it leaves me enough time to do a little tutoring and freelance translation in the evenings as well as continue my studies part-time."

"What about that woman trouble you had? Any news on that front?"

"The woman hasn't shown."

He would have to see that Pranaitis carried a pistol in the glovebox when they travelled. But first he would have to get the man a little more training.

A pistol was only useful in defence against an attack that came with a warning. The cobblestone had come out of nowhere. Who had been talking to him with that stone?

Kedainiai was a very old city with a modest medieval centre. It had a few blocks of stone houses and a square off to the side of a big baroque stone synagogue. Jews constituted a large part of the population of every town and city in Lithuania, and they made up about a third of Kedainiai. Lithuania had always been a mosaic of Lithuanians and Jews, as well as Poles and Russians and Karaites and Tatars. People of all nationalities and religions had coexisted here, more or less peacefully, for hundreds of years.

But that was the state of things in the old world of czars and kaisers. The war had convulsed all the old empires, and the new landscape had not settled yet. It was shifting imperceptibly all the time now, and was still susceptible to catastrophic seismic upheaval.

12

THEY ARRIVED late in the day at the stone gatehouse of the Lukiewicz property, and a liveried grandfather with dirty gold brocade on his epaulettes came out to unlock the gate. He was a very old man who must have been born into serfdom, like Johnny. Until 1861, country estates, called *dvaras*es, came with whole villages of peasants. The people were part of the property. The Lukiewicz estate was over two thousand acres along with another three hundred acres of forest nearby, and the government was going to expropriate most of it and others like it and redistribute the property to landless peasants. Not surprisingly, landowners didn't like that much. Poland's proposed land reform was far less drastic, so it was no wonder an estate owner in Lithuania might have Polish sympathies.

After passing through the gate, they drove for half a kilometre along an oak-shaded lane bordered by a stream on their left. Upstream were a mill and a raceway and beyond that a millpond with grassy banks and a pair of swans on the water's surface. There was a park on the right until the lane curved to show a lawn and the old *dvaras* house itself. It was a neoclassical mansion with eight wide French windows across the two floors. Hewn stone made up the base and the walls above it were stucco. A tower from the back corner overlooked the rest of the house.

As the car drove up to the entrance, the front door opened and a man came outside to greet Adamonis, followed by three hunting dogs and a schnauzer, all of which barked at the car and leaped about excitedly.

"Don't be afraid of the dogs," the man called over the noise. He said something to the dogs, and they sat down in a row, like circus animals, or servants who had been transformed into animals for their misdeeds. Lukiewicz wore a tweed jacket and a white shirt with a dove-grey tie and a matching hat with a wide band, although it was not quite the season for such light colours. Adamonis had imagined he'd be an old man, as a member of the gentry's rearguard, but he was in his forties with a carefully groomed moustache and a slightly distracted expression. If his look was slightly urban, his handshake was decidedly proletarian. This was a man who used his hands for some purpose besides holding a fork and a wineglass.

Strangely, he had a very large moth sitting on his shoulder, mostly grey, like his hat and tie, but with dramatic red lines down the length of its body and at its wing tips.

"If you let the dogs sniff your hand, they'll treat you as one of theirs. Do you mind?"

Adamonis gave each of the sitting dogs his hand to sniff, working his way along the canine reception line. The schnauzer gave his hand a lick. Then Lukiewicz said a word and the dogs rose and bounded ahead into the house, disappearing down the corridor before the two men. Pranaitis took the car around the back.

The moth sat there on Lukiewicz's shoulder as a brooch might sit on the breast of a woman. He noticed Adamonis's fixed stare.

"Is something the matter?" Lukiewicz asked.

"Just above your lapel."

"Is there something there?" he asked.

"A moth. Largish."

Lukiewicz looked over calmly. "A sphinx," he said. "*Chaerocampa elpenor*. Let's just leave it where it is for now. It's the safest place."

"Is it alive?"

"I don't think so. Still a bit early in the season. I was working with my collection and this must have fallen down."

The house was laid out on a centre plan, with a corridor and a staircase ahead of them, and rooms on either side. The hall was decorated with several racks of antlers and hanging from one of them a hunting horn and farther on a leather vest and farther still a powder horn for one of the old-style muskets. It was a hall worthy of Baron Munchausen, not this refined man who walked among the trophies like a museum curator.

"Would you like to see my menagerie?" he asked. "There's still a bit of daylight on the west side of the house and they'll look better now than under lamplight."

Adamonis was taken through a door on their left, into a large room with a glassed-in extension that must have been an orangery in the past and was now a mock aviary. Lukiewicz set the moth on a table. On the walls were many species of birds, from very large ones including a stork and a grey heron all the way down through an owl and honey buzzard, and further down to small birds, including partridges and grouse. Some were arranged as if in flight and others as if alighting.

If the walls were devoted to birds, the desktops were devoted to small animals, from moles to hares, while the floor was given over to fox, wolf, bear, and a massive bison head on a stand.

The room had a slightly sinister atmosphere with the last rays of the sun coming in through the window. This part of Europe had been remote from the rest for centuries, and many of these animals had survived only here, some dangerously close to extinction and others perhaps gone already from this place too. In Russia a room like this could soon contain a stuffed Lukiewicz, a member of a noble species almost completely extinct.

"Did you collect all of these?" Adamonis asked.

"Some. My father was a collector and he taught me taxidermy. It saved my life. We had a much larger collection at our other estate, the big one in Byelorussia, but this was all I could save before the Bolsheviks invaded and before the Poles returned. Please come into the sitting room. Aleksandra prepared us something to eat."

Adamonis followed him down the long corridor to another room on the right side of the main hall, a kind of sitting room where the shadows were growing long. In one corner stood a green ceramic woodstove with tiles that reached all the way to the ceiling. The stove had a cast-iron door with a bas-relief chariot drawn by three horses and carrying a man with a drawn bow. Beside the stove stood a table on which sat a barrel of vinegar—Adamonis could smell its astringency and wondered who could have put it there when it belonged more properly in a kitchen. But in the old estates an ancestor might have set something down temporarily and left it there so long its placement became tradition to subsequent generations. In the centre of the room stood a long table with a linen tablecloth and upon that an assortment of foods. There was a chaise longue on the other side of it, lumpy by the looks of it, and cabinets, two with glass doors that displayed blue ceramic bowls and plates. Books lay on various tables, and there were overstuffed book cases, and in front of them a stand where one could read standing up. In addition to vinegar, the place smelled of age, of old leather and dust with a hint of wet dogs.

They were getting ready to sit when the chief maid came in, dressed in a black dress with a ring of keys at her waist, while carrying a tin with a long spout from which she poured oil into a lamp on the table. She removed the glass and used a match to light the wick, and as she did that, she said, "Praise the lord" in Polish, and although they had been speaking in Lithuanian, Lukiewicz reflexively responded in Polish with, "For ever and ever, amen."

The light illuminated a cold meal of baked pheasant, marinated mushrooms, and boiled crayfish, potato and beet salad and bread and wine. Adamonis asked to wash his hands, and the maid took him to the water closet. He passed by the kitchen where half a dozen men stood in the shadows, day labourers waiting for their pay.

Across all of Russia, houses such as this had long since been burned or pillaged. Near the end of his time in the czar's regular army, Adamonis's radicalized soldiers had helped to torch them. Not many remained in Lithuania either, and the coming land reform would cut the economic base out from under them. When Adamonis returned to the sitting room, Lukiewicz was pouring honey wine into a glass and Adamonis felt a bit sad for this man who was going to lose so much. He even felt some sympathy for the allegiance to Poland, if Lukiewicz actually did have such feelings.

"How is it that taxidermy saved your life?" Adamonis asked him when he had seated himself and they began the meal.

"I had been a student in St. Petersburg, and I was so devoted to collecting animals and insects that, after I graduated, I neglected to find a job. Although we are an old family and held various properties, my father was not much like the other layabouts of our class who thought of themselves as 'gentlemen.' He was an engineer, a very practical man, and he became annoyed with what he saw as my laziness, and we had a falling out. He cut me off for a time, and I had to make a living somehow. Luckily for me, the universities in Russia were changing after the uprisings in 1905. They paid less attention to classics and more to science and every biology lab needed preserved animals. I started out supplying them with anatomical objects, cats whose veins and arteries were filled with red and blue latex. Feral cats were easy enough to find in the streets. Animal skeletons were popular too. I was so successful that I had a small operation with three employees, and I made quite a living from taxidermy until the war. Everything fell apart then. Luckily, my father and I eventually reconciled and I could return home, but not to my birth home, which lies on the Polish side, in Byelorussian Poland, now. I came here instead."

The honey wine was very mellow, very old. It was barely sweet and had just a faint aroma more like the memory of honey than like honey itself.

Adamonis cracked open his first crayfish, pulled out the flesh, and dipped it in mayonnaise before putting it in his mouth. Crayfish were delicious, but they made for messy eating, and one couldn't help but share a certain amount of good fellowship with a man who was eating them with you.

"And what was your life like then, back on your childhood estate?"

"My childhood was wonderful, less so my school years. I would have been just as happy staying on the property my whole life, fishing and hunting with the locals. It was an interesting place, alive with wildlife and various peoples, a kind of crossroads. There were Lithuanian villages and Byelorussian villages and the Catholic Church services were all in Polish. People didn't distinguish themselves by nationality so much as by religion—Catholics, Orthodox, and Jews."

"It sounds like people who didn't know who they were."

"They knew themselves well enough. But things started to change coming up to the war. You had to choose who you were going to be in the new world. Two of my brothers decided they were Poles and one decided he was Byelorussian. I haven't seen them for some time."

"What did you decide?"

"Why, I'm Lithuanian of course. Otherwise I wouldn't be here."

"But don't you have some nostalgia for the old days? Isn't the family seat in Polish Byelorussia? You could go there instead."

Adamonis was baiting him slightly. Lukiewicz could return there, or he could bring Polish rule here.

"The old world is dead. I have a fondness for it, but it's the fondness of my childhood. The class we belonged to feared the Russians or licked their boots. The men were practically illiterate and Jewish managers ran all their business affairs. The ruling class couldn't arrange anything but parties. I remember parties that ran all night, with somebody's aunt at the piano and later a village band that might know six or seven pieces and played them in endless repetition. As the night grew longer, the nobles' drivers would start jangling harnesses and cracking whips out in the yard to get their masters' attention, but they hardly ever left before dawn."

"It sounds like a lot of fun."

"Parties like that are not for me anymore. They would exhaust me. I still hold card parties here sometimes, mostly because some of the neighbours expect it of me. I get half a dozen grandmothers smelling of lavender and wearing twenty-year-old dresses. Some younger men and women too, of course, but they want to stay up late. Sometimes I find them still talking when I come down in the morning, but they consider me old and they are hushed when

I am around them. Some university professors come in the summer to stay in some of my rooms. These activities remind me of the parties of my childhood, but without the extravagance. The old days were wasteful. Half of those nobles were mortgaged to the hilt and the craftier ones were misers. They had no idea of progress."

"And you do?"

"I'm not sure of progress in general, but I am sure of science. We've lived here forever, but we barely know the natural world around us. The peasants know more about the flora and fauna than the gentlemen do. Science is opening our eyes. Everything you see here in this house belongs in a museum, or a botanical garden, not a country house. I'm just a steward until we can open the proper institutions. We need to move forward."

He sounded sincere, but Adamonis would not be doing his job if he didn't ask.

"My sources tell me there is a conspiracy here. That your neighbours intend to bring in the Poles."

Lukiewicz smiled. "My neighbours can barely bring in the hay. They gather to play cards and grumble. That's the extent of it."

"And you don't grumble too?

"Listen, I won't like to give up this place. But I have an idea. We need a nature reserve, and maybe part of this land could be turned into a park. As for me, I'm not going to sit here in this place and hunt and fish for the rest of my life. I've been talking to friends. Kaunas University doesn't have a proper biology department. That kind of work interests me."

Lukiewicz was fighting to keep his eyes open by the time they were eating cakes and drinking brandy. Adamonis spent the night in an ancient bed made up with linens woven on the estate, spun from flax grown on the estate, and his head on a pillow filled with down that had been plucked from geese raised on the property. Except for the French wine and Russian caviar, the old estates had been economies contained unto themselves.

In the morning, Adamonis and Pranaitis toured the farm buildings. In one of the barns there stood a car, and beside it a whole row of old-style horse-drawn carriages and sleds, some of which probably had not been used for fifty years. Aside from the car, they were something between junk and museum exhibits. And outside among the outbuildings and in the fields a good two dozen people went about their business of working on the *dvaras* grounds. On the one hand, they would lose their jobs when Lukiewicz lost the property, but on the other hand, some of them would get farms of their own or go to look for work in the city.

On the way back to Kaunas, Adamonis tried to picture the card games at the Lukiewicz estate. The landowners would talk of what concerned them most, and the coming expropriation would obviously be their main topic of conversation. Could these conversations have been the source of Novak's case? There were so many more pressing threats than this unlikely one. It was even harder to imagine that a cabal of card players had somehow found out he was en route to the estate and thrown a stone through the car window to convey their displeasure. But he did not close his mind to the possibility that he had found a lead to something, even if he was not quite sure what it was.

13

THE WINDOWS were all wide open to a fine spring day and the clerks had put paperweights on their files to save them from being scattered in the breeze.

On his passage through the department Adamonis came upon Pranaitis, holding his head in his hands like a man in a melodrama. His ashtray was full and he smelled of alcohol. Pranaitis was wearing a sweater and a tie instead of a suit, the kind of outfit a man might wear on a Sunday at home.

Adamonis asked Pranaitis to come to his office.

Pranaitis sat in the chair across from the desk with his brow furrowed and splotches of colour on his skin where he had been rubbing his face with his hands. Adamonis asked for tea to be brought in, and when it arrived, Pranaitis thanked Miss Pinigelis, but left his cup and saucer untouched on the edge of the desk.

Adamonis asked Pranaitis some questions about his work, about certain tendencies in the German press both within the country and without. Pranaitis was remarkably good on this subject. Adamonis let him talk for a while, and eventually, Pranaitis tried to pick up his teacup, but he rattled it against the saucer and spilled a few drops on his lap before putting it back and looking to Adamonis with stricken eyes.

"If I was your defence lawyer," Adamonis said, "and you were on the stand, I'd advise you to compose yourself and keep your hands on your lap."

"Am I under investigation for something?"

"Not yet, but you're wearing your troubles on your face. And the way you're dressed is like a red flag. Why aren't you wearing a suit?"

"I'm having it turned inside out, and it's not ready yet."

Kaunas tailors did this sort of thing for men with worn suits who could not afford to have new ones made. A suit turned inside out did not shine the way a worn-out suit did, but it didn't last long either.

"What's the problem?"

"It's a personal matter. I'd rather not say."

"Your personal life is affecting your working life. What's wrong?"

"It's a question of support. It's costing me money and I don't have enough to live on."

"But you have enough money to buy vodka. By 'support' I assume you mean the woman and her son. Has Felicia reappeared?"

He nodded glumly.

"She wants too much money. I can't support her and myself."

"Yet married men work for us."

"I won't marry her."

"Why not?"

"She's a crazy woman, hysterical. She has screaming fits. She pulls my hair and her own. She's threatened me with a knife more than once. And besides, I promised my father I'd never marry her."

"What's your father got to do with this?"

"She was a maid in our house at the farm."

Adamonis considered the man for a while. Pranaitis father's maid was a single mother, certainly poor, and she had no other means of support, but Pranaitis wasn't permitted to marry beneath him.

He could fire Pranaitis, but the man was useful both as a driver and as a German specialist and firing him would do Felicia no favour. Adamonis was a pragmatist. Maybe some good could be wrung out of this situation.

"Take this piece of paper," Adamonis said, pushing it toward him. "Write down Felicia's full name and address. I'll do two things. First of all, I'm assigning thirty percent of your salary to her for the next three months. It won't be enough for her to live on, but it will help her get by if she finds other work. Second, I'll send her for mental assessment to the spa in Birstonas. It's quiet there and they have good doctors and they'll find a babysitter for the child. The department will pick up the expense."

After this gesture, Adamonis expected some sort of relief, but Pranaitis looked down at his hands, too deep in his misery to appreciate his good fortune.

"And one more thing," Adamonis said.

Pranaitis looked up.

"I don't want to smell alcohol on you at work. Do you understand?" Pranaitis opened his mouth to say something. "And if you thought of denying it just now, think again. Your breath against a candle flame would go off like a torch."

Adamonis wasn't sure if he had done the right thing or the wrong thing, but at least the poor woman who had been following Pranaitis around would get some medical attention and a little money. It crossed Adamonis's mind that they were building a new society but in its construction they were using materials from the past. It was hard to say how the new structure would hold up.

14

ADAMONIS worked late that night, scanning briefs to form a mosaic of the threats to the country at that moment from Poles and communists, from internal corruption, and from the meddling of half a dozen countries with various interests. When he finally rose wearily from his desk, he stood for a moment to consider which he needed more— sleep or food. He had forgotten to eat that afternoon and now his hunger trumped his fatigue. It was after eleven. A more settled man would have gone home and eaten there. If he was lucky, a solicitous wife might cook something fast such as cheese blintzes if she had waited up for him.

An ideal Mrs. Adamonis appeared in his mind at times like this, in moments when he was not preoccupied by work. More than anything, this nonexistent woman would need to understand that his life was irregular, like that of a policeman, or a sailor, or a doctor who might be called away on short notice day or night. He envied his sister's family, which seemed so busy and happy and yet, he admitted to himself, slightly dull.

He could imagine a wife all he wanted, but this woman might well have thoughts of her own. Would she like to dance and stay out or would she be shy and uncomfortable at parties? He would not be able to tell her about his work. Would she resent that or understand? In the end, these were fanciful thoughts. Simply to have a wife who sat across the table as they drank tea and ate buttered bread would be a very good thing, as would the warmth of her body beside his under the sheets.

He sighed. He wanted that sort of life, in a way, but his work swept him onward. How could he look for a potential wife when he was busy looking for spies?

Adamonis left the office, followed at a distance by a pair of Chepas's shadows. There was a corner restaurant near the opera house, one that did not have a permit to stay open after curfew, but whose transgressions were overlooked by the police. Night owls needed a place to eat, even if the city would not issue the right permit. Laws were necessary, but one had to pick among them in order to survive. Kaunas was a nightly ghost town, and he was making his way was down Freedom Boulevard when a policeman came up to him and asked for his permit to be out after hours.

Adamonis understood the man was only doing his job, and so he opened his briefcase and took out his permit. The policeman was an earnest, simple man, likely the first one in his family to be living in a city. He kept looking up at Adamonis as he read over the document carefully. His lips moved as he read.

The policeman looked up again, startled when Adamonis's shadows approached. Chepas's men followed him at all times in the evenings and sometimes during the day ever since the incident of the broken car window.

"It's all right," Adamonis said to the policeman. "They'll show you their permits too."

He left them behind.

The Rose Café lay four steps down, in a half cellar: twenty tiny tables with candles lit on some of them. Certain people preferred to keep their faces in shadows. It was a Saturday night, so no alcohol was available, at least not officially—priests felt drunkards would not make it to mass the next morning. There was no menu, just a few regular dishes of sausages, borscht and cabbage soup, cheese, and pickled cucumbers. Sometimes there was a pork stew or boiled fish. Most people ordered *gira*, a fermented drink a bit like beer, but not nearly as alcoholic—it tasted like liquid dark rye bread.

Adamonis was very hungry and "his" waitress, Aldona, knew him well enough to set down a satisfying dish—a bowl of cabbage soup and boiled potatoes—before asking him what else he wanted. She had been a village orphan, but possessed enough spark to work her way up in the new world; he imagined she was sleeping with the owner and would probably end up owning the place. He admired her resourcefulness and she must have sensed this because sometimes she paused to tuck a lock of hair under her kerchief and smile at him. He asked for smoked meat and bread and cheese and a shot of vodka in his glass of *gira* to aid his digestion that late at night.

Once he had eaten the soup, he lit a cigarette to wait for the next dishes. Some of the people in that place would not like to be seen by him, and Adamonis did them the kindness of ignoring them for a while to give them a chance to slip away if they needed to. The last person he had expected to meet there was retired General Vasilyev, the hero of independence whom he had met in Novak's office. Vasilyev was in his reservist's uniform, which he straightened as he came up to Adamonis, offering a brief salute before taking the hand offered to him.

"Mr. Adamonis," he said.

"Yes."

"We met briefly in Novak's office."

"That's right."

"And do I understand you're the head of military counterintelligence now?"

It was not the kind of question one answered in public. Vasilyev waited for a while, received no answer, nodded his head as if recognizing his own indiscretion, and sighed.

"I find myself in a bit of an uncomfortable situation here." Adamonis invited him to sit down. "I came in a while ago and lost track of time. Frankly, I find it boring to be at home too much, so I got into a few conversations. The next thing I knew, it was past curfew. Now, if I go out, the police will take me to the station and there will be all sorts of explanations to make."

"You don't have a permit to go out at night?"

"I do, but I left it at home. Now there's no way to get it."

Vasilyev was drunk and Adamonis had dealt with drunks all his life and occasionally been one himself. He forgave drunks, within limits, and he had to perform favours all the time, and this one would do no harm. Aldona showed up with a plate for Adamonis and the general patted her familiarly on the thigh. She smiled tightly, but stayed when Adamonis asked her to, and she confirmed that the owner had a couple of rooms upstairs where the general could sleep on the couch until morning.

Neither she nor the general was particularly happy about this solution, but in politics, one simply did the best one could.

Adamonis suggested Vasilyev join him in something to eat, but food didn't interest him. Adamonis offered him a drink, and Vasilyev agreed to have another *gira* with vodka. He peered through the gloom at various faces. He was a gregarious man, Adamonis had heard, but with dips in his moods, and he seemed to be in one of them now. But that didn't stop him from talking. Adamonis discovered that Vasilyev had had a family once but lost them during the war. He lived alone on what must have been a very good pension, because if it hadn't been for him, Lithuania might have been part of Russia and would now have been suffering through the same famine.

Vasilyev began to speak intensely, even garrulously, and then stopped and thought for a while, as if struggling with an idea.

"What do you think of business as an occupation?" Vasilyev finally asked.

"I think the wheels of commerce should be helped to turn in this country."

"Yes, that's what people are saying. There are opportunities now. But my people were landowners in Russia, and I've been in the army since I was a cadet. The workings of business are not entirely clear to me."

"Then maybe you should look for a government post."

"The fact is, I'm a little too famous in this country to be an assistant undersecretary in some ministry, and I've become *persona non grata* in the officers' club. Russians like me were welcome when you had to fight the Soviets, but I'm beginning to feel less welcome now."

"Maybe you should learn the language."

"At my age?"

"You're not old."

"No, but new languages come slowly when you're not young anymore. Anyway, the army is out of the question. So what should I be doing here?"

"Good question. I don't know."

"Do you know how old I am?"

"No."

"Forty-eight, but already on a pension. Too old to learn a language easily, but too young to be retired."

"Then you have to do something else."

"Exactly. I've been offered the distributorship of French cognac in this country. I like cognac. I drank it all my life, but I'm not sure I could sit with restaurant owners and try to convince them to buy a bottle or a case. It feels beneath me, somehow. What is a man to do?"

Adamonis didn't have an answer to that. Everyone he knew had hated the war and wanted it to end, but once it did, the new seas they sailed upon were uncharted. Vasilyev was unmoored. Adamonis suggested that there might be a future in one of the private Russian-language schools, and Vasilyev nodded at this advice, but without enthusiasm. Adamonis finished his meal and then helped Aldona lead Vasilyev to a room upstairs. Adamonis didn't want him to make a pass at her, for Vasilyev's sake as well as his own, so he made sure Vasilyev was settled on a couch and Aldona back downstairs in the restaurant before leaving to return to his sister's house.

15

SCAFFOLDINGS rose and hammers banged in a frenzy of rebuilding in the provisional capital of Kaunas. So much dust had not been raised since the Germans' Big Bertha guns turned the Russian forts around Kaunas to rubble in 1915. But in the interim, even the most fortunate of families had trouble finding places to live. The Woolleys installed themselves on the far side of Freedom Boulevard, in a ground-floor apartment in a house that had been abandoned during the war. They were having it renovated while they lived there. When Adamonis went over to call on them, he met Johnny in the courtyard, where he was overseeing the installation of a rain barrel. The workmen were taking a tea break, the two men in caps with hand-rolled cigarettes and Johnny with a pipe between his teeth, which he removed when he saw Adamonis.

"You might not want to go in there at the moment," said Johnny.

"A family fight?"

"Not exactly, but renovations are going slowly. And by the way, thieves have been sniffing up and down the street ever since they moved in, but I've frightened them off."

"You don't miss much."

"Not a thing."

"Stay near them. They can use all the help they can get."

Adamonis tapped on the door and a maid let him inside and led him to the living room, where Woolley and Lily were taking tea on a silver service at a small table with only two chairs. The rest of the furniture was covered in sheets and half the plaster was missing from one of the walls. They looked like a lord and lady down on their luck. Lily asked the maid to remove a sheet from one of the other chairs and as soon as she did so, she raised a cloud of dust that set Woolley off coughing and he charged outside after waving at them to carry on without him.

Lily poured tea. She had a paisley wrap over her shoulders to keep out the chill of their old house, but even under these trying circumstances her bright eyes were warm with an edge of her habitual mischief. She had a scarf over her hair, worn slightly off centre, giving her a piratical air.

He felt awkward for a moment and wondered at himself. After his years in the army, Adamonis found it easier to read men than women, but even so he saw the trace of an ironic smile.

"You'll have to excuse my Robert. His sinusitis has been acting up and he can't bear the dust."

"You don't keep horseradish on hand?"

"It only worked that once. So how did you ever find time to get away from the bureau of statistics?"

"We finished counting rain barrels and now we're moving on to Americans, so I came over here to start my next sum."

"And do I count as an American, or is it just Robert?"

"You must have an American passport, so I suppose you count as one of them."

"Did you know I'm applying for Lithuanian citizenship?" she asked.

"No. Whatever for?"

"If Robert decides to invest here, it will help."

"Are you getting on all right?" asked Adamonis.

"We'd get along better if we saw you more often."

"You and Anele see each other."

"I meant you. Have you been avoiding us?"

Adamonis was startled by the question.

"No, no, not at all, I've just been working."

"Well, work a little less and see us a little more. Robert likes you and you can help him to adjust. You should take him out for a game of billiards one day. Could you do that for me?"

"Lily, I said I'd do anything I could for you two. Is anything wrong?"

"It's a struggle at the moment, while we're living like this, and I want to make it nice for Robert here too."

"I don't see any raspberry canes in the yard. Aren't they what you came back for?"

"I want to get out to the countryside again, but there hasn't been any time. We have to get settled first."

They talked for a while, her manner playful at times. Lily was a little imperious, but he liked her and this slightly demanding manner was a sort of act, he thought, to see how much she could get away with. Eventually Woolley opened the door halfway and looked inside.

"Has the dust settled yet?" He seemed nothing like the dancer and drinker of the party. He was like another man altogether, more like the diplomat he had once been, a clerkish sort of person. And since his sinusitis had returned, he spoke through his nose again, like a man with a cold. When Adamonis asked him how he was doing, Woolley talked as if a dam behind which the words had been accumulating for some time finally was permitted to break.

"How is it possible to live in this town? I'm giving it all the chances I can for the sake of my wife, but honestly, this place is like a cross between the Middle Ages and a comic opera. Do you have any idea how long it took to get a rain barrel?"

"I don't."

"Two weeks. It's either a Sunday or a Catholic holiday or a Saturday or a Jewish holiday. The Catholics won't work one day and the Jews won't work the other. And when they finally do come to work, especially inside, there is no place I can get away to. I thought this city would be like a miniature Vienna, but there seem to be no normal cafés in this town, just restaurants and hotel bars. People eat cucumbers in the street and the country people come here without shoes. If a man had a mind to open a shoe business, he could probably do very well, except the people who don't have shoes don't have any money either. The people here look European, but I believe they are Asiatic. And how many Jews are there here anyway?"

"About a third of the town."

"Where did they all come from?"

"I think they've been here forever."

"Never mind about the Jews. Let's get back to vegetables. Aside from cucumbers, there seem to be no vegetables in this town. Meat is cheaper than tomatoes and anyway, all the meat we get in a restaurant is flavoured with onions."

Adamonis would have to befriend Woolley for the sake of Lily. He wasn't looking forward to it.

"It's a new country," Adamonis said. "It will take time for things to become normal here."

"If they ever do. This state is an artificial construction with powerful neighbours. Tell me one thing above all else. Should we feel safe here?"

"Of course you should. Why not?"

"I'm wondering about this army of yours. How many men does it have and what will it do if the Poles decide to attack, as every second person we meet here says they might."

"They'll defend the country."

"But how? I've heard it's a ragtag bunch."

"They fought on three fronts in the last few years and did all right. Would you like to inspect the army?"

"Maybe I would. I'm no soldier. I'd just like a few details so I can feel at ease about the safety of my wife."

"Vilimas has friends among the officers. I'm sure he could arrange some sort of visit among the troops."

"I'd like to go too," said Lily.

"Are you interested in military matters?" Adamonis asked.

"Not a bit. But I'm proud of this little country and I'd like to see some of the young men who defend it."

"I'm sure it can be arranged."

"But remember," said Lily. "You're the one we want to see more of."

"Everything in this country is peculiar," said Woolley as he surveyed the billiards table in the Hotel Metropolis. "I've never seen a table quite this size and I've never seen a rack full of white balls. What are the rules?"

"Simple," said Arturas Martynas. "Whoever sinks eight balls first wins the game. The red one is the cue ball."

"Why can't the cue ball be white, the way it is in America? And the table is huge!" said Woolley. "The balls barely fit the pockets."

"This is how the game is played here. What did you play in America?" asked Adamonis.

"Eight ball, mostly. In Austria they liked English snooker, but the pockets were bigger."

Adamonis had taken an early lunch to introduce Woolley to Martynas, who was living at the hotel for a few days yet again because he and his wife had found it unbearable to be in the same apartment together. He no longer brought his own sheets and regretted he had not invested in the hotel's renovation because more and more foreigners were staying there, they had a decent kitchen, and service was improving. At a side table the barman provided snacks of tongue in aspic, herring, fried cheese with black pepper, and rye bread, and since they were early, only champagne to drink.

Adamonis put the bill on his tab because he had not been paid for some time. Money was not really a problem for him while he lived with his sister, and the sums were more than enough when they eventually came through. But things were more desperate for those who worked for him on lower salaries. Miss Pinigelis had sat down suddenly in his office one day, and when he finally pried the truth out of her, he discovered she had not eaten for a while because of arrears in salary.

He could not have his staff fainting from hunger. A miserable and disreputable tavern operated around the corner, and using ministry promissory notes, he had the place emptied and cleaned up and turned into a canteen for his department's employees. It served soup and bread and dumplings, simple comfort food the employee could also take home. The modest cost of meals was deducted from their salaries whenever their pay finally came in, and the canteen still made a small profit.

Martynas was surprisingly limber for a short, stout man, and he could lean over the billiards table with one foot in the air behind him and still sink a difficult long shot. Clearly he was a man who had wasted a lot of time in his life. Woolley was a reasonably good player.

"What sort of business do you intend to get into?" Martynas asked after they had played awhile, gotten to know one another, and drunk a glass of champagne.

"I have an open mind," said Woolley. "I did consider building, but from what I've seen of the tradesmen here . . ."

"Infrastructure is your best bet," said Martynas. "People don't have much money yet. You could try export because the food is so cheap here, but you'd have to suffer foreign tariff barriers."

"Your government doesn't have any money either," said Woolley.

The red cue ball clicked against the white ones, sometimes sinking them but more often just rearranging their pattern on the table.

"But it will. We have three million people here and once the taxation is regulated, there will be a steady flow of money."

"I'm beginning to wonder if that will ever happen," said Woolley. "It's a wasteland."

"I prefer to think of it as a frontier," said Martynas, "or a fresh new world where anything is possible. You just need the imagination and the energy to create the right business. Maybe I can help. I have a little capital of my own. I understand you have some resources as well. We could look around this country together and see where the best opportunity lies."

"I'm not opposed," said Woolley, and as if to underscore his commitment, he sank a ball.

"And you, Mr. Adamonis," said Martynas. "You're an intelligent man. We're in a potential paradise here and as a man named for Adam you'd be likely to have some good luck."

He demurred. Martynas had a very partial memory of the biblical stories.

Adamonis was fascinated by the variability of Woolley's character. Drunk, he had been a clown. At home, he
sounded peevish. At the billiards table, he seemed cau-
tious, as every businessman had a right to be, but without
the zest of an entrepreneur. Woolley was curious about
the country, asking many, many questions about its farmers, government, and army. It did not help that Woolley
still spoke through his nose, which gave that unfortunate
nasal twang to his speech. It was tempting to dismiss him
as a fool, but this did not explain his success in life and his
success with Lily.

16

"ARE YOU ALL RIGHT?" Miss Pinigelis asked from the door of Adamonis's office.

He had just completed a presentation on the structure of military counterintelligence to a commission of ministerial assistant deputies, and he was straightening his papers in his office.

Adamonis looked up at this question. It was unusually familiar, and yet he was grateful. They worked very closely day and night, but ever since he had noticed her hunger and established the canteen, she was slightly tender toward him in a way he was unaccustomed to anywhere but at home, and even there his sister administered rough sympathy, as if she were the older sister instead of the younger one.

"It's those tiresome presentations," Adamonis said. "When I'm really working, I don't feel tired, but standing before a delegation of bureaucrats somehow wears me down."

"We're bureaucrats too."

"Don't I know it? But we can't let the rubber stamps and dust weigh down our hearts."

"My heart isn't weighed down," said Miss Pinigelis. "If

you read a little poetry in the evenings, you'll find it helps to maintain your spirits."

Miss Pinigelis was a blessing, a beautiful cross between a nurse and a bodyguard, a wonder in a white blouse and grey business suit with a skirt that fell to halfway between her knees and ankles. With tight curls and an expression that moved between charming and stern, as the situation required, she could usually be counted on to work late if the situation demanded it. She wore the same suit daily, having no other, but she varied her blouses and her modest jewellery. This afternoon she was wearing a silver brooch on her lapel, which gave a little sparkle to her outfit. Indeed, she seemed to sparkle generally.

"There's a Captain Silvester outside who's keen to see you privately."

"Who is this Silvester?"

"Assistant to our military attaché in Moscow. He was actually among the men in the meeting just now."

"He didn't say anything then. Do you think it's important?"

"He looks very serious. You'd better see him. Should I bring in tea?"

"No, I've had enough today. I think I'll burst if I take any more and it will just make him stay longer if he has a cup in front of him. Show him in."

Captain Silvester was in uniform, a solidly built bald man whose eyebrows were arched slightly, giving prominence to remarkably direct and wide eyes. He had come, he said, to flesh out the picture of the activities in the Lithuanian embassy in Moscow, a city with many tensions. The offer was slightly odd. Silvester was not following the usual channels for this sort of information. Adamonis asked him to take a chair on the other side of his desk rather than at his small conference table. If the meeting became tedious, Adamonis could point to one of the briefs in a stack and claim he needed to get on with his work. He did not turn on a lamp although it was getting dark in the office. His window faced north and the room became shadowy later in the day.

Lithuania had reasonably good relations with the Soviet Union, at least on the surface, primarily because the Soviets detested Poland, which had beaten them so badly in the field the year before. Even so, the Soviets tried to run communist cells within Lithuania, just to stay in the game. But the Soviet Union itself was still chaotic, Silvester pointed out, from the after-effects of the German war, the revolution, and everything else.

Famine continued in Moscow, men and women were dying of starvation on the streets. The Lithuanian embassy was a small island of relative prosperity in this devastated land because the ministry of external affairs supplied everything from pencils to sausages by diplomatic courier train cars running out of Kaunas.

Silvester was talking too long, stalling somehow. Adamonis turned on his desk lamp to better illuminate the man's face. There was some kind of struggle going on inside him. Adamonis offered him a cigarette and he accepted, but Silvester wasn't a regular smoker. He didn't inhale the smoke, expelling it in puffs from his mouth like a teenager trying on a grownup habit.

"Why are you telling me all this?" Adamonis finally asked.

Silvester laughed, reached forward from his leather chair to butt out the unfinished cigarette, and then looked up at him.

"It's a pretty serious matter. I wonder if the affair won't frighten you off. I heard you could be trusted, but it's difficult to begin."

"I can't do anything until I hear what you have to say."

"I want this country to be clean, you understand? I'm sick of corruption."

"I share your feelings."

Silvester stood up and walked a half-circle around the room as he gathered his resolve, and then he came forward and leaned across the desk, shook Adamonis's hand as if they were striking a bargain.

"Please sit down," said Adamonis, and Silvester did as he asked.

"Something has been going on at the embassy for months."

Some embassy staff seemed to be doing too well for people on government payroll. Paintings and silverware, bottles of old brandy and even furniture moved through the building, and probably many other goods. This black market game was dangerous, at the very least an embarrassment. Worse, if they were caught, the traders could be blackmailed and turned into Soviet agents.

"Does the station chief know this?" Adamonis asked.

Silvester shifted in his chair, paused, and shifted again. "He must."

"And the military attaché, your superior?"

"I think so. And he's not the only one."

Silvester explained the boxcars regularly left Kaunas for the Moscow embassy, each of them closed with a diplomatic seal granting the shipment immunity at the border. But not all these boxcars ended up at the embassy or even in Moscow proper. Some were diverted to another site and unpacked using false bills of lading. Besides office supplies and food, these boxcars carried other goods, primarily saccharine but also cocaine and morphine.

Saccharine was in high demand on the black market because it was so light and easy to trade. In a way, saccharine was worse than cocaine because in times of famine it gave the illusion of sweetness but had no calories in it. A man could die of starvation with a sweet taste on his lips.

"Can you give me a list of names?" Adamonis asked.

"I have no concrete proof, you understand. Who would have to be the witness against them if any charges were laid?"

"You."

"I can't spy on my colleagues. I don't think I'm capable of that level of duplicity."

"It wouldn't be duplicitous. The smugglers are the duplicitous ones."

Silvester was afraid. He might hate what was going on, but he did not want to ruin the careers of his colleagues. In a small country, enemies had a way of reappearing.

"Haven't the Soviets noticed any of this?" Adamonis asked.

"That's what's so interesting," said Silvester. "They must know it's going on because they seem to know everything else, but they're letting it pass."

"They'll let this go on until they find the right moment to blackmail the smugglers," said Adamonis.

"Exactly. Well?"

"So you think your ministry knows about this."

"Oh, yes."

"Do you think the minister of external affairs is involved in this personally?"

"I can't see how the operation could be carried out without him."

That gave Adamonis pause. Whatever he thought of the cabinet, and some of them were certainly fools, most were also idealists trying to recreate an ancient state in a modern world. But now this.

"I'll start this investigation from my end," Adamonis said. "When do you return to Moscow?"

"In two days. I'm visiting with my mother for a while."

"I may need to contact you again. If you find out anything else after you return, you can write to me from Moscow through the diplomatic post."

"No, I can't. The Soviets have a way of finding out everything. Even here in Kaunas, I'm not sure I'm not being followed. That's why I joined the commission this afternoon, in order not to be seen coming here on my own. I even have a couple of friends waiting for me outside so I'm not seen to be leaving alone either."

"I'll have my men watch you in Kaunas," Adamonis said. "Tell me where you're staying."

17

LANDA coolly turned his chair away from Adamonis and looked away. It was not exactly the reaction that Adamonis had expected.

"Aside from the Woolley embarrassment, you've done well in this position," Landa said. Adamonis could barely hear him. "Do you know what you're getting yourself into?"

"I think I might have some idea."

Landa swivelled in his chair and looked at him as if Adamonis had just admitted to a serious illness. "I'm not so sure you do. Have you thought about where the goods come from before they're packed in Kaunas? Germany, I expect, and I'm pretty sure no duty was paid on them on the way into Lithuania, so there's smuggling on both ends."

"That's a matter for the police."

"Not really. You don't want to do just half the job, do you? Nail the source first. You could bring in your sister organization in the ministry of the interior."

"You mean Novak?"

Landa didn't seem to hear him.

"If you could stop the goods from coming in, you'd stop the black market in Moscow without creating a scandal."

"They'd just find other goods to sell," said Adamonis.

"And by the way, I do mean Novak. His agency might know about this already. Would you like a cigarette?"

Landa offered him a lacquered box. The cigarettes inside were a luxury brand of some kind with black paper along the length and gold paper at the filter. The government had recently banned the importation of cigarettes to grow the local market. Landa spoke as if reading his mind. "I hope these cigarettes are still good. I've had them for some time." Adamonis lit up. The tobacco did not taste stale at all.

"Novak's agency doesn't have the brain power to uncover this sort of smuggling."

"Oh, come on. Novak's people do some good work too." The smoke from their cigarettes was rising to the ceiling and hanging there. Landa leaned back in his seat and put on a professorial tone. "I'd like you to consider something else. How often is your pay late?"

"All the time."

"Now imagine what it must be like to work in the Moscow embassy. You managed to create a canteen for your department because you had a problem that couldn't be solved by regular means. The same may be true there. But their lives are much more tense than ours. Imagine for a moment that you have agents in Moscow and you're the one running them. Agents won't wait to get paid. They're risking their lives for the money. So if you're supposed to be the paymaster, how do you pay them? You and your canteen. See what I mean?"

"We don't know that's true."

"We don't know it's untrue. This is a shaky government with no money trying to build a new country. Stability is very important. If the Poles ever did want to march on Kaunas, nothing would suit them better than a cabinet in disarray."

"What are you saying?"

Landa leaned forward, as if to share a confidence.

"Muckraking."

Landa looked very young and very old at the same time.

"You're going to make enemies of powerful people. Foreign spies all around us and here you are, chasing your own people. Most ministers are Christian Democrats and they'll see this investigation as political."

"It's not."

"It will be whether you like it or not. Ask yourself if it's worth destroying everything for the sake of a few bad apples."

"Who talked about destroying anything?"

"Investigate some more. But don't do anything until you speak to me again."

"And you'll cover my back?"

"I'll do what I can."

Adamonis went down the stairs from his office to the cellars, where the judicial advisers had their offices. The place was always packed with stacks of legal cases tied up with ribbon and furred with dust.

When Adamonis asked for their head counsel, the man needed to be roused from an armchair where he had fallen asleep and let several pages from his current brief fall to the floor. He wasn't embarrassed at all. He wiped his eyeglasses on his handkerchief and pushed his long white hair away from his eyes as Adamonis explained what he might need to do. It took the head counsel a while to take it all in. He assured Adamonis he'd be breaking no laws if he seized the illicit goods while they were under diplomatic seal, but told him to be sure he had solid proof rather than allegations before he presented him with a case. He could then put the wheels of justice in motion along with the prosecutor.

"And how quickly do the wheels of justice turn?" Adamonis asked.

"In due course."

Head counsel did not exactly fill Adamonis with confidence. He had been in his position since czarist times and was like a badger, so deep in his administrative burrow that no political storm could discomfit him.

Anyone Adamonis used in the matter might be subject to some ill winds as well, so he asked Johnny and Pranaitis to start familiarizing themselves with the routine of the railway yards. They were low enough down the hierarchy that they wouldn't suffer if a political storm broke.

18

ADAMONIS was studying some dossiers when Pranaitis put his head into the office.

"You'll need to be leaving soon if you want to make it to the wedding."

There was no end to paperwork. Adamonis had so little time, but the country wedding of one of their clan had given Anele an opportunity to bully him unmercifully until he agreed to attend over the weekend.

Pranaitis lingered by the doorway.

"Is there something else?" Adamonis asked.

"I was wondering if you'd need to have the car overnight if I drove you to the wedding first. I was hoping to take a lady friend to Pazaislis. I could come back the next day to pick you up."

Pazaislis was a former Benedictine monastery, now a convent popular with visitors, who rented rooms from the nuns. It lay on the way to the country wedding. There were so few cars in the country that even ministers' wives loaned theirs out to friends, and drivers gave rides to people walking along the roadside.

Miss Pinigelis was waiting by the car with Pranaitis when Adamonis showed up. He had mixed emotions, pleased for them, yet a little sad too, an emotion he managed to quash.

Miss Pinigelis joined Pranaitis in the front seat while Adamonis sat in the back. He spent his time looking through some of his briefs, but noticed that the two in the front held hands when Pranaitis was not changing gears.

The monastery was only a dozen kilometres outside town, beyond a park on the Nemunas River. When they passed through the woods and drove out into the open land, the nuns in white headdresses and grey habits were like doves across the landscape, working the fields. The monastery complex had a baroque church, a little dilapidated, and cloisters on either side. Miss Pinigelis said goodbye and went to register for the night on the women's side, and Adamonis took a moment to step into the church itself.

The space was compact for all its crumbling baroque grandeur, yet it was also very high, three storeys, one level upon another up to the dome on top, with intricate scrollwork and many religious figures in bas-relief between the windows. Two countrywomen with kerchiefs on their heads muttered prayers from the front pew and a couple of men were kneeling separately.

Adamonis was not a religious man, but he did not object to religion. Churches had been happy places for him when he was a child, places where his parents met their friends. He had been restless during long masses in his childhood, but now this church was a calm and quiet place, except for the muttering of the others.

He thought of Pinigelis and Pranaitis in the front seat, shyly holding hands when they thought he couldn't see them. This sort of feeling was not like him at all, and yet the odd mood carried him as he stepped back out into the sunlight. The birds in the nearby orchard were singing, a chorus of rebuke for a man who read dossiers in the back of his car when the rest of the natural world was in full exultation.

Unable to concentrate on his papers, Adamonis looked out the window at the fields, forests, and villages. The countryside was only a generation away and still exerted a nostalgic gravitational pull.

The roads became progressively worse while they drove toward the Adamonis clan's home village, not much more than a hamlet. They lurched through lanes where geese honked behind wattle fences and they drove by thatched-roof houses where dogs and children ran alongside when the car slowed. Not much had changed for decades, maybe even centuries. They had to stop for a woman grazing her cow in the rich grass of the ditches. Adamonis wondered if the modern world back in Kaunas was nothing more than a dream and if reality lay here.

It was an unusually warm day. He rolled down the window and the scent of lime blossoms was thick in the air and when they drove past overhanging branches, Adamonis turned to look back to see the snow of falling petals. They came up a hill and through a copse of trees and the landscape below opened into fields with the clan's hamlet by a stream in the valley. Traditional music played in the distance, by a trio of violin, accordion, and drum doing a scratchy march.

The nine houses in the hamlet all belonged to cousins and uncles. At each end was a large house, very big indeed, with a steep thatched roof. Behind one of them stood a massive oak under which were tables covered with linen tablecloths. The trio played at the edge of a nearby orchard, whose tree trunks were painted white and whose branches held the small fruit of early summer. The grassy field nearby was mown close to the earth and set aside for dances.

Perhaps seventy of his relatives both close and distant as well as their hired hands lived in this hamlet, and twice as many had come from surrounding villages for the wedding. He had missed the morning marriage ceremony, but he arrived in time to see the wedding couple coming back from the church on a wagon decorated with wreaths of flowers. A parade of wedding guests followed behind them, many of the women in traditional colourful folk costumes, and now they fanned out around the tables set for the meal.

He watched all of this from beside the car with a brief-case in his hand and Pranaitis at his side. A flock of country children came, flying toward the car to inspect it. The children crawled all over the exterior and he let them examine the car until one of his aunts showed up to take him to a room that had been set aside for him. Adamonis took a handful of candies from his briefcase and threw them onto the grass to distract the children and to give Pranaitis a chance to turn around and go back the way he had come.

City cousins were like visiting royalty to those who'd stayed behind on the farms, so he was given a clean, bright farmhouse room for the night while some of the lesser visitors could expect to sleep on hay in the barn. The walls were papered in a bright floral pattern and the room held a chair and small table with a white pitcher and basin upon it, and the bed had a patterned natural linen cover laid between high foot- and headboards. He set down his brief-case and hung up his spring coat as well as his hat because most of the men he'd seen were bareheaded. Then he sat down for a moment to breathe in the smell of the room, old wood and lamp oil, and to look through the window at the party outside.

His newlywed mother and father had lived for a while in this house, and for all he knew, had slept in this very same room before they moved to Kaunas. They had all continued to come to this place over summers throughout his childhood and youth, right to the end of high school, when he left for St. Petersburg. He had played with many of the wedding guests as a child, but he hadn't seen some of them in almost a dozen years.

"Does it take you back?"

Anele stood at the door. She was dressed in a wine-coloured dress with a dropped waist. She had her hair parted in the middle and wore a headband with her hair gathered in a braided bun at either side of her head.

"You look like you're dressed for a dance at the Hotel Metropolis," he said.

"I bring a bit of the country when I'm in the city, and I bring a bit of the city when I'm in the country. It's good for them here to see what the greater world looks like. God only knows they don't get away very much."

"Do you miss this place?" he asked.

"It's good for the children."

"But not for you?"

"It's all right. Our parents left this life behind. There's no going back full-time. But you know, you might be able to find someone appropriate for your own life here." He did not understand. "A country wife is what I had in mind."

He laughed. "One who can spin and weave? Milk a cow in a pinch?"

"Your secretary grew up on a farm and now look at her. She's very urban. There are plenty of lovely young women like her who could adapt just as well, but for the sake of your children, don't choose a first cousin."

"Maybe I've overstayed my welcome at your house."

"That's not what I mean. You're welcome there for as long as you like. For a lifetime, if you want. But you're my brother and you're in danger of turning into an old bachelor. Irregular hours and skipped meals. Drinks with compatriots in the officers' mess. Cigarettes burning in the ashtray all the time and sudden departures in the middle of the night. It can't be healthy."

"No."

"Then why do you live that way?"

"I'm trying to help build something. It takes time. You know that."

"Let someone else do it. What you do is dangerous and you've spent all those years in danger during the war. If you give up everything for the machinery of public life, not even public life, just life in the shadows, you'll turn into a shadow yourself."

"We're living in a precarious world here. Once the public sphere is in order, I'll be able to think of myself."

"There is no order in the public sphere. You'll be like the conductor on an infinite train, checking the tickets of passengers in car after car after car. There's no end to it. And in the meantime, it's a beautiful day, filled with eligible young women."

"For heaven's sake, you make it sound like I'm going to buy a cow. Did you go shopping for your husband?"

"No, I was lucky. But I didn't let the opportunity pass when it presented itself."

"And I won't let the opportunity pass if it presents itself either. So let's go outside and make the best of it."

He rose to go, taking two bottles of Bénédictine from his briefcase to contribute to the festivities.

It was, as Anele had said, an excellent day, with music playing and children running around and many women, both young and old, all dressed in their best clothes. He walked over to the sweets table, which bore mountains of *krustai*, crisp pastries light as air that broke with a *snap* and dusted your vest with powdered sugar. There were dark honey cakes, a punch bowl filled with fruit compote, apple cake, poppy seed cake, a napoleon, and the crowning wedding cake, the tree cake, almost a metre and a half high. A tall, wiry woman with a very long wooden spoon in her hand stood at the table with her arms crossed and a fierce look on her face.

"No cake until after the meal," she said.

"Right."

A few bottles of homemade liqueur already stood on the table, and he was reaching up to put one of his Béné-dictine bottles beside them when he felt a smart *whack* across his hand and dropped the bottle on the grass.

"I said no cake until after the main meal."

"I was just putting a bottle of liqueur on the table."

"No cake, I said."

This violent cake guardian was either not entirely sober or not entirely sane.

"Didn't you hear what I said? I almost broke a bottle of French Bénédictine thanks to you."

"I'd say I was sorry if I was sure what you say is true, but weddings like this always bring out the riffraff. How do I know those bottles aren't filled with water?"

"You'll never know now, because I'm not leaving them here. That's for certain."

"Exactly! A ruse, just as I expected. It would be a shame if the family came here after the meal and found all the cakes were gone."

It wasn't his habit to waste time with rude people and lunatics. He was partly amused by the woman's cake monomania and partly appalled that she might be related to him in some way. He went instead to another table, the gift table, and placed the bottles there so the bride and groom could decide when to drink them, and then he wandered over to the dance floor. The bride and the groom were dancing a very long dance indeed, and an aunt was making the rounds with a bowl, encouraging people to put money into it for the young couple. He raised a few eyebrows when he put in a handful of banknotes. His back pay had finally come in and he felt flush. He had no sooner put the money in the bowl than he was struck a powerful blow across the back with the flat of someone's hand. He turned in anger and was seized in a bear hug by one of his cousins who lifted him into the air and squeezed hard, shook him so his ankles practically knocked against each other.

"Well, cousin, you didn't break, so there's some country bones left in you still, but you're as heavy as a stuffed pig, so you must be sitting at a desk all day long."

This was Adamonis's cousin Stan, a strapping boy he had grown up with in the summers of his childhood, an arm wrestler, a competitive tree climber, a darer. The eldest brother of the bride, he was dressed in a fine country suit and tie that barely managed to hold him in. When he laughed, his shoulders shook, and he laughed often.

"But you look reasonably good, for all your fat city ways," said Stan. "Just think, if your father had stayed behind on the farm, about a fifth of all this would be yours now. Cow shit, horse shit, chicken shit, muddy earth, and work from dawn until dusk. Are you sorry he left it all behind?"

"It's beautiful now."

"Yes, it is. It's a beautiful day. A day off from working in shit. Have you had anything to drink?"

"I haven't even eaten anything yet."

"All the better! The first shot needs to be had on an empty stomach. It increases the effect."

Adamonis went with him to what might as well have been designated as the men's table, where there was a barrel of beer and a crowd of men and much more hearty slapping on the back. He was given a shot of vodka and a mug of beer. He had a quick drink and then wandered out among the dancers and eaters and children to say his hellos to other cousins and relatives he had not seen for years.

The warmth in the air offered promise and the music was almost charming, at least from a distance. Adamonis was walking near the cake table when he heard the cry of another victim of the long wooden spoon, and looked that way to see Lily holding one wrist with her hand.

As it happened, cousin Stan was standing nearby and he had seen the whole thing. He walked up to the cake guard, snatched the wooden spoon from her hand, and broke it across his knee. She burst into tears.

"I was only trying to protect the sweets," she said.

"You're jealous of the bride and should be ashamed of yourself. Now get away from here or I'll spank you."

"You wouldn't dare."

"I'd lift your skirts and slap your bare bottom."

Stan turned to Lily, and Adamonis came up beside her too. She was nursing her wrist but smiling admiringly at Stan. He reached for a *krustas* and offered it to her.

"Please take one of these and consider it medicine for your wrist."

"I will."

Stan bowed ironically and made his way back to the circle of men.

"Why, Mr. Justas Adamonis," she said, biting into the pastry, "you mean they let you out of your office to come to weddings?"

"They open the cage and let us fly free from time to time. Where's Mr. Woolley?"

"Up to some business deal with Arturas Martynas."

Lily was wearing a traditional costume of linen blouse and skirt, with a woven apron, sash, and vest.

"You've gone native," he said.

"That's what I came here for, remember? To revisit my childhood."

"But I didn't realize you were going to stay."

"Why not?"

"Are you having a good time?"

"The sound of the country music is sweet."

"Please, the band sounds like a headache. I have to say I'm astonished by your ongoing romance with the countryside. Nostalgia doesn't usually last once you've returned to the place you've been dreaming of. It's a dream you wake up from."

"So what keeps you here?"

"I suppose it's home, after all."

Even in national costume, Lily stood out from the others because she was an American and she carried herself in the free manner of Americans. Anything was possible for them. Lily's hair came down to her shoulders and in the breeze it blew back a little to reveal a long, smooth neck.

"Do you want to go back to the scene of your heroism?"

He wasn't sure what she meant.

"The place where you saved me when I was a little girl." He was looking at her hair moving slightly in the breeze. "You're blushing," she said.

"I'm too old to blush."

"Never. I think I've uncovered the sensitive side of a very busy man. Come on."

The well she was talking about lay two house yards over from the festivities, and they walked there across the grass. The hay had been mown for the wedding, but in the other yards it was already a few inches tall and yellow and red wildflowers whose names he did not know speckled the green way. A horse behind a fence neighed at them.

They came to the yard with its well, with its bucket set on the rim and a wooden cover to keep out debris.

"It's hard to imagine you were ever small enough to fit in the bucket and go down."

"Open the lid," she said. "As I recall it, the water in this well was very sweet."

He did as she asked and then lowered the bucket, let it fill, and raised it back up and rested it on the rim. There was a tin cup hanging from a string. She dipped the cup into the water and tasted it, smiled, and looked up at him.

"It's delicious. Try some."

She reached out with the cup and held it as he sipped. The water was very good, very cool on that warm day. She set the cup down.

"This is belated thanks," she said, and she leaned forward and kissed him on the cheek.

She waited, and when Adamonis said nothing, she looked down to her feet. "I think I really am hungry now," she said.

They returned to the party and took plates to serve themselves from the feast. In the mix of relatives and old friends, Lily was swept into the company of women and he into the company of men who went to see the traditional opening of a special cask of liquor. This was an oak cask of *starka* that had been buried by the groom's father when he was born. It was vodka flavoured with apple leaves and linden blossoms. The barrel was a metre high and the wax over the bunghole was still thick. Stan brushed off the earth and brought a spigot that he jammed into the bunghole. He let the rust-coloured liquor run into a pitcher, and the father of the groom poured some into a glass and held it to the light to examine its clarity. This liquor did not burn at all, but went down smoothly, leaving an aroma of wood and herbs and ever so slightly of the earth from which it had been taken.

The women serving at the food table heaped Adamonis's plate with warm suckling pig and potatoes and cabbage and laid a buttered piece of heavy black bread on top, and told him to return for sausages and goose once he had eaten his first plateful.

The food was heavy but the liquor was strong and the two balanced each other as he sat with the men, who asked him a hundred questions about life in Kaunas as if it were as far away as Paris. Was it true, they asked, that the children wore shoes even in summer? And did men sell ice cream from boxes around their necks, and if that was true, how did they keep the ice cream from melting? Then they spoke of their farms and the price of pigs for export to Germany. In this conversation, between mouthfuls of food, he was offered drinks he could not refuse: *sermuksnine*, a liquor flavoured with rowan tree berries; *stumbrine*, a fragrant vodka in which a blade of aromatic bison grass had been placed; and when he complained that he could drink no more, a shot of *trejos devynerios*, an infusion similar to Bénédictine, but not so sweet, and tasting of the fields.

He needed to get away from the overly generous relatives, and he walked toward a copse of trees. A few men lay propped against small haystacks, snoring through the early evening. Fearing that someone would call to him with an offer of food or drink, he made his way just inside the trees and behind some bushes, and there he found a pine needle bed, which was still warm from the day's fading sun, and he sat down and loosened his tie. Then he lay back and closed his eyes.

19

WHEN Adamonis awoke to the sound of a voice, the light had faded and the air had cooled. The smell of pine was thick about him; his head had cleared, yet he felt elated, still lifted by the alcohol but not so much as to be weary.

"I saw you go in here an hour ago, but I never saw you come out. I thought the wolves had eaten you." Lily was sitting down on the pine needles beside him.

"How long have you been here?" he asked.

"A little while. All the young men want to spin the American on the dance floor. Except for you."

He felt drunk on the smells of the forest and the air was charged with more oxygen than he was accustomed to down in the city. He could think of no other explanation for what followed.

"I've wanted to take you in my arms from the first moment I saw you," he said. "I've just been waiting for the opportunity."

He didn't know what made him blurt this out, but even a man who kept most secrets couldn't keep them all.

"What's taken you so long?" she asked, and then looked away.

He put his hand on her shoulder, hoping that she would turn to look at him. She didn't turn, but she reached up with her opposite hand and put it on his. He reached forward to turn her chin. They were very close, and the only thing to do was to kiss her.

He had not had a woman's lips on his for some time, and he wondered now why that was. They kissed gently, tentatively, but after a few moments they pulled away. They looked at each other, and kissed again, and then lay back in the pine needles. When they had been kissing for a long time, they pulled slightly apart, and she stroked his face.

He should have done nothing to spoil that mood, but by reflex, aware of dangers, he articulated one of them.

"What about your husband?" he asked.

She shook her head. "Why do you ask about him? He's a very cold man."

"But he's your husband."

She sat up, annoyed. She ran her fingers through her hair as if waking up from sleep.

"I suppose you're right. I owe so much to him. But."

"But what?"

"He is what he is."

"He indulges you. He brought you to this country. There can't be much in this place for him."

"Why do you want to talk about him?"

"Because I'm jealous of him."

"So you want me?"

"More than anything else, above all else. Come on. Lie down beside me. I want to kiss you again."

"Even though I'm a married woman? Doesn't the chief of counterintelligence have a reputation to preserve?"

"Why are you saying that?"

"I know more about you than you think," said Lily. "And I know you have a good heart."

"Have you looked into it already?"

"I could feel it from the first time we met. You like to be in control of things, to be the bluff host. You had to work so hard to get where you are and you had to toughen yourself during the war. But you're masking part of yourself. That's not the real you. There's more to you inside."

"How can you see inside of me?" he asked.

"I just can. From the first time we met—I mean as adults. I looked across the crowd of people when Robert and I stepped out of the car. I looked right at you. Do you remember?"

"I was surprised. I didn't remember you then."

"I was a girl the last time we met."

"But you're not a girl now."

"No."

She lay beside him again. Her blouse was buttoned to the very top, and he reached up there awkwardly to undo the button. She helped him, and they were making good progress when he became aware of a commotion back at the party. The music had stopped and a car horn was sounding.

He sat up. People were calling his name.

"What is it?" she asked.

"Someone's looking for me."

"You could ignore it. You could say you drank too much and were sleeping somewhere in the fields."

"It's the car horn. Pranaitis has come for me. Something's up. I have to go now."

"And leave me here?"

He stood and brushed the pine needles from his clothes. "You can't come out with me. Wait ten or fifteen minutes. I'll be gone by then."

"You're leaving?"

"I have to. Will you be all right by yourself?"

"Oh, I can take care of myself all right. Don't worry about that. But I wonder when I'll see you again."

"As soon as I can."

He helped her up and he brushed the needles from her clothes, as best as he could in the darkness. He reached forward to do up the buttons on her blouse and he was about to say goodbye when she pulled him to her and kissed him again.

20

STAN led a band of cousins looking for Adamonis with torches in their hands. They searched among the drunks who were sleeping across the landscape, and in that search they came across two couples that were unhappy to be interrupted on that warm night.

It never occurred to any of the country guests that it was odd for an employee of the bureau of statistics to have a car appear for him in the middle of the night. The bureau of statistics was unimaginably remote and powerful, and that it should be a cover for another department was beyond comprehension.

Anele was waiting for her brother by the house and had his briefcase ready for him.

"Were you getting to know someone?" Anele asked.

"I had just fallen asleep."

"With a tube of lipstick? Wipe your cheek. I'm a little surprised, actually, but in a good way. Not that many country girls use lipstick."

"I guess the nation is modernizing faster than we realized."

A good forty awestruck revellers were milling around

the car by the time he made his way to it. Pranaitis was standing by the door.

"I'm sorry to interrupt you, but I got a phone call."

"That's all right. You can tell me the rest in the car." Pranaitis took the driver's seat and Adamonis walked around to join him in the front. They were about to pull away when Stan tapped on the window.

"Here's a little something for the way back," he said, and he passed over a half bottle of *starka* and a two-litre bottle of beer. Not to be outdone, his wife passed Adamonis a heavy package of smoked meat, farm bread, a cheese, and a pot of butter. Country people never let anyone leave without a gift of food. And to them, this would be an especially memorable event, a wedding at which one of the guests was so important that a car came for him in the middle of the night.

"Well?" Adamonis asked.

"I got a call from Chepas while I was at the convent. Mr. Landa wants to see you right away."

"No more detail?"

"No."

Adamonis settled into his place and braced himself as Pranaitis drove as fast and as best he could, the deep potholes playing the headlights up and down the walls of trees at roadside.

"Just keep us out of the ditch. I'd rather arrive late than get stuck out here."

Whatever his other failings, Pranaitis was good at the wheel. Once they hit a flatter stretch, Adamonis offered to light a cigarette for him, but he shook his head and stared straight ahead. Adamonis's emotions veered as wildly as the headlights. He thought of Lily, how things might have turned out if he had not been called away.

"Miss Pinigelis will be waiting for us at the monastery," said Pranaitis.

"We can't afford to go looking for her."

"Don't worry. She'll be ready."

Pinigelis had walked out the long laneway from the monastery and was standing at the side of the road in her raincoat with a small bag at her side. She didn't wave, just picked up her satchel from the road when they drew close and got into the back seat when she saw Adamonis was in the front.

"What do we do first?" she asked as soon as she was in the car and they were moving again. She was leaning forward, hanging over the centre of the seat, so close that he could feel her curls brush by his ear.

"Where does Landa want to meet us?" Adamonis asked.

"In his office. Chepas is waiting for us in our own office and Miss Pinigelis and I will be there too. We'll be ready if there's anything you need us need to do."

It was the tail end of the night when Adamonis came down the hall toward Landa's office. Most of the lights were off in the corridors, and a skeleton crew of half a dozen men sat scattered among various desks outside. Landa had his office door open with only the desk lamp on, a low light that didn't illuminate his face directly.

"I wanted you to get the news from me before reading it in the morning papers," said Landa. Adamonis had barely entered the room and he sat down in a chair without taking off his hat or his coat. Landa waited awhile before going on. "Your Captain Silvester was shot and killed this afternoon."

"Where?"

"In his apartment in Moscow. Now listen, I know what you're going to think. But there's more you need to know. He was having an affair. There was a married woman with him and when her husband found them together, he shot him."

"So they know who did it?"

"The husband doesn't deny it. He doesn't even regret it. How well did you know Silvester?"

"I only met him once in my office."

"How did he strike you?"

"A boy scout. Who else would have gone to the trouble to blow the whistle?"

"A boy scout with a selective conscience. He didn't have one when it came to personal matters."

"Maybe that's true and maybe it isn't. The public and private spheres aren't the same."

"No, but sometimes there's a link."

"Do you have any more details?" Adamonis asked.

"Not many. The ambassador called the minister of external affairs, who called me. What I wanted you to be clear about is this—they have the shooter and they have the motive. We shouldn't jump to conclusions."

"What did the minister say?"

"He was furious. He claimed Silvester had damaged our reputation abroad."

"So he blamed the dead man. Do we know anything about the killer?"

"His name is Zeludkov, an officer in the Red Army."

I wish I could have a conversation with him."

"Impossible, obviously."

"Second-best would be to interview the staff at the embassy."

"Not much chance of that either. What if your old friend Dzerzhinsky looked you up? Besides, you have too many ongoing cases now."

Adamonis looked at Landa, but most of his face was in shadow.

"I didn't know you kept such close track of all my cases. Maybe they knew Silvester was on to them. Or he might just have worn the wrong attitude. A self-righteous man would stand out in a den of thieves."

"That's a bit extreme, isn't it? Our Moscow embassy as a den of thieves? It's dangerous to start suspecting everyone. It's a disease in this business."

Adamonis took off his hat and opened the front of his coat. It was too hot, especially as he had rushed in and been sweating. But he kept on sweating.

"I've been in this business awhile," he said.

Landa wouldn't like that. Even though Adamonis could not see his expression, a young man would feel the sting of this sort of remark. Adamonis had to be careful not to alienate Landa, but he couldn't simply give in to his superior's sensitivities.

"I think we need to simplify the equation," said Adamonis. "We can't know who had a hand in the killing aside from the assassin himself, but I think we can assume Silvester was killed because of what he told us."

"Slow down. First Moscow is a den of thieves, then a cabal of murderers, and now the minister is involved as well? Why not the whole cabinet? Can't you see where this line of reasoning is taking you?"

"They make me very, very angry. To enrich yourself is one thing. To kill a man is another."

"Control yourself. Are you sure you want to carry on this investigation?"

"Of course."

"More is at stake now. If you still want to chase this down, do it very, very carefully and make sure you have a solid case. Is there anyone in your inner circle you should worry about?"

Adamonis considered. "Chepas is the only one who worked for any length of time before I was hired. Miss Pinigelis has relatives on the other side of the demarcation line with Poland, but I'm not sure the Poles could be connected to this in any way."

"Just play very close to the vest. If the minister of external affairs really is involved, and I'm not admitting that, he might have other eyes in your office. And one more thing. If you do chase this down and people in high places get accused of corruption, they'll turn on you and accuse you of corruption too. So make sure your private affairs are squeaky clean."

"No need to worry."

"You know, even if you succeed at this, there will be consequences."

"What kind of consequences?"

"Unpredictable ones."

Pranaitis, Chepas, and Pinigelis were waiting in his office. Pranaitis had placed the farm package on the table, and Adamonis had him untie the string and Miss Pinigelis found some plates and cups. The dark rye bread was dense and the crust was hard, but the bread itself was moist. The butter smelled very fresh, as it always did when the cows were eating spring grass. Stan's wife had soured the cream before churning it to give the butter extra tang. The smoked meat was fragrant and salty, and Pinigelis took great care to slice it thinly and then placed the slices on the buttered bread. Pranaitis poured out the beer, which foamed up in the cups.

The morning light was beginning to come through the window. They would have to go home to bed soon.

Adamonis proposed a toast to the deceased Captain Silvester and they remained silent a moment in his memory.

"What has Johnny found out about shipping?" he asked Chepas.

"He's been hanging around the rail yards, helping out the loaders there. They've taken him on as a kind of mascot.

He brings them their tea from the station for the sake of the tips and he sits with them on their breaks. They talk to him. They hope for diplomatic shipments to Moscow because they always get big tips of their own when the ministry inspector comes down to put a diplomatic seal on the cars."

"Do they know when the next shipment is due?"

"No. They come irregularly."

"Well, keep him down there and have your shadows check up on him from time to time. I don't want him coming around this office or my home for a while. He's too noticeable in that coat."

Adamonis invited them to finish their beer. He had Miss Pinigelis divide the rest of the farm food among the three of them. He knew Anele would be bringing in a parcel at least as big as the one he had had. Then he opened up the half bottle of *starka* and poured it out in the cups where the beer had been. They toasted the late Captain Silvester one last time, put on their coats, and went home to bed just as the sun was coming up over the rooftops of Kaunas.

Miss Pinigelis's typewriter was clacking loudly outside Adamonis's open office door and he was deep in his briefs on Monday morning when he received a phone call from Lily. He asked her to wait a moment and stood up to close the door. His working world fell away.

"Are you back in Kaunas already?" he asked. "A country wedding usually lasts three days and sometimes more."

"I wanted to find out if you were all right."

He had never received such a call. He had been wondering if he should telephone Lily, but he couldn't be sure he wouldn't get Woolley instead of her. "Dear Lily. It was a very long night and today is probably going to be a long day, but you've lifted my spirits with this call." He had spoken in his best official voice, but now it was hard to know what to say next. Lily caught the tone.

"Thank you for saying so, Mr. Adamonis."

"I don't mean to sound officious. About Saturday night . . ."

"It was a wonderful night," said Lily. "Don't you dare apologize or blame it on the alcohol. I'm just sorry it ended so abruptly."

He was startled, but pleased. "So am I. Is Mr. Woolley back from his travels?" he asked.

"Robert's still away for a few days. I'm wondering when I might see you again."

"As soon as I can get away."

"Today?"

"No. Not today."

"Tomorrow?"

"I'm not sure."

She paused. "I understand," she said uncertainly.

"Oh, Lily, I'm not sure you do. Something is going on at the office. I might be tied up for a while."

"What kind of thing?"

"I can't say."

"Why not?"

"Matters of state. I'm not sure how this is going to play out, but I can't leave the office for a while. As soon as I'm free, I'll call you."

"Robert will be back in a couple of days. It would be better if you could find the time before he returns."

"I'll do my best."

"Just one thing."

"What?"

"I'm not used to being so forward. I hope I'm not embarrassing you."

"I'm not embarrassed at all. I just wish I could get away."

21

AS THE TRAIN from Kaunas rolled into the town of Kybartai, construction workers were replastering the train station walls and laying new cobbles on the road. The town had been flattened during the war, but because it was the main border crossing with German East Prussia, it was rising again in the new season of peace.

Adamonis had not seen Lily much in the days after the wedding. One or the other couldn't get away for more than a few minutes at a time. As for his working life, the tiny country he was serving consisted of interwoven Gordian knots that he was endlessly trying to pick apart. No shipment was being prepared for the Moscow Embassy. Perhaps someone was frightened after Silvester's death and had decided to lie low for a while.

The passengers who were getting off in Lithuania now disembarked, but others remained. Adamonis and Lily sat across from each other in the train compartment at the window seats, sharing the view through the glass. It was not much of a view, just the platform and a kiosk where a young woman sold coffee and sandwiches to travellers. Lily studied this woman as carefully as he did. The woman at that kiosk, whatever the other difficulties in her life, was free. She was young, hardly more than a girl, and when work was done she'd go home in the evening to her husband or her boyfriend, tired, but with news to share with a loved one of the travellers she had seen that day.

Adamonis didn't look at Lily directly, but he couldn't ignore her altogether either. He glanced at Lily and then to the seat beside her, where Woolley sat with his head tilted back and a bloody handkerchief pressed to his nose. His nose.

When sober, Woolley talked about little else besides his nose, his sinusitis, and how much he suffered in Lithuania. He disdained the local specialists and was on his way to see one in Königsberg in German East Prussia. Adamonis had business of his own there, and so Lily and her husband joined him for the trip. Pranaitis sat beside Adamonis, annoyed that he'd been taken away for a few days from his new love, Miss Pinigelis.

To be with Lily in the company of her husband was particularly irritating to Adamonis. The more he thought of Lily, the less he liked to think of Woolley. Maybe it had been a mistake altogether to travel like this. It would have been better to continue to see each other in snatches, to have at least a few moments together in private for rare kisses.

The train finally moved, but only a short distance, to the town of Eydtkuhnen on the German side. Adamonis's counterparts were expecting him, so the documents check was perfunctory.

If the German town had been more impressive than the Lithuanian one, the differences between the two countries was even more dramatic and a little depressing as soon as they rolled into the countryside. The Prussian fields were exquisitely drained—there were no wet patches or bare spots in the fields. Potato plants stood in military rows and even the wheat seemed to stand taller than it did back in

Lithuania. The houses were mostly brick and the roofs were covered in tiles. Not a single thatched roof was to be seen. It was a wonder how a country as well run as this one could have lost the war.

Woolley finally removed the handkerchief from his nose and dabbed at his nostrils with his finger.

"No blood anymore," he said. "I suppose we must be in Germany."

Königsberg was a mass of red brick, with a river wending its way through the city and buildings far taller than anything in Kaunas. Even brick and stone could be bullies, and Adamonis felt the city loom over them like a reproach. The city had a castle with an impressive tower and a cathedral that could hold the entire population of a Lithuanian provincial town. For all his German, Pranaitis had never been to a German city of this size before, and he was agog at the grandness of it all.

"Try not to look provincial," Adamonis said to him, but he intended the comments for himself.

Woolley and Lily were going to check into their hotel and look around the city. Adamonis had immediate business and an invitation for dinner that evening, and Woolley had a meeting with his doctor the next morning, so they agreed to meet for lunch after Woolley's appointment the next day. Adamonis and Pranaitis took a tram to their suburban guesthouse, a place their German counterparts had suggested because the bigger hotels would have the requisite larger number of foreign spies. Adamonis was slightly suspicious of the Germans' preference, but he let it pass. Allies were not exactly the same as friends.

The Königsberg counterintelligence office was the nexus for all of East Prussia, which was an island cut off from the rest of Germany when the Polish Corridor was driven up to the Baltic after the war. If the purpose of architecture was to impress the lesser mortals, the building in which they

met did a good job—it was tall and heavy, like a stone wedding cake, so much so that one felt the Germans had been
there forever and would be there until the end of time.

The Lithuanians were expected, and were led into a
boardroom where a dozen old wolves of the security appa-
ratus were seated, presided over by their chief, Commissar
Ohme, a block of human flesh with a moustache that could
have been lifted off the face of Bismarck. Adamonis envied
him. He had been in his job for twenty-eight years and the
other men at the table for not many fewer. Ohme knew
all there was to know about the comings and goings in
his town and his men were calm and had well-tried skills,
utterly unlike the inexperienced young Lithuanians and
old Russians who worked in Kaunas.

The Lithuanians were junior partners in this meeting,
virtual arrivistes. The Germans had won the war in the
East and occupied not only Lithuania, but also Estonia,
Latvia, and parts of Byelorussia, Poland, and Ukraine. To
the lasting distress of the Germans, the victorious Entente
allies in the West had made them give it all up, and then
they scarred Germany's territorial integrity in the Treaty
of Versailles. The two Lithuanians represented a fragment
of what would have been German eastern territories only
a few years earlier.

Their meeting had to do with mutual interests, the
suppression of the communists, and, wherever possible,
sharing information about the Poles. The Germans could
never quite accept the loss of the Polish "corridor" and
the city of Danzig. The Lithuanians had their own issues
with the Poles. Thus the enemy of their enemy was their
friend. Or should have been.

The Lithuanians came bearing gifts, lists of German
communists who were in hiding in Lithuania. Ohme provided the Lithuanians with a gift as well, the complete
names, addresses, and passport numbers of a convention

of Lithuanian communists who had met in Prussia earlier that year. They were off to a good start.

As the meeting went on, some of the Germans were going out of their way to be friendly, to the point of being avuncular. They spoke of their experiences in Lithuania during the war; some of them had been stationed there during the occupation, and then wanted to hear stories of how things had been in Southern Russia and Ukraine, where Adamonis had been stationed during the revolution.

And then the Germans wanted to reminisce some more. One spoke of the houses he had seen in Lithuania where the residents were so poor that they did not even have chimneys, just openings in the eaves. Another talked about how the cows in Lithuania were very small and did not give much milk. Finally, one said he had never seen so many undernourished horses in his life as he had there.

What had started off as friendly banter was turning into some kind of baiting that Adamonis did not find acceptable. As far as he was concerned, the meeting was over.

Commissioner Ohme protested, but a couple of the other men at the table were smiling behind their hands. Ohme walked down the stairs with Adamonis and Pranaitis, half-heartedly saying that there were matters that still needed to be discussed, and then stood outside on the sidewalk with them, his manner now surprisingly warm.

"I'm sorry you're leaving so soon," he said. And then he shook Adamonis's right hand while placing his left upon Adamonis's shoulder, as if they were old friends. Adamonis bristled. This was an obvious and naive method of identifying him to shadows who did not know what he looked like. Ohme was testing Adamonis, tagging him as if he were an amateur. They parted ways.

"Stick very close to me," Adamonis said to Pranaitis. "I'm going to need you to do exactly as I do without hesitation. I might surprise you, but you mustn't hesitate. Do you understand?"

Pranaitis did.

They walked over to a streetcar stop in front of the North Train Station, and stepped onto a full tram, pushing their way through to the back where there was an open platform.

"Now watch who gets on," Adamonis said.

Two shadows entered and paid the conductor. Adamonis nudged Pranaitis, and then as soon as the streetcar began to move, he vaulted over the rail of the open platform. Adamonis caught Pranaitis by surprise, but he was able to keep up. The shadows were in the middle of the tram, blocked in by the other riders, and had no chance of catching up. Adamonis hailed a taxi, which he instructed to drive them to within a block of their guesthouse.

"Why were they following us?" Pranaitis asked.

"Commissioner Ohme is sending us a message," he said. "We're in Prussian hands and he wants us to know it because he wants us to feel like junior partners. When we get to the street of our guesthouse, we'll find other shadows there. I want you to go ahead and ask the first man you see for a light for your cigarette. When you get it, look him full in the face for as long as you can. Then go inside. I'll follow a little later."

Pranaitis did as asked. Adamonis waited five minutes and then walked onto the street, a quiet road with a small park across from the guesthouse. There was a young mother sitting on a bench with a baby in a perambulator at her side, the top covered with a veil to keep off insects.

The young woman on the bench was reading a book. The perambulator was new, maybe bought that very same day. Adamonis walked up to her and sat on the bench and said hello, to which she responded coolly with a nod.

"How old is your baby?" Adamonis asked.

"Just three months," she said, without looking up from her book. A more sensitive man would have read her mood and said nothing more. But Adamonis chose not to be a sensitive man.

"They're darlings then, aren't they?" he said. "I have a child that age back at home and I miss him terribly. Could I take a look at yours?"

"He's sleeping," she said, looking at Adamonis now with a hint of alarm.

"I'll be very quiet."

"I don't want to uncover him."

"Come now, aren't you proud of your child? Isn't he pretty?"

"I have to go now."

She stood with the book still in her hand and rolled away, bumping over the curb and crossing the street with the perambulator at a fast clip. No child awoke as she made her rough retreat.

Pranaitis was sitting in the lounge on the ground floor of the guesthouse with a glass of schnapps at his side.

"Well?" Adamonis asked.

"Just as you said."

Adamonis eyed his glass. "If we go to dinner with them tonight, we'll be expected to drink, but you mustn't get drunk."

"I was just calming my nerves. And why do you say 'if'?"

"I think we need to send a message back to them. We've been insulted and they need to know it. We've already sent one message by leaving the meeting early; we sent a second message by losing the shadows. Now we wait to see what they do when we send them our third message by not showing up for dinner."

Adamonis leafed through newspapers and smoked cigarettes as the afternoon faded into evening. Guesthouse patrons came by and sat for a while, read or smoked and then went out. Their landlady asked if they intended to eat with her other guests in the dining room, but Adamonis declined the invitation and asked only for coffee. Pranaitis studied the pattern of his armchair, rubbed the wooden trim with his thumbnail, and glanced from time to time at the newspaper.

Their dinner with the German hosts was supposed to be at seven. At seven fifty-five, a car pulled up in front of the guesthouse. Commissar Ohme himself stepped out of the back and knocked at the door. The landlady let him in and brought him to the sitting room. Adamonis butted a cigarette carefully, and rose slowly.

"I'm so sorry," Ohme said, taking Adamonis's hand in both of his. "Arrogance is our weakness, but you must forgive us. It's hard for us to reconcile ourselves to our territorial losses, and we take it out on our friends. Won't you come to dinner after all?"

"We aren't dressed."

"I'll wait."

The German intelligence officers from the day's meeting were chastened and polite. Those who had smiled most egregiously were not among the dinner guests. They gathered in a hotel dining room bright with chandeliers. It was a dinner like something from before the war, with many wines and many courses and many implements at each side of their plates. Adamonis had eaten at some very fine banquets with Russian officers during the war, but he was not so sure about Pranaitis. No sooner had they drunk a toast at the long table than Pranaitis reached forward to his finger bowl and practically washed his hands and then rubbed his face and dried it with a napkin as if he'd just come in from the fields.

Adamonis sighed. If they had managed earlier that day to present themselves as more than upstarts in the world of diplomacy, Pranaitis had now reestablished their place as peasants. But barely a moment had passed from when Pranaitis practically bathed in his finger bowl than Ohme himself, the massive presence to Adamonis's left at the head of the table, did the same.

They tasted their way through sorrel soup to filet of sole, goose liver pâté, a salad of assorted poultry, stuffed roast sirloin of venison, and roast pork as well as wines suitable to each of the dishes. Pastries followed. The Germans were sending a message of their own. Their empire may have been shattered by the war, but its remains were still very grand indeed. There had been many toasts and some speeches, but when the coffee and sweet Tokay came at the end of the meal, Ohme turned to Adamonis while all the others seemed to be wrapped up in their own conversations, leaving them on an island of intimacy at the head of the table.

"Have you ever been to Memel?" asked Ohme.

"Klaipeda is a very fine city," Adamonis said.

They each used different names but they were talking of the same place, a flourishing Baltic port city that had been part of Germany before the war but was a protectorate of the allies now. It was part of the territorial clipping of Germany that occurred after the Treaty of Versailles. The Germans wanted it back, but they were unlikely to get it. The Poles hungered for the city as well. Klaipeda was also adjacent to Lithuania. It was an ethnically mixed territory, like many other places in the East. Peoples in that part of the world did not live within clearly defined borders and about half the region's inhabitants spoke Lithuanian. The Lithuanian state had more than a little interest in Klaipeda and its territory.

"The war has had many unfortunate outcomes," said Ohme. Adamonis had watched him drink half a dozen glasses of wine and two shots of schnapps, but his words were measured and careful and very sober. The room was hot, but there was no sweat on his face. "Klaipeda, as you call it, is unfinished business. The Poles want it and the French are inclined to give it to them, but I don't think this outcome would be in the interests of Lithuania or Germany."

"There's a French garrison there," Adamonis said.

"Just a skeleton presence for symbolic purposes. Are you fond of Tokay?"

22

ADAMONIS and Pranaitis met the Woolleys for lunch the next day at the Hotel Pension Sieger, in the dining room with tall windows that overlooked the square in front of the North Train Station and flooded the place with light. Robert Woolley sat with a large white plaster over his nose. He looked like an unlucky boxer doing a little sunbathing. Lily was at his side. She had a habit of touching Woolley's hand to get his attention, a gesture that Adamonis found slightly irritating.

They ordered a light lunch of fresh and smoked sausages with potato and beet salad and beer, but Woolley was in pain and would only drink chamomile tea. Adamonis asked him how his treatment had gone.

"My sinuses are a disaster," he said, not surprisingly in a nasal voice, "but at least the specialist here used boiled instruments to clear them and irrigate them. In Lithuania they just rinse the instruments with alcohol. Anyway, I feel terrible now and I have two more days of treatments to go."

"And we have a crisis at home," said Lily.

"What kind of crisis?"

"We've waited a whole month for a new water heater for the bathroom, and our maid called the hotel this morning to say it finally arrived today, but the workmen need to knock out a wall to install it. I'm afraid they'll make a mess."

"Why not have the workmen wait until you get back?"

"For people who need to make a living, they don't seem all that keen to work. I'll have to chase after them for weeks to get them to return. I really should go back today."

"But you just got here, and Mr. Woolley still needs—"

"Robert says he can get by on his own. There will be other opportunities for me to come back to Königsberg. He likes it here."

"Yes," said Woolley, leaning forward. "Immanuel Kant walked these streets and so did E.T.A. Hoffmann. What famous person ever came from Kaunas?"

Adamonis did not want to play this game, but Woolley pressed him.

"Adomas Mickevicius," said Adamonis.

"Nonsense. He was a Polish poet, not a Lithuanian."

Lily broke in. "Robert says this city reminds him of his days in Vienna. Anyway, there's a train this evening and I think I might like to take it."

"But you'll only get in to Kaunas tomorrow morning."

"Exactly," said Woolley. "It's a problem." He leaned forward and rested his hand on Adamonis's wrist. "I wonder if I could ask a favour of you. I don't feel good about letting Lily return to Kaunas on a night train. Do you think perhaps you could send back your aide, Mr. Pranaitis, to accompany her?" Woolley's sincere eyes above his bandaged face looked ridiculous.

"I can do better than that. I've finished most of my business and we can return together. I'll see her home myself."

"Are we leaving?" asked Pranaitis.

"I am, but you aren't."

"I'd be happy to go too."

"I'm sure that's true. But you need to have a little polish on you after that trick with the finger bowls last night." Pranaitis reddened. "I want you to stay in this city for another two days. I want you to practise the art of observation. You are to eat in reasonably good restaurants and observe how people comport themselves. No working-class taverns, by the way, and no more than three drinks with any meal and no drinks without meals. I want you to do this and write up a report of your observations and to have it on my desk on the morning of your return. Other cultural differences are to be noted as well."

"Like what?"

"You will do the noticing and I'll do the assessing."

"Do you mean your business is done here?" asked Lily.

"It is now."

"I'm very grateful," said Woolley, and he sipped at his chamomile tea.

The first-class compartment held only one other passenger, a young German customs official returning to Eydtkuhnen. He was a genial man who liked to eat, and as soon as the train left the Königsberg station, he cut slices of smoked sausage on his lap and offered them to Lily and Adamonis off a clean white handkerchief. Lily declined, but Adamonis took two pieces. He also offered schnapps from a flask, poured into a small glass, which he wiped carefully with his cloth. Lily declined the schnapps too. She was dressed in a dark grey travelling suit and a cloche hat, and she carried only a small leather bag for the return trip. She had been very quiet on joining Adamonis at the station while Woolley complained of his fatigue and pain and left soon after. Lily barely looked at Adamonis, but she had taken his hand when he offered to help her up the steps into the car. She wore gloves.

Civility demanded that they speak German with their fellow passenger and he was effusive and generous in his praise of Lithuanians, whom he imagined the Germans were helping to civilize. Lily said very little and looked out the window into the night. They were in a nonsmoking compartment, and Adamonis stepped out after an hour and took his briefcase with him. In the corridor he saw the conductor and asked him if passengers normally boarded the train along the way.

"Not many," the conductor said. "Sometimes we get a merchant or two at Eydtkuhnen, but not generally at this time of night."

"I'm travelling with my cousin," Adamonis said. "She's had a great deal of fatiguing business in Königsberg. It would be a good thing for her to sleep undisturbed."

"She should have taken a sleeping compartment."

Adamonis shrugged. He opened his briefcase and removed from it a half bottle of Martell, which he pressed into the conductor's hands. It met no resistance. The man turned and took the bottle with him to the conductor's cubicle at the end of the car.

When Adamonis returned to the compartment, Lily was nodding vaguely as their travelling companion spoke of his young family and his hopes for his children. Adamonis was afraid he might follow with photographs, but happily, he stepped off the train two hours later at Eydtkuhnen, and more happily still, no other passengers entered their compartment.

"Well," said Adamonis, "that's a relief."

"Is it?" To his surprise, Lily continued to look out the window.

Given Lily's playful and flirtatious personality, her silence was perplexing. He wondered if she had had some kind of change of heart, or if he had said something wrong.

He studied her double image, her face and its reflection in the window. He couldn't read her heart in either of the faces.

Once they had cleared customs in Kybartai, the Lithuanian conductor entered the compartment. Adamonis wondered for a moment if he wouldn't have news of other passengers, but he said instead that there had been an accident on the tracks ahead of them and there would be a delay.

"How long?" Adamonis asked.

"At least two hours. We'll give a couple of sharp whistles ten minutes before we depart if you want to get something at the train station canteen."

Adamonis looked to Lily and she nodded. They stepped off the train into a warm night. The station was practically empty except for a couple of people sleeping in the waiting room and a few passengers who had chosen to disembark as they did. They drank coffee while standing at the canteen counter, but the atmosphere was eerie, like a theatre between performances.

"I understand there's a park just outside the station. Would you like to take a walk there?" he asked.

"It's very late." But she didn't decline.

If the train station had felt ghostly, the park was even more so, with occasional gas lamps glowing in a light mist and the paths among the gardens branching like choices with uncertain outcomes.

"You've been very quiet this whole trip," Adamonis said.

"Yes."

"Is there a reason?"

"I'm unsure of you now. The wedding feels like it happened a century ago and you've been so busy that you've hardly seen me. It makes me wonder how much you care for me after all. Anyway, you might think I led you on that night."

"Did you?"

"I acted out of impulse and gratitude. And a little admiration."

"Why would you admire me?"

"You're so sure of yourself. I feel tentative here. I'm not sure what will come next."

"I thought this trip to Lithuania would be an adventure for you. You could come and try on this country of your childhood and then return to life in America if things didn't work out."

"I'd rather stay here than go back there."

"Why is that?"

"Everything is so much more restricted for me there. You think of the Americans as freer than we are, but Robert comes out of society and the rules of behaviour are very strict there."

"You've lived most of your life in America. Aren't you used to it?"

"I was used to the easygoing life with my parents, but Robert's parents are very different. They had higher expectations of him. And then there was the matter of me."

"What about you?"

"Robert married down. I'm the daughter of an immigrant foreman. Sunday dinners with his parents and frosty sisters were hell."

"But he does love you."

"So he says."

"What does that mean?"

"I think he secretly shares some of the feelings of his family. He married me to spite them."

"But there must be more to your relationship than that."

"Robert is a romantic in his own way. He wanted to raise me up somehow, to demonstrate that I could be an equal to his mother. I've become his failed project, and that's part of the reason we find ourselves here."

"But he brought you here. Wasn't that a sign of affection?" Adamonis wasn't sure why he was saying things in Woolley's defense.

"It's more complicated than that. He needed to get away, but he also needs to succeed on his terms. He thought of going West to make a new fortune of his own, but instead he came East. Now he needs to succeed and the stress is making him"—she searched for a word and finally settled on one—"agitated."

The path led them to a lawn with a new bandshell at the centre and they made their way toward it. A gravel path surrounded the bandshell and the stones crunched under their feet as they walked up to the edge of the stage. In the pale light of the lamps, she looked more beautiful still.

She raised her hand to brush away a strand of hair over her forehead and on impulse, he took this hand between both of his and held it. She looked at him uncertainly, but when he kissed her, she wasn't uncertain at all.

When they pulled away, she said, "Even if you're just feeling sorry for me, I'm grateful."

"I'm not sorry for you. I'm in love with you."

"Then why did it take you so long to get close to me again?"

She put her hands on his shoulders as he put his around her back, and for a second he thought she intended to push him away. But instead she pulled him toward her and they kissed again.

The train whistle blew twice. She turned away and looked around to see if anyone had seen them. There was a park guard or a policeman in the distance, but he didn't concern Adamonis.

"Come on," he said.

The moment after his declaration of love felt awkward. She didn't say anything, but she held more tightly on to his arm, and this gave him all the confidence he needed. They made their way through the nearly empty station. The conductor was waiting on the platform beside our car.

"I thought I'd lost you," the conductor said.

"Could that have been two hours?"

"No. They cleared the tracks sooner than expected. We're leaving early."

Lily and Adamonis sat down across from each other again. Adamonis closed the door to the compartment. When the train began to move, he asked her if she was tired and she admitted she was. He closed the blind on the door and turned off the compartment lamp. It was far from dark. Light bled in from the corridor around the edges of the blind. Imperfect though the dark was, it seemed to free them somehow.

Adamonis crossed over and sat beside her. She let him take her hand. It wasn't cold at all. He lifted it and touched it to his lips, and in a moment they were kissing again. In the weak light he could see that her eyes were closed and as they kissed her mouth opened a little and their tongues touched. Adamonis felt slightly out of breath and pulled away, but she pulled him back toward her.

"This is wrong," she said.

"No, I think it's right. I love you very much."

"I don't know what to think."

"Then don't think."

The slight rocking of the train and the *clack* of the wheels on the rails were a background hum interrupted by the opening and closing of a door in the corridor. They froze as someone walked past their compartment. They heard the door open and close at the other end.

"Quickly," she said, "before I change my mind or someone else comes."

23

ADAMONIS managed a large network of operatives who worked looking outward at the movements of suspects throughout the country. But they also looked back to him, like hunting dogs making sure their master was in sight. He was a focus of attention throughout his working days and those days bled into most nights of the week. And when he went home, Anele took over surveillance of him in her house.

So how was he to see Lily?

He had built himself a reverse panopticon, and now he would have to find a way to become invisible sometimes.

Anele sensed something and came at him one morning before he left for work. She was dressed in a white smock and she held a dental pick in her hands.

"Have you finally found someone you're fond of?"

Adamonis was startled—he froze with a sheaf of papers halfway into his briefcase. "Anele, you have a patient back there in your chair."

"The idea came upon me suddenly. You have found someone, haven't you? That's why you want to move out."

"Not at all. I just need to be closer to the office because I come and go in the middle of the night. The Hotel Metropolis will be better suited to my needs and the ministry is willing to pay for it."

"But something has changed."

"Of course it has. My work is getting more intense."

"It's more than work. There's something new in you. You seem more human somehow, fallible. Maybe even happy."

He put the papers into his briefcase. "Was I unhappy before?"

"Dedicated, I'd say. Maybe weary sometimes. I believe I heard you humming to yourself this morning. That's new."

"Is humming a crime?"

"You've never hummed before." She paused and transferred the pick in her right hand to join the tiny dental mirror in her left. "How was Lily on the trip to Königsberg?"

If Anele hadn't been his sister and involved in dentistry, Adamonis would have considered her for work as an interrogator. "Lily was fine."

"She's your cousin. Remember that. You have to protect her."

"A distant cousin, barely a cousin. I'm sure Lily can take care of herself."

"I'm concerned about you too."

"So I see."

"You need someone to keep an eye on you. You need to be moored a little more firmly or you'll drift away."

Adamonis was glad to escape from her.

Back in the office, Adamonis noticed a sense of well-being in Miss Pinigelis too, a sort of glow that she had not worn before. Lovers, like saints, bore their halos.

After Adamonis moved into the Hotel Metropolis, he felt young again, a kind of *flâneur* who ate in various hotels and often took the opportunity to try restaurants and bars as well as dance halls to see who was going there and how citizens were entertaining themselves. On one of these combined lounging and reconnaissance rambles, he found himself in the Versailles restaurant, a striving former cafeteria that had rechristened itself with a French name and raised the prices. The Russian manager had found a dozen girls at loose ends on Freedom Boulevard and created a Russian gypsy chorus out of them. Business had picked up after the curfew was lifted and society began to bloom, although not always in a manner the founders of the nation had expected.

The night Adamonis went to the Versailles, the Russian manager was keeping a close eye on the girls, who were expected to encourage the customers to drink between sets. What they did after work was their own business. Adamonis admired the entrepreneurship of the establishment and he was touched by how amateurish it all was. A shy young man came onto the stage to act as master of ceremonies. Poor boy. The latest language laws demanded that, at very least, the announcements had to be made in Lithuanian, but most of the businesspeople barely spoke the language and knew Polish, Russian, or Yiddish much better. As the only employee who was also a native speaker of the language, the young Lithuanian announcer had been seconded for this role from his responsibility as the coat check boy. Fresh-faced and nervous, he looked to the ceiling and he looked at his shoes, and then he said, "And now Miss Larisa will sing 'My Heart Belongs to the Steppes.'" He practically tripped over himself in his rush to get off the stage and the audience roared with pleasure at his embarrassment. Miss Larisa sang with the accompaniment of a violin, and as for Adamonis, he ordered a dish of herring and mushrooms, and a glass of beer, lit up a cigarette to await the food, and looked around.

For all its shoddiness, the Versailles was a popular place, with five and six chairs pulled up to tables intended for four. The customers were upper-level ministerial workers, many businesspeople, a few criminals, and an assortment of bohemians, although they tended to prefer less-bourgeois places, as did the Jews, who had their own cafés. The ethnic layers did not blend easily in Kaunas. Adamonis would have stood out at a Jewish café, and so he let his Jewish informers function as his eyes in those places.

Retired General Vasilyev, the anecdotist and aspiring businessman, was sitting alone in front of a carafe of what looked like brandy, sipping from his glass from time to time. He looked at neither the stage nor the people and seemed to be lost in thought. This was a subject that reminded Adamonis of his days of training in espionage, when his teachers used to take him to restaurants and make him deduce what lay in the minds of the customers. It was the kind of training that got into his bones after a while. It didn't take a seasoned observer to see that General Vasilyev was suffering through some kind of inner turmoil. Adamonis walked over to his table. Vasilyev didn't see him coming and jumped a little when Adamonis tapped him on the shoulder.

"Did I disturb you?"

Vasilyev broke into his more habitual smile.

"Not at all. Actually, I could use a little company. Will you join me?"

Adamonis did as he asked and Vasilyev called for another glass and poured some cognac into it. It was a very good brandy, but not like dry French cognac at all. It was rich and dark, and reminded Adamonis of caramel.

"What am I drinking?" Adamonis asked.

"Armenian brandy."

"It wouldn't be Dvin, would it?"

It was. Adamonis had tasted Dvin once or twice before the war. It was known as exceptionally good, the best outside France. Armenia had gone through terrible times during the war and after it. As far as Adamonis knew, there were no trade routes between Lithuania and Armenia.

"I'm surprised the Versailles has this," said Adamonis.

"I helped to get in a couple of cases."

Armenia was de facto part of the Soviet Union, but there had been no official peace treaty signed yet. It seemed very strange that there should be trade routes out of Armenia that made their way to Lithuania.

"What's on your mind?" Adamonis asked.

"It's the matter of my business. There doesn't seem to be much of a market here, but I wrote to some of my old contacts in Moscow and I might be able to do more trade there. What do you think, could someone like me risk a couple of months in Moscow?"

"They just went through a famine."

"That's true, but you know how it is. One group starves and the other group throws dinner parties. It's always like that."

"But aren't you *persona non grata* there? You led the Lithuanian army against them."

"Perfectly understandable at the time. That's the past. Why should they hold a grudge?"

"Don't rush into anything and please discuss it me with me before you make any concrete plans."

The waitress brought Adamonis his herring and mushrooms and he and Vasilyev talked of other things. Vasilyev ran through his latest repertoire of anecdotes and Adamonis laughed when it seemed appropriate.

24

LANDA was sitting behind his desk, finishing notes on a report, and he asked Adamonis to sit down and wait a moment. Adamonis considered him, a young man older than his years, his brow now lined more deeply than it had been a year ago when they first met. Landa had lost some of the enthusiasm of a nation builder.

Adamonis considered Landa and he considered himself. They believed they were working toward the greater good, yet each would have had a hard time defining the greater good beyond preservation of the nation and a reasonably just society within it. They were scaling a mountain of aspirations, and vertigo could seize them at any moment.

Landa signed a document and put the cap on a bright blue fountain pen of a kind Adamonis had never seen before.

"A Parker, a new American pen from my American uncle," Landa said. The luckier Lithuanians had relatives who had emigrated to America before the war and to have an uncle abroad was like having a trump card. Yet Landa had never spoken of an American uncle before.

"I have some news out of the Moscow Embassy," said Landa. "Silvester's assassin has been released from prison."

"Found innocent?"

"There hasn't been any trial. He's been reassigned to the East and is supposed to return when the investigation resumes."

"When do you think that might be?"

"Most likely never."

"So was he a paid assassin?"

Landa laughed. "They don't like to pay people over there. It's cheaper if you have some knowledge that gives you control over them. It might really have been a crime of passion if his wife was having an affair with Silvester. I'm beginning to think Silvester's revelation and his death could be a coincidence." Adamonis looked at the pen that Landa had set on the desk, and Landa saw him looking. "But this doesn't affect the investigation. Is there anything new from the train yard?"

"I think we must be getting close. The ministry of external affairs has asked for two boxcars to be set aside for a shipment to Moscow."

"Is Johnny still down there?"

"He practically lives in the place. Some people think he's a railway employee."

"I need you to keep me well-informed. Let me know the moment the cars start to be loaded."

Adamonis brought up the matter of retired general Vasilyev.

His superior seemed to be relieved to have the subject changed. "It's funny you should mention Vasilyev," said Landa. "He's been petitioning the ministry of the exterior for work, and at the same time asked the chiefs of staff to reinstate him in the army. But he's a Russian, and let's face it, now that we're established, we can't have foreigners in sensitive positions anymore. Poor man. He's still full of energy and he has nothing to do, so he trolls with offers and hopes someone will take the bait."

"What kinds of offers?"

"He's suggested he could draw up a new mobilization plan for us."

"The army must have one already."

"It does, but there's so much work and so little time that the plan is very rough. We could use some expert advice and as far as I know, the chiefs of staff are happy to have a freelance offer like that. Especially from someone who was successful on the battlefield."

"So we can't put him in the army, but we can let him formulate our mobilization plan. How does that make sense?"

Landa lit a cigarette and sat back in his chair and then looked at Adamonis through the smoke. "Do you suspect something?" he asked.

"He's drinking Armenian brandy. There is no way he could have access to Armenian brandy under ordinary circumstances."

"Maybe he found a cache of it somewhere. Left over from before the war," said Landa.

"Maybe. But he's talking of going to Russia."

"Russia? What for? He'd be behind bars in a moment."

"He doesn't think so. He thinks they've forgiven him. I'm going to have him followed."

"He's a hero of the republic and he's friends with Novak." Landa leaned forward to butt his half-finished cigarette. "Slow down. For all we know, Novak's assigned a bodyguard to him and the last thing we need is to cross wires. Get more evidence first. If this goes wrong, you'll be hung out to dry and I won't be able to protect you."

"I'll take that risk."

"It's not such a small one."

"I'll use my best men. You'll be the only one outside the department who knows." Landa considered the statement. "I also wanted to speak to you about my meetings in Königsberg," said Adamonis.

"I've read your report."

"And?"

"You're not the only one who's been approached with hints about Memel. The German ambassador has spoken to the president and the prime minister. Their military attaché has mentioned Klaipeda twice."

Landa smiled at having caught himself out using both the German and Lithuanian names for the city.

"So the Germans are encouraging us to take the region?" asked Adamonis.

"Our government thinks we could use a victory for a change. We're still smarting after the Poles took Vilnius, and there's some risk they might want Klaipeda as well. It's not in the interests of Germany to have East Prussia entirely surrounded by Poland and it's not in our interest to give the Poles another victory at our expense."

Landa went on to speak at length about the Klaipeda region, as if he wanted to establish some distance from the earlier conversation about Vasilyev.

25

GENERAL VASILYEV ambled down Freedom Boulevard and then turned onto a side street where shops with farm supplies and hardware huddled one beside another. There were no specialized sporting goods stores, but these shops carried a little of everything among the hammers, nails, and sunflower seeds, and in one of them he found a good bamboo fishing rod as well as a Scottish fishing vest with many small pockets. He bought hooks and bobbers, expensive braided line, and a tin of worms. He walked out of the shop wearing the vest and an Austrian hunting hat with a jaunty feather in the band. The vest caused some heads to turn. Clothing such as this was barely known in that part of the world. He made his way down to the Neris River, rowed out to a shallow spot, dropped his anchor, and threw in his line.

Vasilyev rarely caught fish, and did not seem adept at taking them off the hook when he did. The fish flopped and sometimes fell overboard and he occasionally pricked his finger with the hook. Still, he persisted, and took the boat out every Monday. From time to time another fisherman would show up in the spot and the two would chat across the water. In the manner of genial fishermen, they sometimes exchanged cigarettes or other small items. Chepas's followers had binoculars, but they could not make out exactly what the exchanges consisted of. The other fisherman was followed to his apartment in the Old Town. He worked at the train station as a porter and occasional boxcar loader.

Adamonis felt somewhat sorry for the retired general, but part of him could imagine Vasilyev all too well in a classroom in Moscow, where he would lecture recruits while employing a sense of humour about the novice country, an amateur country whose defences he'd managed to infiltrate.

Anele and Lily were joining Adamonis for lunch in the Metropolis Hotel. It had a few dining rooms, and he chose the finer one, with its neo-baroque mouldings and freshly painted walls and linen on the tables. Kaunas was changing quickly, and the restaurant was evolving into the sort of place where ministers' wives came dressed in furs and carrying little dogs. Someone had heard of English tea dances, and in the afternoons at that hour, the ladies congregated again in the interests of various charities. It hadn't been easy to pull Anele away from her dental practice in the middle of the day, but it was the only way he could see Lily in public.

They came in together chatting and barely nodded at Adamonis as they sat down and finished a discussion about one of their farm relatives who was in town to see a specialist about a poorly mended bone. On the one hand, Adamonis was impressed by Lily's ability to be so calm and easy, but on the other hand, it made him a little troubled that she could hide their new relationship so thoroughly.

Adamonis asked after their husbands. Vilimas was expanding his museum and Woolley was travelling the country, working out where the river ports should be situated for the new barge business he had planned with Martynas.

But Woolley's sinuses continued to bother him and he was returning to Königsberg for more treatments in a few days.

"Maybe this time you'll get to see the sights of the city," Adamonis said.

"No, I won't be going with him," said Lily. "I'll be returning to the countryside for a few days to help nurse cousin Joana. They're going to have to break her arm and reset the bone and I know she'll be in pain."

"So this is where you're living your new life?" asked Anele. "In this hotel where you're paying three times what it would cost to make a meal at home? You're among foreigners and businessmen here. No chance for any rest at all. You were better off staying with us. You had a refuge there and someone to watch over you."

"But I have a refuge here as well. I have a suite of two rooms, both a sitting room and a bedroom. I'll take you up there for dessert and demonstrate how regular my life is."

"Bachelor life," said Anele. "A bar and a billiards room downstairs and diplomats and functionaries coming and going all the time. Not much better than a barracks, just with finer furnishings and room service. You disappoint me."

"Isn't that taking family concern a little far?"

"You're a feather in the wind, and while the war was on, you couldn't help it and were blown around. But you continue to live an irregular life even in peacetime. Doesn't family life hold any appeal for you?"

"Of course it does, in good time. But not yet."

"Time is running out. You're in your thirties now. If you wait much longer to have a family, your children will have a grandfather instead of a father."

"Lily," said Adamonis, "defend me from my sister."

"I think Anele is right. You're living a wild life now, but one day you'll wake up and find you have nothing but memories."

"I wouldn't mind having some good memories when I'm old."

"For that to happen," said Anele, "you have to live long enough to get old. Now what are we going to eat? I'm starving."

It was an excellent meal of veal *zrazai* and Russian salad of beans, peas and potatoes, a mild counterbalance to the rich mushroom sauce of the *zrazai*, and he wished the conversation were as good, but the two of them had become like schoolgirls, sharing little jokes and ignoring Adamonis or making fun of him from time to time.

Adamonis called for the waiter and asked for coffee, pastries, and Bénédictine to be brought to his rooms, and they were starting to make their way upstairs when the waiter, a well-meaning but clumsy young man, came rushing up to Anele and announced that there was a phone call for her at the registration desk of the hotel. The three of them walked over to the lobby and Anele took the call, discovering she had a patient with a very bad tooth who needed her back at the office as soon as she could get there.

"Tell him to hold a shot of vodka over the tooth and you'll get to him when you get to him," said Lily.

"No, I had better go," she said. She turned to Lily. "You go on up and inspect the bachelor quarters and report back to me on what you've seen."

"Oh, I don't want to go without you," said Lily. "Maybe another time."

"Nonsense," said Anele. "The coffee and pastries are already up there. If you don't go up now, he'll just go back to the office and the waiters will eat everything themselves."

"At least come up and look at the rooms, Anele. It will just take a second," said Adamonis.

Anele did as he asked, but left after giving them quick farewell kisses. Lily and Adamonis were left in his sitting room, the cups of coffee steaming on a tray on the coffee table, the pastries and Bénédictine set out. Lily began to pull off her gloves.

"There is just one thing I want to know," she said. "How did you manage to arrange this with such good timing?"

"Do you think I ensnared you?" he asked.

"If I didn't want to be caught, I wouldn't be here. I'm just impressed with how you can make things happen. Is there anyone who watches your apartment here?"

"Just from the outside of the building. I demand privacy inside."

"Then we have a good spell of time, if you can spare it."

He wanted her very badly and was glad when she asked his help to undo the clasp on the back of her dress.

They were on the second floor; sheer curtains blocked the view from outside but let in considerable light and she let him undress her with all the confidence of a married woman. They had managed to see each other a few times since the Königsberg trip, but they were always rushed and at least partially clothed. This afternoon together now felt luxurious, and he admired her after she had undressed. She was thin in the American way, although she had lived in the country for some time now. Her breasts were small, like a teenager's. She seemed happy in her nakedness, and laughed and turned around to display herself, and then helped him finish undressing and made him stand in the light.

"You're every bit the soldier," she said, "at attention, I see."

"Alert to your every command."

"Turn around and let me get a look at the rest of you."

She ran her hand over his right shoulder blade.

"You have quite a scar here," she said. "Where did it come from?"

"A saber during the war."

"On your back?"

"He caught me by surprise. I wasn't running away, if that's what you mean."

"I didn't mean that at all. I'm just happy it didn't do any worse. Now turn around again."

She continued her examination of him, and he felt delight at this familiarity. She touched him on the chest. "And this scar here, just below the collarbone?"

"An old bullet wound."

"You've been very lucky, Mr. Adamonis. That's a bullet that could have gone through your heart."

"My heart is actually on the other side."

She placed her palm over his heart. "It preserved your heart for me."

She wrapped her arms around him and held him. He was intensely aware of the pressure of her cool breasts on his chest and her warmer belly, pressing.

Later, Adamonis stood and walked to where the coffee was cooling on the table. He took a small glass of Bénédictine and brought it to her, and she put the pillow against the headboard and sat facing him, sipping from the glass. She looked lovely. He sat in a chair facing her, lit another ciga-rette, and drank a little of the liqueur as well.

"Now is a good time to talk," he said. "We have to think for a moment."

"What do we have to think about?" she asked.

"The two of us. What we're going to do. How you'll leave Woolley."

She froze, looked at him, and set her Bénédictine down.

"Not so fast, Mr. Adamonis. We've just started this thing. I don't even know where we're going yet."

"I'm offering you a direction."

"Let's not rush. What exactly did you have in mind for us?"

"A life together."

"We're together now. Can you imagine anything better than this? Would you want me serving you soup on a Sunday afternoon instead?"

"I didn't mean instead. I meant this too."

"I need to get to know you better. I want you to share some of yourself with me, to trust me so I can trust you."

"You can trust me."

"So you say. You'll have to prove it over time."

"Whatever you want, it's yours."

"Tell me a little more about yourself," said Lily.

"What do you want to know?"

"Tell me about your work."

"You must know I can't talk about that."

"In a general way, silly. Are you still in danger? I worry about you."

"I'm not in danger, no."

"Not ever? Doesn't the enemy want to put you out of the way?"

"What good would that do? Someone else would just take my job."

"But maybe someone less competent. I'm sure the Soviets would love to see a fool in your position."

"And the Poles as well."

"Are they still a threat?"

"That's no secret. Just read the papers. People still get killed in skirmishes along the demarcation line. Something could erupt there at any time."

"And then what would happen?"

"Why, we'd be at war again."

"So you see, I do have something to worry about. The Poles outnumber you ten to one and they aren't distracted by the Soviets anymore. If they ever came through, you'd be arrested for sure, if not hurt in battle before that."

"Lily, why are you spinning this story? Anything could happen at any time. We could all be swept away by something. Besides, I'd know if the Poles were going to attack."

"How?"

"Because they'd mass soldiers at the border and we'd receive news of it. Then we'd mobilize too."

"But how would your agents get news to you? There are no telephone lines between Poland and Lithuania."

"I'm not sure why you're asking me this."

"Because I think I want to live here now. Robert and I might make a life here, and I want to be sure we're in a safe place."

"You're safe enough for now," said Adamonis. "Just trust me on that. Now tell me, how will I manage to see you again?"

She looked at her watch, seemed startled by the hour, and stepped out of bed and began to dress.

"I'm going to see the country cousins again soon. Find a way to go there too. Robert doesn't like villages, so he won't want to go. And compose yourself better. Your face almost gave you away over lunch. You're supposed to be the chief of counterintelligence, for heaven's sakes."

"You haven't said you love me."

"I do. I love you very much, but you're still guarded around me. Keep your secrets in public, but in private open your heart a little more."

26

ADAMONIS's phone rang angrily well before dawn. He imagined, for a moment, the voice of an outraged Woolley on the other end of the line, but it was Pinigelis, who was on night duty back at the office. Chepas had something to report. Adamonis should come in right away.

Pranaitis was there along with Miss Pinigelis. Chepas was practising invisibility again, and Adamonis didn't notice him until Chepas rose to shake hands. Adamonis could smell mint on Pranaitis's breath and something alcoholic lay behind it. But Pranaitis had been off-duty, so.

"Where's the shadow?" Adamonis asked. "I want to hear this from his own lips."

"I was the shadow," said Chepas.

Vasilyev had left his apartment at one in the morning. It was easier to move around now that the curfew had been lifted. He came down from the suburb where he lived and walked past Soboras to the top of the boulevard where a park lay behind a low green fence with a gate that led to steps up a hill. Vasilyev stood by the gate and looked around for some time before opening it and going along a path that led to a park restaurant that had long since closed for the night.

Halfway up the hill, he turned suddenly and looked around, but Chepas was creeping along quietly behind bushes, and he was unseen.

Above at the darkened restaurant with its empty terrace, someone appeared from the dimness. The two men met and greeted each other and then stood and talked for a while. When the two men separated, Chepas saw the other walk past the restaurant to a fence, where he swung aside a pair of loose boards and left the grounds.

"Who was the other man?" asked Adamonis.

"The fisherman."

"Who works at the train station?"

"Yes. They may have exchanged documents and Vasilyev might still have them. This could be a good time to bring them in."

Adamonis declined. It was more likely that Vasilyev had given documents than received them, so there wouldn't be any incriminating evidence to be had from him. He sent his staff all home to bed.

The following day Adamonis went to Landa, who stared out the window for a long time after he received the news.

"Do you think Vasilyev is masterminding the smuggling operation?" asked Landa.

"I don't know. They may be separate cases or they may overlap. We expect the railway cars to be loaded at any moment."

Landa shuddered. "What a mess. Vasilyev is some sort of spy and at least one of the ministers is involved in a smuggling operation. This is getting too big. It should go to the chiefs of staff and our own minister."

"I was wondering if we could hold off on that," said Adamonis. "We don't know who else knows about it. If we take the information up, one of the bastards might get wind of it."

"Interesting word. But do you have any idea of the scope of this? This nation is barely five years old. Some of the men in that cabinet were fighting for independence for decades and some of them went to prison for it. When the time comes to write the history of Lithuania, some of these men will have statues of them built on public squares. And think of Vasilyev himself. He saved us from the Red Army. His reputation has to be worth something, even if he's slipped up now. You have to allow for a certain amount of human weakness."

"But how much? We're being read like an open book and somewhere someone is laughing at us."

"We have to live with human nature. People are a mixture of weak and strong and we have to respect them for the best parts of themselves. We should let the cabinet decide what to do."

"The cabinet has been compromised."

"And what good do you think it will do for the nation when all of this hits the newspapers? We'll look like a country run by petty thieves and fools."

"Which is exactly what we're trying to stop. I don't want to live in a corrupt society. Do you?"

"Of course not. But the question is how to uproot the weeds without destroying the whole garden. And think what kind of hell is going to descend on you and me if any of this goes wrong. Even if it goes right, powerful people will be angry with us."

"Are you afraid?"

"Don't be insulting. Can't you think of some intermediate step we could take?"

"Like what?"

"Let Vasilyev or the Soviets know he's being followed. They'll spirit him out of the country and his reputation will be secure. We'd still have the general in our gallery of heroes."

"No good. If ever they needed to embarrass us, they'd bring him out for show. Then the country would look like a collection of fools and you and I would be the worst fools of all."

"But what if something happened to Vasilyev?"

"Like what?"

"What if he went West?"

"It won't work. We pay him a big pension, but the money wouldn't go far abroad. Out in Paris he'd have to drive a cab or be a doorman, along with the other White generals and former Russian princes. He knows that. He won't go there unless we send him on some sort of diplomatic mission, and why would we want to do that? And what about Captain Silvester? There's one dead man in this affair already."

Landa nodded and continued to look at Adamonis.

They both knew an accident would solve many problems. He looked at Landa, who was fussing with his new Parker pen on the desk. Adamonis rubbed his forehead to loosen the tension. He had chosen not to cross that river, but had come so close to it that the tips of his boots were wet.

"Do you think you might not be tempted to do something dodgy yourself if you were in a desperate situation?" asked Landa.

"Never. Listen, I take this upon myself. Let's bust this ring. If we succeed, we'll have done some good for the country, but if we fail, you can say it was all my idea."

"You underestimate the storm. You'll go down for certain, but you won't be alone." Adamonis watched Landa wrestle with himself until he finally set the pen aside, "Do you have some kind of plan?"

Landa agreed to what Adamonis proposed. He had Adamonis write out a letter of resignation, undated, but signed. Landa took the sheet of paper and placed it in an envelope and put the envelope in his desk. Adamonis watched him as he locked the drawer.

"Only the two of us will know this is here," said Landa. "I hope you know what you're doing, for both our sakes."

27

THE DINNER took place three days later in a small private dining room in the Metropolis hotel just as Johnny sent word that the boxcars were being loaded down at the rail yards.

"If the minister gets wind of this, he'll close us down," said Landa. "As it is, within a few days, news of this will get out and the chiefs of staff will want to know what the hell we're doing."

"With any luck, the situation will play itself out by then. In any case, I'll say the operation was my idea. You never knew a thing."

"Luck," said Landa bitterly. "I hate to rely on luck. And anyway, if I claim I knew nothing, I'll look like an idiot."

"But if it works out, you'll look like a genius."

The dinner in the Hotel Metropolis, nominally hosted by Adamonis's brother-in-law, Vilimas, was a fundraiser for the War Museum. Adamonis had arranged the seating so that he could observe Vasilyev two persons down and across the table from him. Initially they stood about drinking champagne and eating caviar. They were a slightly unusual group, just one level below the usual coterie of deputy ministers. This unlikely gathering of men became all the more unlikely as Woolley walked into the room.

"What's he doing here?" Adamonis asked Vilimas.

"Lily thought it would be good for him to mix in local society some more, so she asked me to invite him when she found out about the party."

"How did she know about it in the first place?"

"Anele must have told her. Don't you think business-men are good to have around?"

"All right. But from here on, no more surprises. And when you speak, please stick to the script."

"I was hoping you'd let me improvise. I'm good at speaking in public."

"Just read the words I wrote out for you, please. You can add something if you want. But please don't subtract anything."

Woolley made Adamonis uncomfortable in a manner he was unaccustomed to feeling about himself. To shake off this feeling, Adamonis went directly to his side.

"Mr. Woolley," he said. "I haven't seen you since Königsberg. How is your health?" Woolley shrugged and spooned himself a little caviar upon black bread. "How long have you been in this country now?" Adamonis asked.

"Well over a year."

"Not tired of us yet?"

Woolley gave Adamonis a piercing look, ambiguous, and he thought for a moment that Woolley might suspect something.

"I haven't exhausted the business possibilities of this place. It's hard here, in this poor and backward country, but Mr. Martynas has been very helpful and I think we might be developing something."

"In barges?" Adamonis asked.

"Exactly. The roads are horrible here and the rail line is overcrowded. With all the farm exports going to Germany, there's a bottleneck. We could ship more cheaply by boat, but the infrastructure for shipping on the river is very poor."

"And what about competition?" Adamonis asked. "The route from Kaunas to the sea has been used for centuries."

"We'd start considerably higher upriver. I wish you and the Poles could sort things out—we could ship right from the headwaters if you weren't involved in this ridiculous dispute of yours. And by the way, you would let me know if any of the ports I picked were close to potential Polish conflict zones, wouldn't you?"

"I couldn't possibly do that."

"What a pity. And I've seen some plans for lovely wide boats with shallow drafts."

"I didn't know you were knowledgeable about boats."

"My people come from Worcester and it's only a couple of hours to the sea. I sailed a lot when I was young."

They were asked to sit down and Vilimas rose to make a short speech, this first one not scripted by Adamonis. He talked about the glorious, if brief, recent history of the country, and how the War Museum had grand plans for expansion that he would go into more depth about later, after dinner. Adamonis was seated beside Woolley, who had learned no Lithuanian in a year, and he translated Vilimas's words for the American.

After this speech, the table broke into several conversations. Vasilyev was telling one of his anecdotes to his neighbour, and it must have been a good one because the neighbour sputtered over his soup.

"Let me ask you a question," Adamonis said to Woolley when the soup bowls were being removed. "Why do you bother with this country at all?"

Woolley looked at him abruptly, more agitated by the question than he had expected.

"What do you mean?"

"There's not much here for you. A man like you must certainly find this a dull place."

"That's true. It's exceedingly dull here. Do you know the foreign diplomats stationed here are paid a hardship bonus?" he asked.

"That's my point. If you're looking for a place to invest, there must be more promising places than this one."

"You don't sound like much of a patriot."

"On the contrary, that's exactly what I am. It's the only reason I'm here, but I find your presence more perplexing."

"My wife wanted to come here."

"So she did, but it's been quite a while already. She must have gotten over her nostalgia by now."

"She seems to like it here well enough."

"But you stay here reluctantly."

"You seem to be provoking me, Mr. Adamonis."

"I'm just looking out for the welfare of my cousin."

"The best way you can help out Lily is by helping me with this project. Mr. Martynas and I were thinking of a three-way partnership. The state could be a part owner of the barge system."

"The state has no money to invest in boats."

"But it could help build the infrastructure. I'm thinking of loading docks to take on cargo at various points down the river. At Jurbarkas, for example."

The waiters brought in the next course.

"What is this gelatinous thing?" asked Woolley.

"Headcheese. You must have had it in Austria. They call it *Presswurst* there, I believe."

"It's one of the most barbaric dishes ever put on a plate."

"Don't the Americans eat aspic?"

"We do, occasionally, but it's made of tomatoes or sometimes carrots and served as a side dish. Not like this, with bits of pigs' heads."

"Actually, it's made with pigs' feet in this country."

"Can you imagine what a pig must walk through?"

Adamonis took two squares of headcheese to show his enthusiasm for it. Woolley took two slices of *skilandis*, a very thick smoked sausage. He declined the offer of horseradish, perhaps fearing it might lead to another night like the one in Birstonas.

Vilimas tapped on his glass after the first course was cleared and before the main course was brought in. He was reading from the script that his brother-in-law had provided for him, and as Adamonis had expected, the table listened politely, but without keen interest, about the plans to expand the museum.

Vilimas then reminded everyone that the museum remained part of the army and he spoke very briefly about military reform and significant changes coming in military dispositions to address potential foreign threats.

Adamonis watched Vasilyev carefully during this talk. He may have been a good general in the field, but he would not have made a good poker player because his lip quivered slightly at the news of new military dispositions and his face reddened. Even Woolley seemed to pick up interest as Adamonis distractedly translated for him.

Vasilyev looked at his watch. It was already ten o'clock. Vasilyev's neighbour was telling anecdotes, but the retired general merely nodded from time to time.

When the meal finally ended after midnight, Adamonis went up to his room in the hotel and undressed for bed. Adamonis planned to sleep soundly; he expected the next day to be a long one.

28

LILY appeared at the dining room entranceway just as Adamonis was finishing his breakfast tea in the Metropolis café.
He had been thinking of her, and he hoped his thoughts
had summoned her. He rose as she came to his table.

"What a wonderful surprise," he said. She was wearing
the sort of jacket women travelled in and seemed slightly
flustered. "Is everything all right?"

"It is and it isn't. I've come for a favour."

He asked her to sit down and ordered tea for her.

"I'm supposed to go into the country today to take care
of our cousin, but our car has broken down and the driver
says he can't get another one on short notice. I was hoping
I could borrow yours."

It was not a good time. He offered the loan of it, but he
couldn't lend Pranaitis. When he told her that, Lily spent
a long time blowing the steam off the top of her teacup
and looking at the brew as if she was searching for something inside it.

"I was hoping," she said, "you might join me."

The boxcars were almost ready to go and Vasilyev was
sure to act soon. He told her it would be difficult to get
away.

She looked up from her cup. "Difficult or impossible? I need to talk to you."

"We could talk here."

"No. I'd like to do this in private."

He told her to go back to her house and wait for him.

The department sensed that something was going on and the secretaries and clerks looked at Adamonis keenly as he made his way past them to his office. Inside, he found Pranaitis, Chepas, Pinigelis, and a couple of adjutants. He turned to Chepas first.

"Vasilyev's been given the bait and I think he'll act soon, certainly within the next day or two. I need all your shadows ready. Above all, we have to seem calm and unconcerned. I don't like the buzz out there on the floor. I want you to walk out of here as if something has been called off. I do need someone hidden in the park restaurant before dark and I want someone watching the fence by the park from the outside. What's happening at the train station?"

"The boxcars are loaded, actually," said Chepas. "They're just waiting for a functionary from the ministry of external affairs to seal them, but there's been some kind of holdup. They're waiting for something."

"Do you have the staff to cover both the station and Vasilyev?"

"I think so."

"I want to know as soon as there's movement."

As they were speaking, the substitute secretary who had been watching Miss Pinigelis's desk outside their door came in.

"Mr. Landa is on the phone. He wants to speak to you."

Adamonis had everyone leave the office and picked up his phone.

"Do you have any news?" Landa asked.

"It's too early but I expect Vasilyev to act soon."

"Whatever you do, your case must be airtight. Do you understand? I want no half measures. No bungling."

"Of course not."

"I'm counting on you. I might want to be there if something does happen."

"Are you sure? You'd be implicated then."

"I'll be implicated no matter what."

Adamonis hung up the phone and called the others back in. He could feel their enthusiasm, but he needed to calm them down.

"Miss Pinigelis," he said. "You will sit at my desk here while I'm gone. You will have the replacement sit at your desk." He turned to an adjutant. "You are to sit here as well. If she needs to go out for a moment, watch the phone. I want each of you to keep a record of anything that comes through. Mr. Chepas, you call here if you pick up any news. Do you understand? I don't expect anything to happen before tonight, but make sure you're available."

"What happens if the train begins to move?" asked Chepas.

"How long will it take the train to reach the border?"

"Maybe a day. It's part of a slow freight run that needs to pick up other boxcars at a lot of country stations. Where will you be?"

"I'll be in touch. I'm going for a drive. Mr. Pranaitis, I want you to get the car ready. Make sure the tank is full and get me two spare tires."

They did as he asked, but Chepas in particular was made uneasy by Adamonis's intended absence and his refusal to accept shadows. Chepas didn't say anything, but Adamonis could feel his puzzled look. When Adamonis got into the car, he told Pranaitis to drive to the Woolleys' house. He helped Lily put her suitcase in the car. There was no sign of her husband.

Adamonis caught Pranaitis's troubled gaze in the rear-view mirror.

"Drive to Pazaislis," he said.

"The monastery?"

"Do you know another Pazaislis?"

Pranaitis looked away and had the good sense not to look in the rear-view mirror again. However, Lily watched both the mirror and the back of Pranaitis's head. She touched Adamonis's leg with her hand, but neither of them acknowledged the gesture and she took her hand away after a moment. Adamonis asked Pranaitis to stop at a newsstand on Freedom Boulevard and made a bit of a show of choosing the newspapers he wanted, and then they rode in silence until they arrived at the monastery. Adamonis asked Pranaitis to step outside the car.

"Go to the main office and stay by the phone," he said, "and give me the car keys."

"You're going somewhere alone?"

"My village. You know the place."

"I could take you there now."

"You could, but you won't. I'll drive Mrs. Woolley there myself."

"Are you sure you want to stay out of touch with the office at a time like this? I don't like to leave you alone."

"I brought along my pistol today. I'll be all right."

Pranaitis gave Adamonis the keys and walked to the monastery office door, but he did not go in. He stood there and watched as Adamonis got into the car and drove off with Lily in the back seat.

After a few kilometres, when they came to a place where there was no one to be seen and nothing but autumn fields around them, he stopped the car. He went around to open her door. The car was in the dappled light under a maple and hay had been cut somewhere nearby and it was scenting the air. Lily slid into the front with him. He was about to turn the key in the ignition when she leaned in to him, and he kissed her, and then he found her hand on his leg again, but this time it wasn't withdrawn.

"Let's find a place somewhere," she said.

"I don't have much time."

He pulled in a little farther along, among some trees, and they got into the back seat together. There was nothing romantic about the back seat of a car, and nothing comfortable either, but she seemed to have missed him badly and he would have done it anywhere at all.

"I needed you today," she said, when he looked at his watch after she rejoined him in the front of the car.

"I need you always," he said, "but today is an interesting day at the office. I'll have to drive fast. Do you mind speed?"

"I like a bit of risk."

They smoked as they drove, and he had needed to be alert because animals wandered onto these roads and potholes were a constant danger. But at least the weather had been dry.

"Robert was very agitated when he came in last night."

"Was he? What about?"

"He said you pretty much told him we should leave the country."

"That's not exactly what I said."

"But that's how he interpreted it. Are you trying to get rid of us?"

"Not both of you."

She looked out the window at the passing fields and then bumped her head on the window at her side when he swerved around a stone. She was quiet for a while.

"What good would that do us if he did leave? This is a Catholic country. There are no divorces permitted here."

"People go up to Riga. There are ways around that."

"But no future, really. All I'm saying is that things are all right the way they are for now. Don't be in such a rush. Not only did you try to intimidate Robert, this talk about the disposition of troops worries him too."

"Why should that worry him?"

"Any movement of troops means you're getting ready for something, but what? Are the Poles mobilizing? Robert is a businessman and businessmen need peace. You unnerved him and then Vilimas scared him by making it seem like there's a threat of war. He needs to know the truth."

"It's a routine matter. He'd be better off concerning himself with his nose."

She looked away and Adamonis thought she was angry, but then he glanced over and saw her shoulders were shaking.

"It's not good to laugh at your husband," he said.

"How can I help it?"

"How can you stand him?"

She stopped laughing. "Now you're going too far. Robert is a good man in his own way. He's the one who brought me here. He's the one who's stayed so long. Indirectly, he brought me to you."

"So now I should be grateful to him?"

"Something like that. Just enough to help him get his business started and rolling." She asked for another cigarette and he passed her one but had to let her light it herself and then asked her to light another one for him. "You're not in any danger, are you?" she asked.

"Why do you ask?"

"You don't usually carry a pistol."

She asked him some questions about politics and his work, but these subjects bored him and he gave superficial answers, even when she probed. Their conversation all the way to their hamlet was strained, as if they had had an argument, but on his drive back to Pazaislis to pick up Pranaitis, he couldn't remember any substance to their argument at all.

The car had a flat tire on the way back. The bolts were rusty and Adamonis had a difficult time changing it and this made him late at the monastery; he arrived shortly before the nuns dined. He could hear them singing their late-afternoon prayers in the chapel and Pranaitis was standing by the door where he had left him.

"Did you never go in?" Adamonis asked. Adamonis knew he had abandoned his post for a woman, just the sort of infraction that would have been punished harshly in the army. But he was the leader here, and no one dared to question his actions.

"I was inside all day and phoned the office a few times," said Pranaitis. "I was beginning to get worried about you."

"No need. Is there any news from the office?"

"Nothing."

Adamonis was relieved. There would be no price to pay.

"Just as I suspected," he said. "I'd like you to drop me off at my hotel and to return to the office. Call me at the hotel if anything comes up. And settle down. You look like a nervous wreck."

"I don't know how you can be so calm about all this."

"What good would it do to show my nerves?"

But his nerves had suffered more than he cared to admit.

Adamonis walked into the Hotel Metropolis and was startled by the brightness of the stained-glass window at the landing of the main staircase. The early evening light, reflected and intensified by a tin roof outside, made the window glow as he had never seen it. And now that he thought of it, two of the images in the glass had been changed. A pair of ancient Lithuanian heraldic images, one a sort of symbol of a castle and the other a kind of double cross, lay within red shields on the stained-glass windows. These would have been forbidden in czarist times and for a moment his heart leaped to see them.

And yet, why was that? He had fought under many banners during the war, some national, some regimental, and briefly under one Soviet. He knew of people who traded banners of allegiance as often as an advantage presented itself. But there was something about this light on the symbols in the stained-glass window that moved him. There was something here that was important to him, something that needed to be defended. This place had been under siege for hundreds of years and many others had defended it before him. Now it was his turn.

Patriotism was the cloak that covered tyrants and politicians, and nostalgia was the disease of old men. Yet there was something to be said for belonging, something to be said against being a lone fish rather than one in a school, a lone bird instead of one in a flock. He laughed to himself. Perhaps it was a desire to be nothing more than a sheep, and sheep had no defence except the attentiveness of the shepherd and his dog.

The rest of the lobby was being refurbished as well. The wooden panelling was now waxed and dusted and the patterned ceramic floor no longer had cracked tiles. Come to think of it, the buckled corridor floors were now smooth as well.

The hotel and the country were evolving. Maybe one day this could be a normal hotel in a normal country.

These thoughts cleared Lily from his mind and gave him a new sense of purpose. He was, after all, in the middle of an operation. He had to push it to the end.

He checked for messages at the desk where he was well known now and addressed by name, and then went up to his room. There he poured himself two fingers of brandy and went to the window to look outside through the sheers. A man was standing on the corner, one of his. He phoned the office and Miss Pinigelis answered. Her calm voice reassured him that nothing had happened while he was gone.

Having felt patriotic on his way up the stairs, he now felt some remorse for driving off with Lily. Acting in self-interest in the middle of an important operation: he wasn't himself. He wondered if the tension in his life wasn't beginning to impair his judgment. His offers to her seemed to spring right out of his mouth without originating first in his brain.

Was this what it meant to speak with one's heart? And if so, what was the use of having a heart that put the rest of him in danger?

Others would consider him lucky to have a married woman willing to sleep with him whenever the opportunity presented itself, and an earlier version of him might have felt the same way. It would have been just another adventure. But he had had adventures enough. He could imagine living a settled life like that of his sister, as long as Lily was part of the picture. He was troubled by Lily, uneasy about the way things were going.

After a late dinner, Adamonis was walking by the bar and, hearing the *click* of billiard balls, he looked inside to see Arturas Martynas playing a solo game. They saw each other from time to time, but they were not close. Martynas was like an insurance salesman who was always trying to get his friends and acquaintances to sign up for a policy. Martynas had schemes, and might end up a rich man, or he might end up in jail. But like all schemers, he had a certain amount of charisma, which made it pleasant to be around

182 / Provisionally Yours

him for short periods of time. Adamonis had had enough of his own thoughts and walked in for a game.

Adamonis chalked his cue stick as Martynas racked up the balls and then he potted the cue ball on the break-off shot. Martynas gave him a look.

"Disappointed in the quality of my game?" Adamonis asked.

"Pleased, actually. My opponent's misfortune is my good fortune. Remember we're playing for money here. I'm eager to win another bottle of champagne."

"I was the one who won the last time we played."

"Your memory must be playing tricks on you."

Adamonis enjoyed this sort of banter. It took him back to the billiards tables he had played on all across old Russia in his czarist army days. There was a certain flatness to the time men spent together in pastimes such as billiards. It took them back to their childhoods when everything was play and one could focus on matters that had no relevance at all to the rest of the world. In that moment when a much bigger game was being played out in the other part of his life, Adamonis enjoyed the simplicity of knocking balls against one another. It was no wonder that some men never married. The surface of a billiards table was so much simpler to understand, he thought, than the depths of the heart.

"How is the barges business going?" Adamonis asked.

Martynas snorted. "It's a question of whether I'll go broke or crazy first, working with Woolley and working in this country."

"Capital problems?" Adamonis asked.

"Exactly. I thought Woolley would be in for the whole shot, but the best he can offer is a third of the money I need. I'm not sure why he's holding out on me."

"Maybe he doesn't want to take all the risk himself."

"That's for sure."

"Can you blame him?"

"Not for that, but for other things. He can't seem to concentrate on the most important part of the game. He runs around the country, or has me do it, picking likely loading depots. Measuring the distance to train lines and decent roads. All of that is fine, but you won't get anywhere without a boat. First we need some boats and in order to get boats, we need capital. You'd think the government would be willing to invest."

"I suppose it can't invest money it doesn't have."

"No, but Woolley goes to Germany for treatments to his nose. The Germans always have money stashed away, even when they pretend to be broke. Anyway, there must be banks there."

"Couldn't you find some investors here too? Say a dozen at a modest sum each? You know everyone."

"I'm working on it, actually. I have a few lined up. Would you like to be one of them?"

"I don't think so. The government is two months behind on my pay and anyway, I don't play where I don't understand the rules of the game."

They knocked the balls about for a long time, each of them winning a game and then losing to the other. As the evening went on, Adamonis kept looking at the phone on the wall.

It was well after midnight.

And then the phone rang.

29

ADAMONIS's offices were never entirely empty day or night. The clerks' hall had half a dozen men and women lingering among the thirty desks, and they turned to watch as Adamonis came in. People who worked in offices developed a sixth sense for unusual activity. A farmer went out and looked at the sky, sniffed the wind, listened to the movement of his horses in their stable, and divined what the day would bring. The clerks and the secretaries had come to read the office atmosphere like human barometers, and they sensed a storm of some kind was in the wind.

There were two others in his outer office, a lieutenant in uniform and an adjutant, both of whom rose when Adamonis came in. Pranaitis and Pinigelis were already there. The earnest young lieutenant was named Dilkus. He had a degree in history and was one of the few well-educated men in the department; Adamonis had an eye on him for promotion. Only the desk lamp was turned on in Adamonis's office, and at first he saw no one, but of course the practically invisible Chepas was in a chair in the corner. Adamonis took his place at the desk.

"All right," Adamonis said. "What do you know?"

Having spent most of his working life as a shadow, Chepas was unflappable, temperamentally suited to long hours doing nothing at all except keeping his eyes open. Adamonis could see those eyes even in the shadows where he sat.

"The functionary from the ministry of the exterior came down to seal the boxcars. But there was a bit of a surprise. General Vasilyev's park contact appeared and had one of the loaders put a small suitcase in the shipment too. They added it to the bill of lading."

"In the presence of the ministry man?"

"Yes."

"Any idea about the contents?"

"The loader said it was heavy for its size. Maybe ten kilos."

"And Vasilyev?"

"No sign of him."

"And the ministry man?"

"He didn't look surprised. Johnny watched the whole loading procedure, and when the functionary left, Johnny walked up to the two railway loaders who were counting wads of banknotes in their hands. They told Johnny about their good fortune. The ministry man had given them each a fistful of cash."

It was a lot of money, not far off an annual salary.

"When does the train leave?" Adamonis asked.

"There are two options. Either in a couple of hours or tomorrow night."

"What's the first major station after Kaunas?"

"Jonava."

"All right then. We wait and see." Adamonis had Miss Pinigelis connect him to the Jonava counterintelligence office and tell the night porter to rouse the section chief. Adamonis told the section chief to be ready with four men and to await his instructions.

"You still have men on Vasilyev?" Adamonis asked, and Chepas assured him he did.

Adamonis told Chepas to make sure to let him know when the train rolled out of the Kaunas station, and then Adamonis sent everyone to rest in the outer office or to find someplace where they could stretch out but be on hand if called.

Around dawn, Miss Pinigelis brought in bread and cheese and a pot of strong tea and Johnny came in. Others could watch the train station now. Adamonis had missed his old friend and poured him two fingers of brandy and toasted him on his success, and then Johnny went to rest in the outer office with the others.

Adamonis felt not the least bit tired; through the open door he could see Johnny's head was resting against a wall where he was snoring quietly. He was an adaptable old man who found his food and his repose where he could. Pranaitis was talking to Pinigelis as he taught her a few German words, and she gamely wrote them down on a sheet of paper. When they reached ten words, he would go back to the top of the list and quiz her. As he ran his fingers down the list, she missed a word, and Adamonis watched him nudge her hand back up the list to the right word. They seemed to be getting along very well.

The train did not leave that morning, a Sunday, and some of the clerks who had spent the night left to go to mass and others came in. The four in the outer office, including Dilkus, stayed where they were, one or the other sleeping in his chair from time to time. Late in the afternoon, Adamonis had nodded off himself, when Miss Pinigelis came in to say there was a phone call from Lily. He picked up the phone and asked Miss Pinigelis to close his door as she went out.

"Mr. Woolley is travelling again. You might be able to give me another ride," Lily said.

"I thought you were in the country."

"I didn't stay. I wanted to be nearer to you, and another opportunity just opened up."

"I can't get away now."

"You're sure?"

"I'm sorry."

"Something big is happening, isn't it? Anele said she called for you at the hotel but you haven't been there. Are you sleeping in the office?"

"I'm afraid I am."

"Maybe I could bring you something."

"No, I'm fine. Miss Pinigelis takes good care of me and there's a canteen next door."

"I'm a bit envious of her."

"Why?"

"I wish I could see you."

"So do I."

"At least tell me you're safe," said Lily.

"I'm sitting at my desk. I couldn't be any safer."

"But will you need to go out? If you do, call me here. Robert is away more than he's home. I could meet you somewhere, just for a cup of coffee. I could come over to your canteen."

"It's not possible now."

"Tell me what's happening." A short silence ensued. Miss Pinigelis opened his door, but when she looked at him, he shook his head and she shut it again. "I love you, you know," said Lily.

"I feel the same way."

"Then say it."

"I'm in my office."

"Can anyone else hear you?"

"I do love you, Lily. It's unbearable for me to be away from you, but I can't see you now and I can't keep the phone line busy."

"At least I have that," she said reluctantly. "See me as soon as you can, then. I miss you terribly."

Chepas called that evening to say the boxcars had left the Kaunas train yard. Adamonis phoned the Jonava office and told the section chief to stop the train at the Jonava station and to uncouple the two diplomatic railcars sealed by the ministry of the exterior.

The evening drifted into the second night at the office. The canteen was closed on Sunday and they were running out of food but had a good supply of cigarettes, coffee, and tea and they fuelled themselves with those. Adamonis's phone rang at four o'clock in the morning. The boxcars had been uncoupled at the Jonava station and they were under guard, awaiting his instruction. He wrote a note to Landa, and had it delivered to his office so it would be waiting when he arrived at the office at eight. He told Landa what he had done and asked him to inform the minister of external affairs to send a representative to Jonava to be present when the boxcars were opened for inspection.

At nine in the morning, Landa came in with his coat undone and a sheet of paper in his hands.

"You've really kicked the hornets' nest this time," he said, and he sat down across from Adamonis. "This is a telegram from the minister of external affairs. It says I am to release the boxcars immediately or be handed over to a court of law."

"May I see the telegram?"

Landa handed it over.

"Isn't it a bit unusual for a minister to write to a director in another ministry?" Adamonis asked.

"Right. Ministers only communicate with other ministers. This should have gone to our boss, the minister of defence."

"It will get to him eventually. Do you think our minister will stand up for you?"

Landa did not answer the question. And Adamonis waited as his boss struggled. It was taking him time to gather up his resolution.

"I won't reply to the telegram," said Landa at last. "But they're going to try to stop us. Get out of this office and take your team with you. Find a place with a phone, but stay out of the Metropolis."

"I can go to my sister's."

"Here is a phone number. Leave a message for me there if you want to get in touch."

"You're staying out of your office too?"

"Right."

30

ADAMONIS summoned Dilkus, the promising young lieutenant who had been waiting in his outer office for two days. Adamonis told him to take four men with him, to open the boxcars for inspection at the Jonava station, and to make a list of their contents. If a representative of the ministry of external affairs was there, to work with him, but if not, to do the job on their own in the presence of local witnesses.

Adamonis was just gathering his papers when Miss Pinigelis put her head into the office.

"There's a clerk from the ministry of external affairs who wants to see you."

There was no way to avoid him.

Adamonis expected an intimidating heavyweight, but the man who came in was a middle-aged functionary in a shiny suit. He was quick to explain he had a young wife, and he had played in the boxcars affair with a small shipment of cocaine that would help support his family. A lot of them were doing it. He was a bit player, one of many, and he did not want to take the fall for the main culprit.

Adamonis tried to stop him at two different points in his rather long story, but it took the clerk twenty minutes to say his piece and another five for Adamonis to frighten him a little and then get rid of him. In the anteroom sat four other bureaucrats from the same ministry, all of them more or less red-faced and avoiding one another's gaze. He did not have time to see them.

Chepas appeared as Adamonis was leaving with Pranaitis and Johnny. Miss Pinigelis stayed behind to answer the phones in case there was news she would then convey to him. Chepas said there was a rustle of activity going through the ministry of external affairs, followed by smoke from its chimneys.

Adamonis and his team installed themselves at his sister's house. She agreed to cancel all her appointments that day so there would be no strangers coming to the door. Pranaitis put the car behind the house. Chepas stood a shadow at each end of the street before going back out to supervise the surveillance of Vasilyev. Adamonis set himself up in the living room and the others were put at the long table in the kitchen, where the cook treated them like farm hands who had come in from the fields and needed to be fed. She heated a pot of sorrel soup and set out bread and butter, smoked meat and cheese and pickled cucumbers.

Anele came into the living room, still in her white dentist's smock.

"You know you're welcome here," she said.

"But?"

"But I need to know there's no danger. Should I take the children to the countryside?"

"Take them to Pazaislis for a couple of days. Or even to the village until the end of the week. But I can't give you the loan of the ministry car. I might need it."

She nodded and left the room, taking off her smock as she went.

As the day went on, Chepas arrived briefly without any news, and then stepped out to check on his men at the ends of the road. Johnny and Pranaitis played cards at the kitchen table and Adamonis called Miss Pinigelis from time to time to learn that more functionaries from the ministry of the exterior had come looking for him and there had been a call from the minister himself, but he would not leave a message. The minister was displeased that Adamonis could not be found. Adamonis looked through his papers and wandered into the kitchen to watch the men playing cards. He walked back to the other room and looked in his briefcase to make sure his pistol was loaded.

Miss Pinigelis telephoned. "Dilkus called. He wants me to give you a message."

"Well?"

"He sounded frightened. He said that he found the deputy minister had beat him to the Jonava station and the man had shouted at him. The deputy said Dilkus could be fired on the spot and taken to trial afterwards. His life could be made hell. So Dilkus removed the guards and left the boxcars as they were."

Adamonis was furious.

"Have the boxcars left the station?"

"Yes."

"Is there anywhere I can reach Dilkus?"

"He left a number."

"Who gave you the order to search the boxcars?" Adamonis asked once he reached Dilkus.

"You did."

"And I'm the one responsible for the order, not you, and you've refused a direct command. Are you some sort of coward who backs down at the first bureaucrat with a temper? You're a soldier. Do you know what it means to refuse a direct order?"

Silence on the other end of the line.

"Now nobody can save you but me. Do you understand? Unless you do this, you can kiss your career good-

bye and I'll make sure you're kicked all the way down to
the gutter. Get in a fast car. Kick the deputy minister out
of his own car if you have to, but do it and get those boxcars before they leave the country."

He hung up.

The proof of Adamonis's case was slipping away. It
would be a race to the last Lithuanian train station at the
border town of Obeliai, if Dilkus made it in time and did
not lose his nerve.

31

ADAMONIS had had too little sleep and too many cigarettes over the last two days and no matter how much lemon tea he drank, he could not clear the scum from his mouth. Even so, he reached for his cigarettes. Pranaitis and Johnny alternately dozed or stepped out to the yard for some air. They went out to relieve Chepas's shadows to give them a chance to eat something. The less he slept, the more Adamonis had time to think about Dilkus, who he hoped was only a fool and not a knave. Adamonis should have gone to the Jonava station himself.

When the phone rang that night, Pinigelis put Chepas on the line.

"Vasilyev's in the park. Someone's with him."

"Meet me at Soboras," said Adamonis. Vasilyev was the bigger prize that Adamonis stayed behind for. Now was the time to bring him in. He sent Pranaitis with the car down to Donelaicio Street, and he took a shadow and went out on foot. There was a park at the end of the street and he walked through it and came to the edge of it and saw where Kaunas lay beyond him below the hill on which he stood. The street lights were off for some reason. Few lights in private houses burned at night because electricity was expensive, and the points of it were like the lights on distant ships upon a vast, black ocean. He and the shadow walked quickly down the steps. He could see the head-lights of Pranaitis's car approaching as he crossed Done-laicio Street, and then Adamonis cut into a cross street until he came to the tall domes of the Soboras church, its mass a darker shadow within the night.

Adamonis met Chepas huddling on the south side of the church along with two others.

"Where is he?" Adamonis asked.

"Gone now. Vasilyev took the man back to his flat."

"Do we know who the other one is?"

"Too dark to tell."

It was disappointing, but maybe Vasilyev had too much information to pass on in a short note.

"Are you armed?" asked Adamonis.

"No."

"I have a pistol with me. Come on. We'll drive up to Vasilyev's."

They drove beyond the Green Hill, past where his sister lived, to a house set out on the fringes of the new suburb-to-be and some distance from the street. Vasilyev lived on the second floor of a house, with a set of wooden steps leading up to his flat. Adamonis posted the two shad-ows at each side of the house. He told Chepas and Pra-naitis to wait for him at the car.

"You're going in alone?" asked Chepas.

"He knows me. He won't feel threatened by me."

The door to the apartment suddenly opened and Vasi-lyev himself came outside. He was framed by the rectangle of light behind him. Vasilyev looked around very carefully.

Adamonis stepped out of the shadows on the street and began to walk toward the house, calling to Vasilyev, "I was passing by and saw you come out and I thought that since you're awake, I'd come for a visit."

Adamonis strode quickly toward him. It took Vasilyev a few moments to pull himself together but by then Adamonis was already ascending the creaking wooden steps.

Vasilyev showed the palm of his hand, as if to ward him off. "I'd invite you in, but I have someone here. You know, it might be a bit delicate." He laughed, but Adamonis kept walking up the steps until he was right in front of him.

"Think nothing of it," Adamonis said, reaching forward to shake his hand. Vasilyev took the hand instinctively and Adamonis did not let go and pushed him inside the flat. "Your guest is exactly the person I want to meet," Adamonis said. He heard Chepas and one of the shadows coming quickly up the steps and Adamonis let them in and asked Vasilyev to sit down at a table.

Vasilyev lived in furnished rooms, one of those places where everything from the couch to the tablecloth was not exactly new, but not exactly worn, yet somehow depressing, the haunt of a bachelor near the end of his middle age. And there was hardly anything there that had any sort of personal imprint. Except for one thing. Vasilyev stared at it, and Adamonis looked at it too. His medal from the Lithuanian government was on display on the ceramic stove.

There was no sign of anyone else. Adamonis sent Chepas and the shadow to look in the other rooms and they soon came back with a short man in a slightly extravagant suit, the lapels a little too wide, the tie a little too rich. Not really in the Soviet style at all. The man had been hiding in a wardrobe. The shadow had a sheaf of papers in his hand, found under clothes strewn at the bottom of the wardrobe.

"What's your name?" Adamonis asked.

"Vitaly Anikov."

"What is your occupation, Mr. Anikov?"

"I am the Soviet cultural attaché. I would like to contact my embassy."

The words were bold enough, but Anikov was very frightened, practically trembling. Adamonis made him sit down and asked him a few questions. Chepas and the shadow did a more thorough search and came up with more papers. Adamonis scanned them and saw they contained a report from Vasilyev about the proposed new disposition of Lithuanian troops.

Vasilyev watched Adamonis and smoked cigarettes from the case Adamonis left on the table.

"You're free to go home," Adamonis said to the cultural attaché.

Adamonis had to tell him twice. Finally Anikov stood and made toward the door, but kept looking over his shoulder. Adamonis followed him out onto the balcony and Anikov kept looking back as he went down the steps, moving slowly outside and watching, as if he expected to be shot. But once he sensed he was away from Adamonis's men, he ran. Adamonis returned to the apartment.

Anikov would be back at the embassy within the hour and the night porter there would call the ambassador at his home. News would spread quickly.

A shadow put his head inside. "There are headlights on the road," he said.

Adamonis reached over and turned off the light in the room. "Let me know if the car stops near us," he said.

They waited, and the car passed. It was not good to stay where they were.

"Let's go," said Adamonis.

They led Vasilyev down the stairs with Chepas in front and the shadow holding onto Vasilyev's collar from behind. Pranaitis and the shadow sat in the front of the car.

"Where are you taking me?" Vasilyev asked.

"To a safe place."

Vasilyev studied the direction Adamonis chose. If they were heading into the country, they might be planning to execute him, but he sat back when he saw they were only going the few blocks back to Anele's house. Adamonis could hear the phone ringing inside at Anele's place, but Johnny did not pick it up. Once they went inside, he sat Vasilyev among his men at the kitchen table. The phone started to ring again in the other room and he went to answer it.

Pinigelis was on the line.

"Dilkus has been trying to reach you."

"Did he get to the train in time?"

"Yes. He's broken the diplomatic seal and gone into the car."

"Do you know what he found?"

"He wants to report to you."

"Give me his number."

When Dilkus and his men had opened the doors of the boxcars, the Obeliai rail yard began to fill with the taste of sweetness as the saccharine from a torn bag drifted out. Within minutes, the night travellers in the station were rubbing their noses and the sound of sneezing came again and again from all the way down the road from the station. Lieutenant Dilkus had redeemed himself.

No one from the ministry of the exterior had been there. Adamonis instructed Dilkus to make a very careful inventory, and in particular to note the contents of a small suitcase. To rouse the pharmacist and the mayor as well as the chief of police, and to have all of them present as witnesses as he went through the contents of the car.

32

CHEPAS and Pranaitis were sitting with their arms crossed along with Vasilyev, who had continued to smoke at Anele's kitchen table. Adamonis's men looked to him as he came into the room.

"We have it," said Adamonis. It was an evening of double success. He had Vasilyev and his documents, and the contents of the boxcars as well, proof of external and internal betrayals.

Pranaitis was up in a moment, shaking his hand. Chepas did not rise, keeping an eye on Vasilyev, but he clapped his hands together and shook them in a gesture of victory.

"You have what?" asked Vasilyev.

"All we need," said Adamonis.

Vasilyev was not taking everything in. He was dazed, but asked for a cup of tea to wash the nicotine from his mouth. "We'll have to go soon," said Adamonis. "I need to take you in."

"Just a cup of tea."

Adamonis had Pranaitis put the water on.

"Can we speak privately?" Vasilyev asked.

Chepas did not want to leave them, but Adamonis said it would be all right. The two men sat across from each other and Adamonis's men went into the living room. He closed the door behind them.

Vasilyev blew across the surface of his cup and sipped from it. He set the teacup back on the saucer on the table. He seemed to have pulled himself together.

"There's one thing you should know," he said. "My mother and wife are alive in Moscow."

Personal reasons. What other motivation could he have had except for money?

"But you didn't go to them years ago, when you had a chance," said Adamonis. "And you didn't get them out. You stayed here and served us and you left them behind. Did you have some other motivation?"

He turned up his hands like a man demonstrating the obvious.

"In the end, I'm a Russian and my loyalty is to my people. I was just living here for a while, but you can't deny I saved this little country in its time of need. You need to put that on the scales."

His reply made Adamonis uneasy. What chance did they have in the long run if ethnicity trumped citizenship?

Vasilyev roused himself from his fatalism. "Listen," he said, "this sort of scandal will do the country no good. I'm the former chief of staff, for heaven's sake. People will lose confidence in the country if they see me arrested. Just let me go somewhere else. I could slip away quietly to South America."

"That's not up to me."

"But it is up to you. Once you put me into the maw of the system, there'll be no exit for me. You could do something for the nation as well as for me tonight. You could do it right now."

"I wish there was an easier way out, but I don't see one."

Vasilyev slumped back in his chair. "They'll probably just exchange me for someone in the Soviet Union."

"You may be right. I have no idea how things will end up."

"There was famine in Moscow," Vasilyev said. "My mother and wife would have died of hunger if not for me. I was sending them money and the Soviet embassy sniffed me out and made me cooperate. And at first the embassy didn't ask for much. I just passed on what I heard in the cafés. Soon, they kept telling me, I would have paid my bill and they'd let me return to my family. To tell you the truth, I didn't want to go back. But they wouldn't release the women. Just think what you would have done in my position."

But Adamonis couldn't permit himself to have those thoughts.

"It's funny how things turn out sometimes, isn't it?" Vasilyev asked. He had no anecdote to add to this observation. There was nothing Adamonis could do but agree with him. He went to the cabinet where he knew the cook kept her bottle, and he poured Vasilyev three fingers of *trejos devynerios*, the herbal liquor that was bitter medicine.

They were getting ready to leave shortly before dawn when the phone rang.

"Landa called," said Pinigelis. Adamonis felt a pang. He should have called his superior as soon as they had Vasilyev back at the house, but the call from Dilkus and the conversation with Vasilyev had delayed him.

"I'll call him back right now," said Adamonis.

"You can't reach him. He's on his way to you now."

"On his way here? Why?"

"He said he wanted to take Vasilyev in himself."

Adamonis passed the news on to his men. Chepas shifted uneasily.

"We should finish this ourselves," Chepas said. "We have the documents from his house. We have the contents of the boxcars being tallied. Once we put Vasilyev under lock and key, then our part is done."

"Landa is my superior," said Adamonis. "I've received an order."

"Not a direct order," said Chepas. "Miss Pinigelis passed it on. You could say you misunderstood."

"We can't afford to alienate Landa. We're going to be in hot water tomorrow, and this puts him in the pot with us. Anyway, you worked with him before you worked with me. Do you have any doubts?"

"I don't know him anymore. He's changed somehow. I've seen a lot of operations go to hell, even at the last moment. If we take Vasilyev in ourselves, we'll be sure we've finished our job."

Adamonis considered what he was saying, and was beginning to think Chepas was right, but then he saw the beams of headlights flash across from behind a curtained window and a car came up the drive.

Landa came in with two men, heavyset types who looked like provincial policemen.

"Good job, good job," Landa said happily, and shook Adamonis's hand without looking at him longer than a moment.

"Can I give you a briefing?" Adamonis asked.

But Landa declined.

"Do you know about the boxcars?" Adamonis asked.

He did. They could talk later in the day. Landa needed to take Vasilyev in.

Adamonis's unease grew when Landa told them it was unnecessary for Adamonis or any of his men to go outside with him. Adamonis's unease grew to alarm when shortly after Landa and Vasilyev stepped outside into the darkness one of Landa's men began to shout, but Adamonis did not make it outside before he heard two shots in quick succession.

33

BITTER COLD descended on the Adamonis hamlet, freezing the rutted muck of the roads, only to give way the next day to a warm front that turned the furrowed fields back to long thin islands between canals of standing water that led nowhere. The days were short and grey. On warm days, the cattle were kept inside to prevent them from sinking into the mud to their bellies.

In the countryside, the seasonal moods of the farmers and their families were reversed from those who lived in the city, where spring and summer brought joy. In the countryside winter brought happiness because the heavy work of fall was done and the storerooms were full of rye and wheat, barley and buckwheat. Potatoes and beets lay in heaps and barrels full of cabbage were turning into sauerkraut as they fermented. Garlands of dried mushrooms hung in one room, and dried apples in another. The fatted pigs would soon be slaughtered and then lengths of sausages would hang in the smokehouse.

Adamonis wondered how Johnny was getting along back in Kaunas.

"You deserve a holiday," Landa had said. "You practically look like a corpse from all the late nights and cigarettes."

"Why did they have to shoot him?"

"He was trying to escape."

"What's being covered up?"

"Nothing at all. Look, Dilkus's report has gone in and the cabinet has resigned due to the scandal. Novak is gone along with the whole government! Think how we've managed to shake things up! There will be a fresh start—a new government and a new minister of external affairs."

"And will the former minister be taken to trial?"

"We aren't the judiciary. Remember that. Our job is to uncover the crimes and then hand the guilty parties over to the courts. You're practically a hero, but the new government doesn't want the newspapers crawling all over you for more lurid details."

"Did you see Dilkus's report?" Adamonis asked.

"Yes, of course. Saccharine and cocaine as well as brandy and silver and any number of things that could be exchanged on the black market in Moscow."

"And you saw what Vasilyev had in that suitcase?"

"Of course, of course."

The suitcase had been intended for his wife and daughter. It contained flour, sugar, coffee, and smoked meat.

"Do you think Vasilyev's women got the suitcase?" Adamonis asked.

"How can I possibly know that? It's out of our hands."

The morning after Vasilyev's death and the seizure of the goods in the boxcars, Miss Pinigelis could not keep out their various clerks and operatives who appeared in the outer offices bearing bottles of vodka and *krupnikas* and soon they had a good fifteen people in the office drinking toasts to Adamonis and the department. Dilkus had not returned from the Obeliai station yet, and in any case he would have to keep the shipment under guard and bring it back to Kaunas as evidence. After a couple of hours, Adamonis had to drive off all the well-wishers and write up his report and begin to move it through the proper channels.

He was still sitting among the overflowing ashtrays and empty glasses in his office when Landa showed up late that evening. He smiled enigmatically as he sat down in a chair opposite Adamonis, and he poured himself a little *krupnikas* from an open bottle on the edge of the desk and sipped from it, and then delivered the news of the forced vacation. Landa wanted Adamonis to hurry because it looked like rain was coming, and he wanted Pranaitis to take Adamonis to his village and return immediately to Kaunas with the car. Once the rains became steady, there was no way in and out by car.

"Why so fast?" Adamonis asked.

"I've told you about the press. There's also the matter of the Soviet embassy, which claims you held their cultural attaché against his will. The Christian Democratic Party doesn't think it was a criminal investigation—they believe you spearheaded a plot to oust them and Novak is furious you never brought him inside the investigation. Let me take care of all this. I'm covering for you. Just take a rest in the countryside until the dust settles."

"I don't want to take a rest."

"This is not a suggestion. It's an order."

When Adamonis stopped by Anele's house to pick up the briefcase he had left there, she was waiting for him in the living room. There were no dental patients and Vilimas was sitting with her instead of being at his office in the museum. Vilimas looked embarrassed, but said nothing. Anele did not rise from her chair when Adamonis came in.

The house was very quiet.

"Where are the children?" asked Adamonis.

"They aren't here. Why do you ask?"

Adamonis was nonplussed. "I'm their uncle."

"But you didn't take them into consideration when you moved your operation here, did you?"

"I didn't think of it at the time because I didn't believe anything dangerous was going on. And anyway, you took them away."

"Because I thought of it. Shots were fired in our drive. A man was killed out in front of our house, and you brought all of that down on us."

"I didn't know it would turn out that way."

"Not exactly, no. But in spite of all my advice you continue to play these dangerous games. It's not enough that you'll bring disaster on yourself, you didn't even have the consideration to protect my children."

"Anele, my job is to protect the country."

"Your first job is to protect your family, and one of them could have been hurt or worse. Your briefcase is on the floor beside the couch. I noticed there was a pistol in it, so you didn't exactly come here unarmed. I want you to gather up anything else you might have in the house and take it all to the damned Hotel Metropolis. And then I'll thank you to stay away from this house unless you're invited."

On the first days of his vacation in the countryside, Adamonis felt as if he had stepped off a rocking boat and could not find his land legs. Exhausted from the days without sleep during the operation, he would lie down on the bed in his low-ceilinged room only to snap awake half an hour later with his heart racing and a sense of vertigo so strong that he sat on the edge of the bed with both feet on the floor until the motion ceased. Then he went to the window and opened the shutters, but the sky was overcast and there was nothing to see outside.

In the evenings, he sat with Stan and his family as they gathered by the fire, where a widowed aunt told ghost stories while the women spun or wove and the men repaired harnesses and twisted hemp for rope. Sometimes Stan's wife read from newspapers, but these travelled so slowly that the news of the Kaunas scandals had not arrived yet. After a while, Stan would light a lantern and go out to check on the animals and take Adamonis with him. In his workshop, Stan set the lantern down and took out a bottle of *namine* and poured each of them three fingers as a nightcap. On the third night, he gave the bottle to Adamonis and told him to put it in his pocket and use it in the middle of the night when he woke up. Stan had heard him walking around.

On the fifth day, Lily came riding in upon a cart loaded with hay. She was wearing a long woollen coat and a headscarf and carried two suitcases, one of them filled with gifts for the relatives and the children: candies wrapped in shiny paper, chocolates and a bottle of crème de menthe for the women and one of French brandy for the men. Adamonis was overjoyed to see her, but the eyes of the relatives were very sharp and he could make no gesture beyond familial kisses and hugs. She was staying next door, but she came to Stan's house that evening, along with half the village, it seemed, in order to read the newspapers she brought from Kaunas.

According to some of the newspapers, Adamonis was a hero, the guardian of the nation. The seizure of the smuggled goods was written up in great detail, but most of the detail was fiction, and the crisis in government was written out like a morality tale. It had been the subject of many Sunday sermons. General Vasilyev's death was written as a separate story, one in which he was killed by thieves whom he had caught red-handed as they escaped. No link was drawn between the two narratives.

Adamonis was the most celebrated relative to come out of his parents' village, the prince of the remote countryside.

The next day dawned cold, with the water in the furrows covered by a thin layer of ice, and Lily came after breakfast to walk with Adamonis into the countryside along a path beside a stream. They walked as cousins might, close, but not touching, the distance hard.

"I've missed you terribly," he said once they were far away from the others.

"I was so worried. I knew something was going on and I was sure you were in danger."

"Trouble more than danger. I might be in more trouble now than I was then."

"I know. I only brought selected newspapers. You should hear what the Christian Democrats are writing about you. I thought your position was supposed to be some kind of secret."

"Not anymore, I guess."

"No. Not anymore. What are you doing out here anyway?" asked Lily.

"I've been banished for a while until the storm dies down."

"And what will happen next?"

"I don't know."

She stopped and looked him in the face. She was intent on the words she was about to say, but her face was very beautiful and distracted him. "Are you listening to me?" she asked. "They should be ashamed of the way they treated you in Kaunas."

"Who is *they*?"

"The government, your department. You've saved the country and they have you out here in the wilderness as if you've committed some kind of crime. You deserve better than this."

"You're very kind, but you overstate my impact. This is just what what I do. This is what I am. A bureaucrat, really. A government employee."

"With a pistol."

"Yes, sometimes. But I haven't needed to use it yet."

"Anele is very angry with you."

"I know."

"Maybe it's time for a change."

"Like what?"

"Go into business. Robert could use your help. He keeps running into roadblocks here. Martynas is all talk and he claims he has contacts, but he can't deliver. Robert needs a stronger man with him. Someone like you."

"Lily, how could I possibly go into business with your husband? I can't stand the sight of him."

"Oh, come on. He's not that bad."

"Maybe not, but he's your husband and I envy him for that. It's not a change in career that I need. It's you."

She turned away from him and walked up a little way along the path. The water in the stream beside them was high and the bushes that grew along the side were half-submerged in moving water with fringes of thin ice. She turned back to him then and held out her hands. He stepped forward and took them in his own.

"I love you too, but things are impossible for us," she said.

"Don't say that. We can find a way."

"What kind of way? I feel a debt to Robert and I couldn't leave him stranded here and besides, there's no divorce permitted in this country."

"We could go somewhere else."

"I want to stay where I am. Don't you? And that makes everything impossible. Can't we just love each other the way we are?"

"But what if I did find a way to solve everything? Would you marry me then?"

She let go of his hands and looked around to see if anyone was nearby. She laughed. "If you could do the impossible, make Robert happy and me as well and have us live here somehow, then yes, I would marry you. But those aren't my only conditions."

"What else do you want?"

"I want you to be open with me. I've said that before. All this skulking around that you do leaves me outside your life. Open up to me. You have secrets, I know, but if we're to marry, there can be no secrets between us. You'd have to open your heart to me and I'd open mine." She laughed again. "I don't know why we're even saying these things. They'll never happen."

It was impossible to kiss her then, because although the countryside looked empty, one could never be sure. She stayed another day, and after she left, Adamonis turned the problem of their relationship around and around in his mind. He could think of nothing, but he would not let the problem rest.

34

"THE DISADVANTAGE of living and working in a small country," Landa said upon seeing Adamonis on his return to Kaunas, "is that you meet the same people coming and going. In Russia, you can parcel out justice and never see the guilty party again. Here, you'll run into him on the street or at a friend's party."

The vacillating fall weather had developed into a particularly cold spell, although they were not in winter yet. The office window behind Landa's head had specks of frost on it and the Finnish ceramic stove in the corner had a fresh fire burning hotly inside.

"We are the trash men," said Landa, "and no one wants trash but no one respects the people who take it out. A bit of stink hovers over us."

"You mean particularly over me."

"I've done all I can in your absence. But remember, you've embarrassed important people, and they hate to be embarrassed. It's all the worse that you're some kind of matinee hero to the opposition parties."

"We set out to clean up this place and make it safe. Remember?"

"Maybe. It all seemed simple at the beginning, didn't it? But the aftermath will follow you for the rest of your career. In any case, let's not dwell on that too much now. This is a success of sorts, a complicated success. Not the last one, I hope. How are you feeling, by the way?"

"I feel fine, except I've put on weight in the country. I thought they were fattening me for slaughter."

Landa chuckled. "That's more likely here than in the countryside." When Adamonis did not laugh along with him, Landa added, "It's a joke, Justas. Take it as a joke."

"All right."

"And what about your sister. How is she?" Landa asked.

"She won't speak to me. Incidentally, which of the two men with you fired the shots? I don't remember it coming up in the newspapers."

"Sergeant Butkus."

"The name doesn't mean anything to me."

"You don't remember? He was one of the men with me when you found the printing press, one of your early successes."

"Those men were useless. I wanted them fired."

"Seniority, you know, counts for something here. I just had them reassigned to intelligence instead of counter-intelligence. And anyway, I'm glad he was there. Vasilyev could have got away."

"A middle-aged man can't run as far or as fast as a young one."

"What's done is done. Let's move on. Unless, of course, you feel burned out."

"Burned out?"

"You looked terrible. That's why I sent you off to the country. But you know as well as I do that this sort of work can eat people up."

"I've been at this for quite a while. I think I'm used to it."

"You're sure?" Landa asked.

"I'm sure."

"Then let's start off with a clean slate. All right?"

"What did you have in mind?"

"The new government is eager to make an impression. There have been too many embarrassments. And while you may have enemies, you have your supporters too. Some of them are in this government and I've been singing your praises."

Landa looked to Adamonis for appreciation, but Adamonis was impassive.

"The people of Klaipeda have grown restless," said Landa. "This can't be permitted to go on."

His meaning was clear enough.

"I wonder what our neighbours think about that," said Adamonis.

"The Soviets and the Germans have no objection."

"I'm a little surprised at the Germans. They believe the city and the region belong to them."

"They believed that of Danzig too and the city was taken away from them and made into a so called "free city." The Germans lost the war. They have no other option but to give up Klaipeda and the only question is who the allies will give it to . The French want revenge and they would never let Germany keep the region, and better us than the Poles unless the allies make it into another "free region" in which case we lose again. There have been too many losses. We need a win."

"How big is the French garrison?"

Landa had a binder ready on his desk, and he opened it up. "The French have two hundred and fifty soldiers and there's a native police force of over three hundred."

"That's not much of an army," Adamonis said. "We could march in with a few thousand men and the city and the region would be ours in a day."

"A Lithuanian army can't march in there. The locals will have to rise up and seize the city from the French occupying garrison. We need someone who can arrange that."

So they wanted him to lead an uprising. It was one way to get rid of him. He asked Landa to give him a little time.

Adamonis was furious that Vasilyev had been shot and he was equally upset that he had been sent out of town after the operation so the facts of it could be twisted, turned inside out, and presented as any one of half a dozen different stories. All of this in his absence. Landa said he was shielding him, but from whom?

A part of him did thrill to the thought of more action. Klaipeda would be quite a prize. There was something impetuous about the plan to seize territory from the French, a mouse tweaking the whiskers of the big cat.

He thought for some time about the countryside surrounding Klaipeda The farmers there were mostly ethnic Lithuanians. After so much time under German rule, though, the Lithuanians were different there, mostly Lutherans rather than Roman Catholics. Did religion matter more than nationality, or did neither one have any weight at all? He did not know. But he mulled over this difference in religions and slowly it came to him that different religions had different rules and these were reflected in the civil statutes.

Lutherans permitted divorce.

When he returned to see Landa, he agreed to take on the mission as soon as it was finally approved, but with conditions.

"*Conditions?*" Landa asked. "Really. And what kind of conditions do you think I can present to our new minister? He won't see you, you know."

"I have a certain interest in shipping," said Adamonis. Landa showed barely any change in expression. "It would be very useful if we could build a couple of ports upriver from Klaipeda to help shipping along the Nemunas. The Germans may have given us their approval privately, but in public, they're going to scream blue murder. They might close the rail link. We have to be ready to ship downriver."

"I didn't realize you were interested in commerce," said Landa.

"I understand the machinery of state runs on money."

Landa looked at him with a sense of recognition. Here was another bureaucrat ready to risk his life for the nation as long as there was something in it for him. Adamonis did not think Landa was disappointed by this insight. Quite the opposite. Now he knew what Adamonis wanted.

"I'll take your interests upstairs and then let you know," said Landa.

35

MISS PINIGELIS was clearing up her desk for the day, her hair loose and covering her downturned face as she packed papers into her valise. Who else would take work home except a woman as dedicated as this? Most of his employees looked upon their work as a provisional stage in their careers. Adamonis could train cadres all he wanted, but they moved on at the first opportunity. She was loyal, and the longer she worked in the department, the more he treasured her.

Pinigelis was scrupulous in her work, but not one of those people who lost their humanity in the dust and stamps of government offices. In less businesslike attire, she would look very good in the café society that was beginning to develop in the city. And he had heard she had some wit, although she was circumspect in using it around him. She responded to his greeting without looking up at him, but when Adamonis asked her where Pranaitis was, she raised her head and looked him full in the face.

"I have no idea," she said. She had been crying and was on the verge of it again. Adamonis was astonished and touched his finger to her tear-stained cheek. He had never touched her before, but she didn't seem upset by this sudden intimacy. Still, he withdrew his hand quickly. And then she looked at him defiantly, unashamed by her tears and somehow even a little proud of her pain.

"What's wrong?" he asked.

"Nothing."

Adamonis had seen many tears in his line of work, more often than he cared to remember, and as a doctor became used to the groans of patients, he was more than a little accustomed to the pain of others. Yet he found himself surprisingly touched.

"Come into my office," he said. She did as he asked and he closed the door behind her and then walked around to his side of the desk.

"Would you like a drink?"

"No. I hate the stuff." She was still standing.

"Please sit down." She did as he asked. "Are you opposed to alcohol?" He poured himself two fingers of brandy.

"I'm opposed to some of the men who drink it. My father could never hold his liquor. He was an embarrassment, and a good number of the men in this country take after him." She looked down at her hands.

"And what of Pranaitis?"

"He's weak and he's foolish and I don't know why I waste my tears on him."

"Is he drinking again?"

"Oh, yes."

"I didn't notice him on my way in. Does he drink alone or in the company of other men? The lone drinker is the one you have to watch out for."

"He drinks in the company of women. One woman, anyway."

So Felicia was back again. How were they ever going to take care of the matters of state when they couldn't take care of the matters of their hearts?

"How much do you know about her?" he asked.

"Enough."

They were already beyond the realm appropriate for a government office, but he couldn't let it drop. It would be like leaving a wounded comrade on the field. Pranaitis was so unpredictable. But if Adamonis fired him, Pinigelis might go with him and what good would that do him?

"Tell me what he's said to you."

"He told me a madwoman has been following him for years. She shows up out of nowhere and makes accusations until he moves on or frightens her so badly that she leaves him alone for a while."

"And what do you think of this story?"

"There has to be more to it than that. A crazy woman would be put away or arrested. She's holding something over him, and sometimes I'm afraid it's the worst thing of all and he's afraid to tell me."

"What would be the worst thing of all?"

"The knowledge they're actually married."

Part of him wanted to smile, but she looked up at him so sincerely that the urge evaporated and he studied her face. Brown eyes and a ready smile, at least ordinarily, and fine features. This woman may have come from the countryside but there was nothing coarse about her. If she had had more money in the family, she might have gone on to university the way his sister had. Intelligent beyond her peers in some remote village that hadn't changed in centuries, she had made it to Kaunas and found an office job, quite an achievement for anyone where she came from. Yet this determination and success had cost her something, the needs of her heart put on hold so she could achieve her ambition. Then Pranaitis came along, but he came with problems.

"They're not married," said Adamonis.

"You know this for a fact?"

"I do."

She sighed and brushed back her hair and wiped her cheeks with the backs of her hands. Then it was his turn to feel a pang because in spite of her unhappy situation, she had something he didn't have.

"Then why is he so troubled?" she asked.

"This woman has a child, and the child is his."

She responded without the least hesitation. "He's not the only unmarried man who's made babies."

How quick people were to save their sympathy for themselves.

"No. So now that you know this, are you relieved?"

"What I can't understand is why he keeps going to her. Do you think he still loves her?"

"I doubt it. I think the child makes him feel guilty and when he feels guilty, he drinks too much."

"How old is the child?" she asked.

"A boy of six."

"You've met them?"

"I've had someone check up for me."

"Could you tell me a little more?"

He could. Adamonis told her that Felicia had been to Birstonas for three months and the doctors there had diagnosed her with hysteria. She seemed to be curable, though. After all, she loved her son, and she had to recover at the sanatorium or they'd take him from her and place him permanently in a parish orphanage. She received part of Pranaitis's pay, but it wasn't always enough, and when she was in trouble, she knew where to find him.

"So what can he do about all this?" she asked.

"I don't know. Maybe nothing. You might have to be the one to do something."

"Like what?"

"Lose your problem."

She absorbed this for a while before speaking. "I couldn't do that. I'm in love with him and he's in love with me. We'll have to run away."

Adamonis finished the brandy in his glass. "You make it sound so simple. Where could you run? America closed its doors to immigration. Russia is a nightmare and Germany is still licking its wounds after the defeat. We're at war with the Poles. You might go up to Riga. It's both close enough and far enough, but it's the first foreign place someone would look. Even there you wouldn't know anyone and you'd have to learn the language and you'd compete against all the Latvians moving into the city to look for work. I don't guess either one of you has any money saved up, at least not much, not on what you're paid here. Imagine a cold room in Riga with your money running out. How would you sustain yourselves there?"

"Where did you get this terrible picture?"

"I'm always thinking about escape routes. The world as we knew it collapsed once before, and it might collapse again. You have to think to the future."

"There has to be some sort of solution. Doesn't love count for anything?"

"Maybe. Let me go look for him. I'll see what I can find out."

36

ADAMONIS dismissed his personal shadows and took Johnny along with him for the walk up to Pranaitis's apartment on Donelaicio Street. Johnny had a sort of calming influence on him. It was good to have a man who brought some of the pragmatism of the countryside with him. And it didn't hurt to have someone to help inure him against the melancholy of a dismally cold late-autumn evening.

Donelaicio was a long street that ran parallel to Freedom Boulevard. It had had some fine, traditional wooden houses on it. Log houses were the norm all the way up to Finland and into Russia because logs kept the heat in better. In the city, the logs were covered with clapboard to make them look finer, and the eaves were decorated with wooden ornaments. But wooden houses, decorated or not, simply wouldn't do for a capital city, even a provisional one. Brick and stucco apartment blocks were rising and if this kept up, Kaunas would eventually lose its village characteristics.

In the almost two years since he'd arrived, they'd gone from a country on the verge of nonexistence to a real place where money was beginning to flow in. Some of it came from émigrés like Lily, who returned with their American dollars and were beginning to build apartment blocks.

"What do you think of all these new buildings, Johnny?" Adamonis felt the chill and wished he'd brought his gloves, but Johnny seemed insensitive to the cold and didn't even have his sheepskin buttoned up.

"Not much."

"Aren't you impressed? Look how tall they're going to be. Some of them will be five and six storeys high."

"I prefer to keep my feet on the earth or close to it. Living up high like that isn't natural."

"Are you afraid of heights?"

"Not me. I climbed enough trees in my boyhood to know what it's like up there. But here's the thing. When you're up high like that, your imagination begins to take off. When I was a boy, I remember thinking maybe I could fly from a treetop like a bird, but I had enough sense not to jump off a limb of some tall oak."

"I don't follow you."

"I'm saying that people get all sorts of odd ideas, and they get more of them if they live in tall buildings. And if you live up high, you might get crazy enough to jump out the window and kill yourself."

"People find ways to kill themselves all the time. They hang themselves from trees or shoot themselves if they're rich enough to own pistols. And anyway, why are you talking about suicide?"

"You're the one who brought it up."

"Have you ever thought of suicide?"

"Not me, but plenty of people kill themselves. My sister was one. She was unmarried and pregnant and drank concentrated vinegar and it burned her guts out. It was terrible. I was going to kill the man who got her pregnant, but he fled to America."

"What a sad story. Do you have any other family?"

"Growing up, I had only her. I had children once too, but they died of measles. Their mother threw herself in a river."

"I'm sorry. I never realized you had such a tragic life."

"A lot of bad things happened to me, but I survived, for some reason. I don't know what the reason is. Maybe God does. War and disease and famine have come through here often enough, yet here I am. I must be serving some purpose, even if I'm no more important than a sparrow on a branch."

"Well, you're more important than a sparrow to me."

"But you're not God."

Adamonis looked at him to see what he meant by this, but his expression hadn't changed.

Pranaitis lived at the end of a short, dead-end street off Donelaicio. Construction was going on at the corner, but just behind it were the wooden houses, a dozen on each side, with their short front gardens protected by fences leaning every which way. Pranaitis lived right at the end in a big, two-storey house that had been carved into rooms to rent. He had his own entrance at the back, with a porch overlooking a rough yard with scrap metal at one end of it and a pair of outhouses at the other end, one of them particularly decrepit and odoriferous with a plank nailed over the door, and another, newer one beside it, stinking just as badly as the first.

Adamonis knocked on the door and heard movement inside, but no one answered. He knocked again and still no answer, and finally he called out his name and the lock on the other side turned and Pranaitis opened the door.

He looked as if he had just gotten out of bed, with his brilliantined hair up in cowlicks around his ears and his face red and his eyes bloodshot. His shirt collar was stained with a thin streak of blood and he had a scratch on his neck that looked as though it had been put there by a razor held by an unsteady hand. The room stank of alcohol.

"Mr. Adamonis," he said, surprised and frightened by his boss's appearance. "I never expected to see you at my door. You've caught me at a bad time."

"So I see. May we come in?"

"My place is a mess."

"I'm sure I've seen worse."

But Adamonis rarely had. Inside was a room trashed by a man in frenzy. The bed was unmade and stank of old sweat and alcohol. The books and papers had been swept from his desk and lay on the floor and the chair was knocked over. Johnny closed the door behind them and stood with his back to a wall, nervously rubbing the fingertips of his right hand with his thumb in a gesture of unease at what was to come.

"What happened here?"

Pranaitis sat down on the edge of his bed and looked at his hands on his lap. "I've had some personal trouble."

"I'll say. I can only admire the brains you had not to come into work today."

"It's my day off."

"And ordinarily I wouldn't care one way or another what you did in your free time unless it affected your work, but this place is a disaster. I'm wondering if you shouldn't spend a few weeks in Birstonas to dry out."

"I've been under a lot of pressure."

"Felicia?"

He looked up at Adamonis then with an expression of anguish. "She was threatening me, do you understand? She said she'd take me to the police."

"She wanted money."

"Worse. To get married. I am not going to harness myself for life to a madwoman."

"Did you hit her?"

He nodded. Adamonis realized the scratch on his neck had not come from a razor after all. The right thing to do was to dismiss Pranaitis. A chronic alcoholic was hopeless. But now Adamonis felt as if he owed something to Miss Pinigelis, even though she deserved better than this pathetic wreck on the bed.

"Where did she go?" Adamonis asked.

"I don't know."

"No. But she seems to have a habit of coming back. I'll think of something, but before I waste any time on this, I need to know about your relationship with Miss Pinigelis."

"I'm in love with her."

"Yes, all right. But how much in love? Do you want to marry her?"

"That would make me the happiest man on earth."

For her sake, Adamonis would need to do something, although he was not sure what solution he could possibly find to the triangle of Pinigelis, Felicia, and Pranaitis. For all he knew, Felicia was at a police station now, showing bruises and putting in a complaint. Adamonis wondered for the second time that day if Miss Pinigelis wouldn't be better off without him, but how did one reason with the human heart?

37

NORTHERN COUNTRIES were like people subject to extreme mood swings, for they were intensely bright and alive with birdsong in the warm months, and particularly dark and gloomy in the winter. Most of the overhead lights in the outer office were extinguished by government decree to save on electricity, and only a few clerks sat bent under their gooseneck desk lamps, scratching at papers. Mr. Landa's secretary was not at her place outside his door and Adamonis half expected Landa not to answer when he knocked. But he heard Landa's voice from the other side, telling him to come in.

Landa had aged significantly in the interval since they first met at the train station. He had taken on gravity whereas back then he had had an air of adventure, the attitude of a man who found himself with responsibilities beyond his range and was amused by the circumstances. His beard was long gone. Landa wasn't amused by much of anything anymore. His hair was short now and he wore steel-rimmed eyeglasses to help him read the myriad of documents that went across his desk daily. He wore a new suit so understated that it had to be expensive, but his face bore an anxious air. "How have you been?" Landa asked.

"The same as usual. Well."

Landa looked as if he was about to say something, but stopped himself. He looked down to shuffle some papers and then looked up.

"The uprising in the Klaipeda region has received final approval." He watched Adamonis to see how the news would go over.

"All right."

"We need to act soon. The Conference of Ambassadors is ruling on the district and they're going to make an announcement on January 10. The Poles want the region and the French are on the side of the Poles. If we wait for the bureaucrats to judge, it looks like the decision will go against us. You're the man who's going to change all that."

Adamonis nodded.

"You'll be running the show, but don't expect anything in writing. We might raise one or two hundred local men in the region, but you'll have around a thousand of our own volunteers dressed in civilian clothes. I can't say the operation is without its risks."

"And afterward?"

"It will be an autonomous region, federated with us. They're all Protestants there and don't want to be tied too tightly to the Catholic Church in this country. "

"What about me?"

"You'd stay there as chargé d'affaires during the transition. Then provided everything works out well and you can handle the post, you might be appointed governor."

A kind of reward then. And in the meantime, the Christian Democrats would be pleased to have him gone.

"How does all of this suit you?" asked Landa.

"Logistics are going to be a challenge."

"I'm sure you're up to it. I'll assign some help." Landa reached for his fountain pen and unscrewed the top. He had deemed the interview over, but Adamonis was not finished.

"When we first talked about this, I asked you about my interest in barge ports being partially financed by the government and you said you'd mention it upstairs."

Landa did not even look up. He started to write on a document. "That's been approved," he said.

There was much to be done and Adamonis would have to hurry. Even so, he found time to descend into the bowels of the building to confer with the head counsel. The lawyer was not well informed about the civil statutes in the Klaipeda region, but he did know that divorce was permitted there.

Adamonis used a telephone in the head counsel's office to call Lily and he asked her and Woolley to meet him at the Versailles Restaurant later that evening. It was a last-minute invitation and Lily hesitated. Judging by the length of time it took her to agree, she had to put up with the protestations of Woolley.

38

IT HAD BECOME DIFFICULT to secure a table at the Versailles Restaurant, but they always kept one in reserve for important, unexpected guests, and Adamonis was now in that category, so they found him a place near the stage. He made his way through a room filled with diners, even though the show had not started yet. A lone accordionist sat on the stage, playing "The Blue Danube," which seemed to be a recurring national favourite.

Once he was seated, as an experiment, he ordered a flask of Armenian brandy, but found out there was none available, and so had a bottle of champagne brought to the table, but left it on ice until Woolley and Lily arrived. He also asked for a bottle of Vichy water as well as a plate of mild cheese, and sliced cucumbers with honey on the side for dipping, a local food that he knew Woolley approved of.

Woolley's expression when Adamonis saw him at the doorway was one of distaste, like the face of a prudish man taken out slumming against his will, but Lily saw Adamonis in the crowd and waved merrily and said something to Woolley and his look softened as they came to the table. Adamonis rose and kissed her on the cheek and the scent of her turned his head for the slightest of moments. He pulled himself together, stood back, and shook Woolley's indifferent hand and they sat down.

"Doesn't anyone in this town know another tune?" asked Woolley. Adamonis called over the waiter and gave him five litas, their new national currency, to pass to the accordionist to silence him. Lily wore a simple grey evening dress. The string of pearls around her neck and a cloche hat were the uniform of women of a certain class. She seemed cheerful and gave Adamonis not the slightest hint in her look that they might have anything but a relationship appropriate to cousins, however distant.

"How is life in the countryside?" Adamonis asked her, for she had been out to their hamlet again.

"I love the country," she said, "but at this time of year, with the leaves down and the earth plowed for winter, I like it better here in town."

"And you, Mr. Woolley, how is your business going?" Adamonis never called him by anything other than his last name, and Woolley did the same.

"I think I'm coming to the end of some kind of rope in this place," he said, and to his credit, he said it sadly. Adamonis had seen only two moods in him, the one of excessive exuberance when he first arrived and the other, more common, seething sulkiness. This melancholy raised some sympathy in Adamonis for the first time.

"Are we celebrating something?" Lily asked as she eyed the champagne.

"We are. I have news."

Adamonis waited until the waiter opened the bottle and filled their glasses.

"To barges," said Adamonis. Woolley made a sour face. "Drink up. I have good news."

They did, and Adamonis saw Lily put her hand on Woolley's as they waited expectantly. Adamonis envied his hand and as if sensing this, Lily pressed her leg against his under the table.

"I've been in a meeting with someone very high up," Adamonis said, "but I can't tell you his name just now. Things are changing in this country and opportunities are opening. Have you seen the construction on Donelaicio Street?"

"Noise and dust," said Woolley, since they did not live far away from there.

"It's the sound of progress, the dust of wealth, gold dust, let's say. Look around this room. Some of the upper-class thieves in this town are drinking cognac and champagne. A year ago they were still drinking *namine* fresh out of the still. I'm saying that the country is beginning to move."

"If you call rich criminals progress," said Lily.

"I don't. Not really. If I were a smart detective I'd put a quarter of this room in jail and decimate the upper eche-lons of the criminal class. There's enough money here now that these thieves who skim off the top are living a good life, and a businessman should be able to do even better."

"I am a businessman and I've been working on this project for well over a year. I can raise capital for the boats but I can't raise capital for the infrastructure."

"My point exactly, infrastructure. Keep this quiet, but I know for a fact that the government intends to build a series of river ports along the Nemunas."

Woolley pulled his hand out from under Lily's. "You know this for certain?"

"As certain as a government can ever be."

"How soon and how many?"

"I can't give you many details except for the fact that it's going to happen. I expect that work should start in the spring."

"In concert with the Germans? They control the coast."

"The Germans will not be a problem," Adamonis said. "Should we drink to your expected success?" Woolley did so, but Adamonis could practically hear the wheels spinning in Woolley's head.

"Mr. Adamonis," he said, "I have business partners with a lot of money potentially at risk. I have to say that I am stretching my own resources as well. I need to know a little more. At this time of year we could put in a bid on a couple of low-priced German barges but they'll be no use to us unless we have river ports and access to the sea. I need to know this is a sure thing. I'm talking about large sums of money, and they depend on your ability to guarantee river ports."

"I'm certain of them," Adamonis said.

Woolley straightened his back and raised his hand for the waiter. He had no Lithuanian, but the waiters spoke all the main languages and it wasn't hard for the waiter to understand the order for another bottle of champagne and a large portion of caviar.

"Mr. Adamonis," Woolley said, "if what you say is true, you've saved my project and you may have saved my fortune, such as it is. And dear Lily will be able to stay in the country as long as she wants."

"Do you still want to?" Adamonis asked her.

"Oh, yes. I've grown accustomed to it here."

"And what about you, Mr. Woolley? You've never liked it here much. Will this be enough to make you stay?"

"I didn't like it because I was bored and there were so few diversions in this place. But the barges will be an interesting project. I'll be building something for myself, occupying my days, and, I should add, doing something for the country in the process. Lily wanted us to help this place start out. My only hesitation is the lack of proper documentation. We have your word, and I'm sure it's good, but

what about the person who gave you his word. Is he good
for it too?"

"Oh, I think so."

"And would it be possible to get something in writing?"

"You'll have to trust me."

"I do trust you," he said fervently. "I trust you both
for yourself and because you're Lily's relative, and I know
you'd never do anything to harm her. You do feel for her,
don't you?"

"I do."

"How deeply?"

"I have only her best interests in mind."

"I'm satisfied," Woolley said. The waiter brought the
champagne and opened it, and laid down a bowl of caviar
set inside a bowl of ice.

"I'll be in your debt for this," said Woolley.

"Not at all."

"It's normal business practice to pay a finder's fee in
these sorts of matters. The sums could be significant."

"Not necessary," Adamonis said. "I live well enough for
a bachelor as it is."

"Please don't write off the offer just yet," said Woolley.
"You can't be sure what tomorrow will bring."

Adamonis was going to say something, but Woolley
held up his hand, indicating that Adamonis should keep
silent. Woolley talked at length about his plans, but he
finally stood up to go to the bathroom. Adamonis waited
until he was out of the room.

"Well," he said to Lily, "are you happy?"

"Delirious," she said. "But listen, I know him pretty
well. He'll be in one of his fine moods for a while, but it
won't last. In a day or two, the worm of doubt is going to
start gnawing at him unless he has something solid to rely

on. Can't you get him some sort of statement on paper?"

"You heard what I said to him."

"I did, but something on paper will settle him down for the winter. Otherwise, he'll begin to squirm and be up nights, worrying the thing."

"Lily, I can't give him anything in writing."

"Why not?"

"I'm already compromising myself by what I've said. If any of this came out, I'd be in serious trouble."

"So you've already stepped out of bounds. What harm could a piece of paper do?"

"Why are we talking about his business? I've just found a way to keep us together. Why can't we talk about us?"

"We can, but to secure us, we need to secure him."

"I have other plans I can't talk about just yet. Do you think you'd ever be willing to make a run for it?"

She sat back. "What do you mean?"

"With me. We could go away together." To Adamonis's dismay, she didn't look as happy about this as he had thought she would.

"And leave him alone here? He'd be better off in America."

"He'd have his business. Anyway, what concern is it of yours how he'll feel? The man had his feelings strangled out of him at birth. There's nothing in him except those mood swings. That dark side of him can't be pleasant to be around."

"But he's my husband."

"And he can become your un-husband."

"Here? You told me it was impossible. And anyway, why would you set him up in business here if you wanted to get rid of him?"

"I can't tell you more now. I just need you to know that if I set him up properly, you'll be free of him. Or don't you love me enough to do something about it?"

"Of course I love you. Haven't I proved it?"

They had been leaning in toward each other and speaking quietly, but she sat back with a look of alarm and Adamonis looked over his shoulder to see Woolley approaching the table, and not far behind him, the Polish landowner Lukiewicz, standing with his hat and gloves in his hand and looking around the tables as if searching for someone he knew.

"Mr. Woolley couldn't have heard you," Adamonis said to Lily. The two men had not seen each other. "And if you really love me, what will you give me in the spring?" Adamonis asked.

"All of me," she said.

Woolley made his way through the tables and sat down. "What were you talking about?" he asked.

"Barges," they said together, and laughed.

Adamonis waved to Lukiewicz, who was still standing near the doorway, clearly confused, like a stork that found itself in a cesspool full of toads rather than in a pond filled with frogs. He didn't seem to recognize Adamonis at first, but then smiled ruefully and made his way toward them. Adamonis stood to greet him.

"You're the last person I ever expected to meet in a place like this," Adamonis said to him. "What brings you to Kaunas?"

"I've been invited to scout a location for a botanical garden and I was supposed to meet some of my colleagues for dinner. Is it always this smoky in Kaunas restaurants?"

"Always."

"It's like living inside a room with a broken chimney."

Adamonis remembered the Woolleys and turned to introduce them.

"Do you speak German or English?" Adamonis asked Lukiewicz.

"I do, but they understand Polish."

The assertion surprised Adamonis, who turned to Woolley. "Do you speak Polish?" he asked.

"Just a smattering," he said, and before Adamonis could say anything else, he stood and introduced himself and his wife in Polish, and then switched to German. Adamonis asked Lukiewicz to join them if he couldn't find his friends.

"I can barely stand it in here as it is," he said. "I'm sorry. I'm unaccustomed to these places. I haven't been in one since my student days. I'll have to go. But tell me, is this the Metropolis restaurant?"

"It's the Versailles. Didn't you see the sign?"

"I can track a fox print across dry earth, but I can't seem to find my bearings in the city. Is the Metropolis far?"

"Not even ten minutes. The doorman can show you the way. Here, let me go with you."

Lukiewicz nodded goodbye to the Woolleys and Adamonis led him to the door where one of his shadows was waiting. Adamonis asked him to take Lukiewicz to the Metropolis and said he'd look in to see him there on his way home if Lukiewicz's party was still in the restaurant when he got there.

When Adamonis returned to the table, the Woolleys were in intense conversation.

"What are you talking about?" he asked.

"Barges," they answered together, and they all laughed.

"What a curious man," said Woolley. "How do you know him?"

"He's very intelligent in certain ways," Adamonis said, "but I suppose he doesn't belong in the city. An amateur naturalist. Where did you get your Polish?"

"When I worked in Vienna before the war, there were endless Polish delegations at the embassy, lobbying for support for independence. It was useful to know some of the language, but I haven't used it in years."

Woolley had become jolly in a way Adamonis had not seen since the afternoon he met him at the Metropolis. Adamonis wondered if he wasn't nervous. He spoke at great length and with great fondness about his days in Vienna. He ordered food and another bottle of champagne, even though they hadn't finished the one they still had. Adamonis had a thought that was barely a thought, a feeling too vague to name, but it faded with the next glass of champagne and the pressure of Lily's leg against his under the table.

39

IT WAS NOT so much that best-laid plans went wrong as that the planning itself was derailed by events both big and small. Adamonis's right-hand man in the mission for the uprising in Klaipeda, assigned by Landa, was so pressed for time that he couldn't visit his dentist to deal with an aching tooth. The tooth became infected and the infection spread to his heart, and he lay in the hospital between life and death while Adamonis had to carry on the organization of nine hundred men in three different units. It was a military operation, but couldn't be seen to be one, and could not be run out of the offices of the general staff. Instead they ran it out of Adamonis's office, and all the necessary comings and goings excited the Soviet embassy, which thought the Lithuanians were about to launch a major operation against its cells.

The government would deny any connection to the rebels if the operation failed, but the government provided the rifles and the bullets, bought cheaply in Germany and found to be not entirely reliable. And if the operation were a spectacular failure, someone would have to take the blame. None of this needed to be explained to Adamonis; he understood the rules. His reward for finding a traitor and uncovering corruption within the government was the opportunity to be killed in battle or scapegoated if he failed. Unless he succeeded. The rules in the new world they were creating were remarkably similar to the rules in the old one.

For half an hour each night, before retiring to sleep in his rooms at the Hotel Metropolis, he luxuriated in his comfort because he knew it would not last. He put his hand against the warm ceramic wall that heated his room, imagining what it would be like to remember the sensation when they went into battle in the cold. He enjoyed his glass of brandy before bed, and he ruminated about his future, and that of Lily and Woolley, problems to be solved after the operation was completed.

Adamonis finished the brandy in his glass and turned off the light in his sitting room. He walked over to the window and looked through the sheer curtain. The street lights were on that night, and out there in the cold he saw Johnny, who seemed to be on his way somewhere. But the man in the sheepskin coat paused and looked up at the window, as if sensing Adamonis was there, and gave a small wave, just in case. Adamonis waved back at him, knowing the gesture would remain unseen. Johnny was no sort of problem, but neither was he a solution. He was a thread of continuity in time that would continue to unspool as the fashions, the institutions, and the rulers changed.

The leading officers of Adamonis's three units resented his leadership because he was not known to them nor active in the officers' club, and as for the volunteers, they were merely volunteers: well-meaning and determined young men, some in it for the adventure, some out of patriotism, and some for a few weeks' pay. There actually were some local enthusiasts ready to rise up in the Klaipeda region itself, but Adamonis's intelligence about them was poor and he didn't know how well armed they were or if they would follow orders.

The chaotic preparations to create a local uprising were similar to most military campaigns, with some complications. But the enemy of a good plan, as Adamonis's teachers in military school taught him, was the dream of a perfect plan.

Adamonis was deep in preparations the next day when Johnny came knocking at his door to say he wanted to speak "on a matter of utmost importance." Where did an old man like Johnny even pick up a word like *utmost?*

Adamonis did not respond at first and made Johnny wait outside while he went over some logistical details with the irreplaceable Pinigelis. They needed to act quickly. A convention of the allies would be deciding the fate of Klaipeda on January 10 or 11, and it looked as if they might make the region into a free city on the model of Danzig. It was a classic maneuver, giving no one country what it wanted, namely outright possession. It would keep the region out of the hands of the Germans, the Poles, and the Lithuanians; the allies could always say to the aggrieved parties that it could have turned out worse for them if they had given it to someone else. But Lithuania had no decent port city and it needed Klaipeda if it was to thrive. And it didn't hurt that there would be unhindered access to the sea for any barges that came down the river with goods.

Adamonis's fondness for Pinigelis grew over that period. Not only did she work day and night, but she managed to do a little separate research for him and confirmed that the civil statutes in the Klaipeda region allowed divorce. Thus the upshot of the annexation of the place the Germans called Memel and the Lithuanians called Klaipeda would be that Woolley could have his barges and Adamonis could have Mrs. Woolley.

Everything depended on how well the Lithuanians did on the field of battle. Every battle was a risk. Things did tend to go wrong in the most unexpected ways.

Miss Pinigelis and Adamonis were bent over a map of the city of Klaipeda, studying the location of the préfecture and the barracks, where the largest numbers of French soldiers were deployed. Adamonis could smell the lemon tea on her breath, a sweet and pleasant scent. She had risen, through her competence, to being an integral part of Adamonis's planning. He could trust her, and her own talent was sharpened by gratitude for the way he was helping her with Pranaitis. Adamonis kept Pranaitis busy driving memos and supplies to the various committees at work on the plan. Adamonis had even made him drive twice into the region itself, no easy task on the snow-blown winter roads. Pranaitis seemed to be keeping himself sober.

Miss Pinigelis stepped out of the office to get some other maps, and when she came back with two big ones rolled under her arm, she told Adamonis that Johnny was still outside and he couldn't wait much longer.

Adamonis wasn't thinking so much of Johnny. The office lights, all bright to help them study the map, illuminated Miss Pinigelis's face as if she were an actress onstage. Adamonis was dumbstruck, admiring her.

"Well?" she asked.

"Yes?"

"Will you see Johnny or won't you?"

"This is not a good time."

"He won't go away."

Adamonis sighed. "Then you'd better bring him in."

Johnny came in with his white sheepskin coat, trailing his ancient smell of the smokehouse.

Adamonis looked back down at the map. "I don't have much time. You'll have to be quick."

"I need you to come with me," Johnny said. There he stood, an old man entirely out of place in the office. Half a dozen soldiers in civilian clothing were working in the outer office, and plainclothes officers had taken over most of the clerks' hall beyond that.

"What? Come with you where?" Adamonis asked, more than slightly impatient with him.

"I can't say."

"You'd better say. I have no intention of leaving this place. Can't you see I'm busy?"

"I see it very well, but what I have to show you can't wait."

"If it can't wait, why don't you just tell me what the matter is and save me a trip?"

"You need to see this yourself. It won't take long. Under an hour. Trust me with this. When have I ever asked you to do anything before?"

The answer was never. Adamonis put on his hat and followed Johnny onto the street. Once they were out there, he readjusted his scarf and put his gloved hands into his coat pockets. It had been a cold autumn and now it was a freezing winter. Early night had fallen, but there was snow on the ground and the sliver of a moon, enough so that they could see all right. Johnny didn't seem to feel the cold at all. Summer and winter, he wore the sheepskin coat indoors and out as if it were his fur.

Johnny took Adamonis up Donelaicio Street, but before they had gone very far, he asked where Pranaitis was.

"Using the car to move some goods for me," Adamonis said.

"You're sure?"

Adamonis was sure. Pranaitis followed his orders to the letter, terrified of his superior and willing to do anything asked of him.

Johnny took Adamonis to Pranaitis's flat, around the back of the house, all shuttered and closed up against the cold, smoke rising out of two of its three chimneys.

"What are we doing here?" Adamonis asked.

"Be patient. You'll see."

He did not take Adamonis to Pranaitis's door, but walked across the trampled snow to the older of the two outhouses at the back of the yard. Johnny reached behind the shack and took out an iron bar with a flat end. With this, he pried out one of the nails on the board that had been set across the door. The board swung down, and Johnny looked around them first, and then opened the door.

Adamonis had been standing near him, but now he was startled and pulled away. Inside was what looked like a woman climbing out of the toilet hole. Adamonis's first reaction was to step forward and help her, but quickly enough he could see her eyes were open and glassy and frost clung to her hat and to the strands of hair that escaped from it. She looked as if she had fallen inside in a ridiculous accident and found herself trapped when she tried to pull herself out. But that didn't make sense. Adamonis looked more closely and saw her thin coat was bunched around her hips and her arms were loose at her sides, the palms turned out toward him, as if in supplication. She had not fallen in and tried to climb out. Someone had tried stuff her down the hole to get rid of the body, but the outhouse pit was so full of excrement that the body would not go all the way down.

The light was poor, but Adamonis stepped in, trying to keep his own shadow from falling across her body. Her dazed face was frozen solid, and he could see dark patches on her throat. Then he stepped back and looked carefully at her hands. There was blood on her right fingertips. She had tried to defend herself.

Poor Felicia. Adamonis wondered where her son was.

Adamonis stepped out of the space and asked Johnny to close the door and nail the board back across it again.

40

FIRST, the government informed the French that the people of the Klaipeda region were clamouring to join Lithuania. As expected, the Lithuanian government received no answer.

Adamonis's men were massed near the border of the Klaipeda region and ready to begin their long walk through the winter night, needing to cross the twenty-three kilometres to Klaipeda by dawn. Along the way, the force would split into three groups, two heading south to protect against potential German reinforcements and the main body marching with Adamonis, toward the city.

He had fought in winter, so he knew the cold as an old enemy, but he couldn't seem to get warm enough that night, even when he had been walking some distance and should have raised the heat in his body. But he was cold somehow, shivering as he never had in the past. He could have travelled by car or on horseback, but he wanted to walk among the men and encourage them, and the sight of him, sharing their trek, would help to keep up morale.

There had been a few details he needed to arrange before the march that night, and one of them was to get Pranaitis to sign some documents. Adamonis had said nothing to the man of what he and Johnny had found in the outhouse. There would be time for that later, if necessary.

"My experience in the independence wars proved to me that I'm not much of a soldier," Pranaitis protested. "I won't be of use to you once the shooting starts."

They were standing in the office of a village railway station, the last place where Adamonis had ready telephone contact with Kaunas before morning. Carriages creaked and groaned outside—they needed some supplies beyond what they could carry, and men stamped their feet and the phone rang incessantly and various people were asking Adamonis various things at the same time.

"You've been at my side from the first," Adamonis said to him. "I need you along for the sake of my luck. Besides, you were in the army, weren't you?"

"A poor conscript. I'm an intellectual, not a foot soldier."

"You once told me that a farmer's son could learn to do anything. This will be a chance to redeem yourself. When you're old, you'll be able to tell your children on winter nights that on a night like this, you walked out with your countrymen to reclaim a piece of this nation. Now sign these papers."

"What kind of papers?"

"They recognize your son as legitimate."

Pranaitis looked at Adamonis as if he had gone out of his mind. "What's that all about?"

"Everyone on the mission has to declare his family status. There will be a bonus after the campaign, and you'll be paid according to the number of dependents you have. I'm doing you a favour."

They were on the verge of leaving and the place was noisy with boots on wooden floors and doors swinging open and shut and men giving and taking orders.

"I can't make a decision like that on the spot. I'm not sure what the implications are."

"The implications are that you sign these papers or you're fired. I've been patient with you and your excesses to this point. This is for your own good. Sign the papers and take responsibility for yourself for a change. And quickly."

Adamonis handed him a pen.

Pranaitis knew better than anyone else that he needed redemption, so he did sign, and Adamonis passed the papers to his adjutant and had them sent back to Kaunas that night. Adamonis instructed Pranaitis to stay at his side.

So went their long walk through the night; after the other two groups split off, there were six hundred men with Adamonis, none in uniform. They wore green armbands with the initials of the Klaipeda Uprising Committee. Adamonis could count on the officers and on the soldiers dressed as civilians, but the band contained all sorts of other men. They would be hard to hold together for any length of time. The men carried bread bags, but they only had four days' worth of rations.

Adamonis had walked out like this often enough during the war years, although less often at the end, when he usually stayed with the high command. He was almost a decade older than everyone but the officers. He wondered what his sister would think of him—an incurable romantic and an incurable soldier, off on adventures though he was well past the age when he should have known better.

The field of battle was unpredictable. For all he knew, the Germans might come to the aid of the French garrison, or there might be a gunboat with reinforcements in the Baltic, or the untrained men among his party might turn and run at the first *crack* of a rifle shot. But for all the cold and for all the uncertainty, he also had a sense of adventure, a sense of going out into the real world instead of spending much of his time behind a desk, as he had for the last two years. Physical action rested his mind, and he needed to rest his mind from thoughts about Lily, to say nothing of his thoughts about Pranaitis.

They arrived unopposed shortly before dawn at a hamlet just outside the city of Klaipeda, a place where the men could fan out into requisitioned farm outbuildings to get a little rest in the hay after bowls of steaming cabbage soup served by auxiliary volunteers. There were indeed locals involved in the uprising. They were not, after all, invading a hostile region. The problem in that part of the world was that many different peoples lived intermingled, and it was hard to make clear border lines. There were many ethnic Germans in the region, very many, and among them Jews, whose allegiance to either the status quo or to the insurrection was unclear.

It was a rather wealthy hamlet, being so close to Klaipeda, and the parish priest had a telephone. While the officers ate in shifts at a long, oak table, Adamonis made a few necessary phone calls. His two southern wings had achieved their objectives unopposed. At Tilsit, the Germans had even provided his men with extra weapons. This was a very good sign, so their southern flank was secure. Adamonis's scouts told him the streets of Klaipeda were quiet and it seemed that they might be able to do all they hoped to do without firing a shot.

The French must have known they were coming because they had their own intelligence, but there were no defensive positions set up as far as the scouts could tell. In one part of his mind, Adamonis also had to keep watch for anyone from within who was watching him too closely, someone who might have plans to take care of him in revenge for the Vasilyev operation. Yet while being vigilant, he had to keep this concern in proportion or he would worry about his back too much while the biggest danger was before him. One could not predict all betrayals.

After a decent rest of a couple of hours, Adamonis had his officer rouse one group of men from where they lay in the hay, bundled in greatcoats and scarves, with caps on their heads and belts of bullets on their waists or across their chests. He sent this unit out to begin the encirclement of the city from the north, if fifty men could be said to encircle anything so large. He also sent a note to the French high commissioner, Gabriel Petisné, inviting him to surrender. Adamonis waited the rest of the day, but received no reply.

After midnight, his northern wing tried to take one of the French barracks, but the French illuminated the night with rockets and let fire with machine guns from within the barracks, and his men fell back with two wounded. The French were not willing to give up the city without a fight.

With only six hundred men, they were really too few to hold the city if it came to a long siege, so Adamonis needed to press forward, and they set out in force that same night. When the next dawn came up, they held four positions in Klaipeda, a city like a miniature Königsberg, with grand wedding-cake buildings and the steeple of the Church of St. John disappearing into the winter mist that came off the sea. The mist was just as well. The French could not see the Lithuanians' movements from that vantage point. Adamonis began to have his men take strategic positions.

41

THERE WERE SKIRMISHES here and there, but the French were not thick on the ground and they withdrew after a few shots. Adamonis took some bridges and the post office as well as the train station, but they would have to take the main French force at the préfecture, where the high commissioner was housed. And they needed to do it quickly because the cold remained bitter and they had already been in the field for three days with no arrangements for resupply. Adamonis wanted the préfecture and he wanted to command the attack himself.

The building stood on a cobbled city street not far from the vast market square. It was three storeys high and the windows were sandbagged with machine guns at two of them and riflemen at others. Adamonis sent a messenger proposing that the French surrender and offering them safety as well as the right to remain in their barracks and the préfecture as long as they gave up their weapons, but the high commissioner was no more willing to give up than he had been two days earlier.

Adamonis surrounded the préfecture and instructed his men to fire on the building, but not to aim for the windows and not to fire too often. Riflemen had only been issued two hundred bullets each and these could not be wasted. The Lithuanians were just to give a sort of warning of what might come if the French resisted.

The French responded with withering fire from their machine guns and two of his men went down.

Adamonis called a ceasefire to pull the fallen men out of danger. The officers redeployed their men carefully to three main points with cover behind buildings across the street from the préfecture. Adamonis also sent a stiffer force to cover the rear of the building. He possessed two light machine guns of his own and he had one of them open fire on the window immediately to the right of the front door of the préfecture and the other to shoot at the door within the portico itself. The door splintered and the French machine gun at that particular window fell silent. They had either killed or wounded the gunner, but another would be in his place soon enough.

Sporadic fire was going on now all along the street. Bullets ricocheted and bits of mortar and stone flew about, sometimes dusting Adamonis in their closeness. He was standing by the corner of a building, a place his officers were encouraging him to vacate, when a rifle came out from one of the second-floor windows. Before it could fire, Pranaitis stepped away from Adamonis's side, aimed, fired, and stepped back, and the French rifle fell from the window and clattered onto the street before them.

"I thought you said you were no good at this," Adamonis said to Pranaitis.

"I can shoot. I'm trying my best."

"Good man. We have to show them we're not going away. Do you think you could try something else?"

Pranaitis was flushed and filled with the success of his last shot, emboldened by his achievement. He nodded.

"I'll get the others to provide covering fire. The front door has been shot half open. Do you think you could get close enough to throw a grenade in there?"

With a kill behind him, Pranaitis was drunk with his accomplishment in battle. He felt he could do anything. Adamonis gave the order, and the Lithuanians let loose volley upon volley of rifle fire as well as the concentrated fire of their light machine guns. The préfecture erupted into a wall of miniature dust explosions as the bullets stuck across the front of the building. Most of the préfecture windows fell silent as the men inside withdrew from the window ledges to shield themselves. Adamonis had a revolver of his own trained in the direction of the building in case he saw a target of opportunity.

"Go now," said Adamonis, and he pushed Pranaitis forward.

Pranaitis charged out from beside Adamonis and ran thirty feet to get within throwing distance of the ruined door. He even had the end of the hand grenade unscrewed and ready to go when a shot hit him in the leg and he fell. Things happened very quickly then. He glanced back toward Adamonis, and gave a very brief look filled with understanding. And then the grenade that had fallen at his side blew up.

Another Lithuanian ran right into the smoke of the explosion, and he did what Pranaitis had failed to do, tossing a grenade in through the double doors, blowing them open. But he was stuck there in the shallow portico, because the French were now firing from their windows, making his way back dangerous. He was safe where he stood, but he would not be for long once the French realized he was there. Now Adamonis would have to storm the doors and begin the worst kind of fighting, moving from room to room, perhaps throwing grenades ahead while hoping that none were thrown at the Lithuanians first.

Adamonis called a ceasefire for a moment, giving the men time to reload and prepare themselves for the assault, but he kept two men ready with trained rifles in case one of the Frenchmen dared to put his head outside the window to shoot at their man in the portico.

Adamonis had his hand raised, ready to command the next attack, when the French stopped firing. Adamonis held his men back, and waited and tried not to look at the grisly remains of Pranaitis, and then after some long minutes, a sound pierced the eerie silence. Even with his ears still ringing, Adamonis could hear the *creak* of a rusty pulley. It made him look up to the top of the building. The French flag was lowered from the flagpole and a white sheet was run up. The French were surrendering.

42

THE BEST HOTEL in Klaipeda was the appropriately named Victoria, and the officers were in high spirits and ready to celebrate to the depth of the hotel's wine cellar, but Adamonis would not permit it yet. To take a position was one thing, but to hold it against counterattack was another. They held their breath for a week and had one stroke of very good luck that may have helped them more than anything. It turned out the French had occupied the Ruhr Valley in Germany on January 10 because the Germans were so behind in paying war reparations. The main focus of Europe was therefore elsewhere.

Soon it began to seem as if no one was going to fight the Lithuanians, and the French were even consoling the Poles, saying that since they had seized Vilnius in 1919, they should let the Lithuanians have this much smaller city and its region.

By the time ten days had passed and Adamonis had some confidence they would be all right, he could finally permit a victory parade. Kaunas issued Lithuanian tricolour ribbons by the hundreds, organized an orchestra, and arranged that the dozen men of Adamonis's force who had fallen would be honoured in the more sombre part of the parade, in sealed coffins at the front.

Kaunas brought in the families of the slain heroes, and with them Adamonis brought Miss Pinigelis. He was staying in the Victoria Hotel in a suite of rooms overlooking the street, and he asked his adjutant to leave them alone once she arrived.

Adamonis's hotel suite consisted of a makeshift boardroom, a bedroom, and a large dining room with a long table heaped with hothouse flowers, sent by various Lithuanian associations in thanks for the liberation of Klaipeda. There were many bottles of champagne and expensive liquors at one end of the table, for the visiting delegations brought gifts and wanted to toast the Lithuanians' success with Adamonis. On the first sideboard, mounds of candies wrapped in various coloured wrappers lay in crystal bowls the size of soup tureens, and on the second sideboard, cakes from napoleons to linzer tortes as well as heaps of gingerbread.

Outside, the crowd was thick on the street and the band was already playing the Rakoczy March, a Hungarian tune that would be seen as appropriately neutral—nothing Polish or German would do, and a general antipathy to Russian tunes made the Rakoczy safe from misinterpretation.

The damask curtains were pulled away and Adamonis was standing behind the sheers, looking out on the street scene when Miss Pinigelis came in. He turned when he heard her, glad to have the light at his back and thus his face in shadow. Pinigelis stood with her hands at her sides, wearing a black hat and an open black coat over her office clothes. Her curls ringed her face, which was very white. She looked at the table heaped with celebratory gifts and then looked away from it at Adamonis. He greeted her from a distance, unsure, restraining the urge to go to her to console her.

She nodded at his greeting, but did not walk up to him. A chasm lay between them. "Thank you for inviting me to walk with his body," she said. "I suppose I should be grateful."

"It's nothing compared to your loss. I'm very sorry things turned out this way. I know how much you loved him."

"I did love him. Foolishly. He was a lot like me. He had come from nowhere in the countryside and made something of himself."

She looked around the room and then looked at Adamonis. He sensed some resentment, and why not? Pranaitis had gone with Adamonis and by doing so had gone to his death. But the luxury of the room also offended her, the way a Calvinist might be offended by the decorations in a Catholic church.

"Will you sit down?" Adamonis asked.

"I think we have to leave for the cortège soon. And then there's the parade after that."

"In a moment, but they won't start without us. You have time to sit for a moment."

"I think I'd rather stand. I want to know a little more. No one told me the details of how he died."

"In the assault on the préfecture. He was very brave, leading a charge, and if it wasn't for him, we might have lost many more men."

"A hero, then?"

"Definitely a hero."

"I didn't think of him that way. He didn't seem the type."

"He rose to the occasion. Extreme situations bring out the best in men."

"And the worst."

"This was not the worst."

"Maybe not for you. But for me."

She had a right to her emotions. In any case, he couldn't stop them and he had emotions of his own, but the conversation had started off on the wrong foot somehow.

"I didn't want to bring this up just now," said Adamonis, "but we'd better get it all over with, to the last detail."

"What do you mean?"

"You need to know something. He was lost to you before he left for Klaipeda. If he hadn't died in the battle, you still wouldn't have had a future with him."

"He said he would stop drinking for me."

"I don't mean that. It's the matter of Felicia. I did a certain thing before we set out. I forced him to sign a marriage certificate, so he was briefly married to Felicia before he died."

She sat down at the news. "I don't understand. Why would you have done that? Why would he have agreed?"

"For the sake of his son. Felicia is not well, a madwoman. But the boy is guilty of nothing. All of the men who went into this battle will be rewarded financially, and the relatives of the dead will receive pensions. Now that poor mother and child will have something to live on."

"Did you know he would die in battle?"

"Of course not."

"But you must have suspected. Otherwise you wouldn't have done such a thing. And he agreed to do it?"

"The papers didn't seem important to him."

"But they did to you."

"I was forced to think of all contingencies."

"So you took him away from me twice. If he'd survived, he would have been a married man. But he didn't. He died for you. Why did you have this need to punish me so badly?"

"I wasn't punishing you. I couldn't have done any of this without you and your help. But listen, the child was going to live barefoot and hungry unless something was done for him."

"If his mother is crazy, he could have taken the boy away. I would have helped him. I loved that man and I would have loved his son. What gave you the right to intervene in his life that way?"

She was very angry with Adamonis, but he couldn't tell her the truth. At least the orphan boy would have some sort of pension. But now she hated him for it.

"Isn't this just a little too neat?" she asked.

"What do you mean?"

"You had him sign papers and he died soon after. If I worked for an insurance company, I would have his death investigated."

"There were many witnesses. He was shot by the French during a charge."

"Why did you take him along in the first place? He was a translator and a driver, not a soldier. Did you intend for him to die?"

"I was trying to do the right thing."

"All of you people trying to do the right thing make me angry. None of the causes in the world are worth a human life. Now we have another strip of land. Why do you think that could be any kind of consolation to me?"

"I know it's nothing to you. I'm sorry. But we're running out of time to talk about this any more now. We'll have to go. The music outside has stopped."

She looked at the table covered with the flowers, bottles, and cakes. She put her hands on her lap and then looked up at Adamonis.

"Then his wife is the one who should be here, not me," she said. "His wife and his son should be walking below. Why aren't they here?"

"We don't know where they are. We're looking for them. But you have the right to walk in the march outside.

You loved him. That should be worth something."

She looked away from him and was silent for a while. And then they had to go outside. He wanted to say so much more to her, to offer her work with him in Klaipeda. But she hated him just now. Any offer would have to wait.

Adamonis did not lead the cortège, but he was in the lead party. Somewhere outside during the march, Miss Pinigelis disappeared and he couldn't go looking for her. He marched with the others to the music of a dirge, and he spoke when his turn came alongside the top-hatted politicians at the memorial for the dead. Some people were touched when Adamonis's voice broke as he spoke of the men who fell in the uprising. Adamonis even wept a little, and he believed the soldiers among the audience forgave him this weakness because he felt so deeply about all that the victory had cost.

They paused for a decent time as the bodies were taken away to the train station to be shipped back home.

Adamonis looked for Pinigelis again, but still didn't find her. She was not in the crowd that made its back to the Friedrich Market Square, this time to the music of the more military and triumphant Radetzky March. And once they reached the destination, a real street party began, with free beer and sandwiches and street dancing. The most popular tune was "The Blue Danube."

43

SPRING finally came, and Adamonis took the opportunity on one of the first fine days of lilac blooms to return to Kaunas from Klaipeda, where he now lived in a suite of rooms at the Victoria Hotel. The celebrations were long since over, and the dining room table which once stood covered with gifts now bore maps, briefs, and petitions, which Miss Pinigelis struggled with but failed to keep in order. Adamonis was provisional governor of the autonomous territory until the proper legislation was in place to make his appointment permanent. He wasn't sure he was looking forward to it. The German inhabitants resented the Lithuanians, Kaunas was slow to deliver finances, and he had to scramble for funds to pay the volunteers who had come into the country with him and refused to leave until they saw their money.

This was the reward he received for his success in battle, a new type of war, a battle against bureaucratic paper, disgruntled local farmers, and sullen policemen who had to take Lithuanian language lessons after their shifts.

There were so many pressing matters in Klaipeda that he really shouldn't have left, but there were so many loose ends in Kaunas that he needed to get back there. He had not seen the clerks in his old department for months, and they stood to applaud him as he walked in, much to his embarrassment. Adamonis stopped by his old office to confer with Chepas, who was his provisional replacement and replacing Landa as well, who had moved up to become assistant deputy minister of finance.

"Landa used to look for hidden enemies, and now he looks for hidden money to tax," said Chepas from his place at the desk where Adamonis used to sit. Chepas had made a point of not cleaning out the desk, leaving it as he had found it in case his old boss resumed his position. It was a generous gesture.

"You don't mind my finishing off this business?" Adamonis asked.

"Go right ahead. But be discreet and keep me informed and try not to let anything go wrong. You know, everyone in power in this town is a little bit afraid of you."

Chepas read his expression and explained.

"There always seem to be unexpected consequences whenever you do something," said Chepas. "You have a reputation for achieving your goals, but there tends to be damage along the way."

By prior arrangement, Adamonis had the car meet Woolley and Lily at their house where the driver packed their small suitcases in the trunk. Adamonis specified that they were not to take too much—just their essentials and their passports, in case they needed to deal with officialdom.

Woolley was dressed in a light linen suit, just the thing for a weekend in the country, and he had a light grey broad-brimmed hat for the outing, all the better to keep the sun off his face. He carried a smart walking stick too, but ever the man of business, he had a small satchel of documents that he brought with him as well. He had not wanted to go into the country with Adamonis at first, but the ministry of transport, thanks to Adamonis, was planning the barge ports, and Woolley could not turn down the man who had enabled his business plan. As for Lily, she was in a dress more suitable for a garden party than a country week-end. It seemed rather filmy to Adamonis, and the brim of her hat, much wider than Woolley's, wasn't very stiff and would flutter in the wind.

Adamonis had not seen her since their meeting months earlier at the Versailles restaurant. Lily had written half a dozen letters in the months since the uprising in Klaipeda, but Adamonis had put her off. He burned her letters after reading them.

He wondered what it would be like to see her again after all that had happened. Lily placed herself between Woolley and Adamonis in the back seat of the car, and as soon as they were seated, he felt the press of her leg against his. The pressure made him slightly melancholy.

"So, are you going to tell us our destination now?" asked Lily.

"Not yet. It's a surprise."

"I have just one hope," said Woolley.

"What's that?"

"I hope there isn't a goose on the menu once we arrive."

"I think they've all been eaten," said Adamonis.

After the Lithuanians' seizure of Klaipeda, the Germans launched a formal protest, even though they had encouraged the operation on the sly. To make their public anger seem more real, they had closed the border to imports for three months, and a gigantic shipment of geese was left stranded in Lithuania, and became the excess inventory of a new government export agency. Lithuania was a poor country and couldn't absorb this sort of loss, and so every goose was assigned a fixed price and every public servant was forced to accept partial payment of salary in the form of geese. That entire winter, hosts served goose and guests ate it, returning the favour whenever they could.

"Have you had a chance to go out to visit the country cousins?" asked Lily.

"There's been no time."

"No. You're an important man now, a provisional governor. Imagine! Soon you won't have time for your family at all."

"But I've made a little time for you."

"Yes, you have, and we're grateful. Tell me what life is like in Klaipeda."

"A nightmare. We should have been more careful what we hoped for. The Germans who live there consider us lower class and the local farmers are furious because they've discovered farm products are cheaper here, and their market is flooded with Lithuanian food and they're losing money. And of course, they can't export to Germany now."

"Was it worth it, in the end? That poor driver of yours lost his life."

"And he's not the only one. A tragedy, really. But there are always some losses, even in a game you win."

Woolley had taken out some papers from his briefcase and was making notes on his lap as they drove along.

"You were damned lucky the entente allies didn't put up a bigger fight and the Poles didn't get involved either. I thought it was touch and go there for a while."

"We were both lucky, don't you think?"

Woolley had been in an admonishing mood for a moment, forgetting what he owed Adamonis.

"Of course, of course," he said.

"How is business?" Adamonis asked.

"We have two barges working already and a third one on order from Germany. I understand that relations with them are normalizing?"

"Yes."

"It's a shame the port construction is so slow, but we're doing fine now and we'll do better once we have the ports all in place. Just you wait and see. People like me will raise the standard of living in this country. I have friends back in the States with capital and with ideas. We could make Kaunas bustle. I don't see why we couldn't open a Rotary Club here."

Adamonis didn't know enough Americans to know if they were all like Woolley. He hoped not. Woolley blew this sort of steam for some time and then fell back into his papers as soon as Lily and Adamonis began to talk of the clan. Lily and Adamonis spoke for a while of Anele, who was beginning to forgive Adamonis and had invited him to visit once his business was done.

"I've heard a rumour," said Lily.

"Oh?"

"You have brought your secretary from the Kaunas office with you to Klaipeda."

"That's right, and a few others of my staff as well. Why should office matters interest you?"

"Your sister said you're rather close to Miss Pinigelis."

"My sister hasn't spoken to me since I left. How could she have any idea of my doings in Klaipeda?"

"Women have mysterious ways of finding things out. Do you have romantic intentions?"

"Lily, you're embarrassing me."

"Do you intend to marry Miss Pinigelis?" she asked.

"Really! I might have had lunch with her twice."

"That's how it all begins, isn't it? Should I be envious?"

"Lily, surely you don't grudge me female company."

264 / *Provisionally Yours*

"Hmm."

Adamonis would not follow up on the subject, and so they spoke of other things, stopping in Kedainiai for coffee, and then driving on. The mood in the car shifted a little after an hour. Both Lily and Woolley looked hard out the windows, but they didn't ask Adamonis about their destination until they drove up to the stone gatehouse of the Lukiewicz estate, and the liveried grandfather came out to fumble with the keys to unlock the gate.

Lily and Woolley looked at each other with alarm.

"Why are you bringing us here?" asked Lily.

"Do you know the place?" Adamonis asked.

"I've been across the whole country on business," said Woolley. "I seem to remember being here once before. Do you remember it, Lily?"

"I don't like this place. Please, don't tell me we're staying here."

"What's gotten into you?" Adamonis asked. "It's a country estate where I thought we could spend the weekend and get a little fresh air. The owner is a hunter and he might take us out on a bird shoot."

"I hate hunting," said Lily.

"You wouldn't have to take part. You could walk in the garden."

They didn't say anything for a few moments as the car drove along the treed lane.

"I remember this place all too well," said Lily. "The owner has rooms full of stuffed animals and bugs pinned to cards on the walls. It's grotesque. I'd be terrified to spend any time here."

"Now, now. A little *krupnikas* will calm your nerves."

"Can't you see she's afraid of this place?" asked Woolley. "Why would you force her to do something she doesn't want to do?"

"Indulge me," said Adamonis.

The car pulled up on the gravel before the house. There were two other cars parked a little way ahead of them. A country maid with a headscarf opened the door and peered at them, and then disappeared, leaving the door ajar. Lukiewicz then came out with his dogs, but Lily would not descend from the car at first.

"Take me away from here," she pleaded.

"Lily, please, you'll see. It will be for the best."

Adamonis eventually got them out of the car and they greeted Lukiewicz quite formally and he led them into the dining room. Lukiewicz began speaking in Polish, but Lily and Woolley answered only in German, so that was the language they settled on. It was late and a cold supper waited for them on the table. There was a veal pâté and chicken in aspic and sorrel salad and pickled mushrooms and beets. The cook fried up some potato pancakes on the side. Through all the political and emotional upheavals Adamonis had lived through, he never took his food for granted. It somehow filled a place in his heart that was too often empty.

To say it was an awkward meal would have been an understatement. For his part, Lukiewicz acted genially, although he was always like an absent-minded professor and seemed to forget about them from time to time to drift off into his thoughts. They sat in that gloomy room while outside the evening stretched on with the impossibly long light of northern spring. So little of it managed to come in and the maid lit the oil lamps before dessert. Woolley and Lily barely spoke as Adamonis asked Lukiewicz about the plans for his botanical gardens and for the changes he would be making to the farm after most of his property was severed and parcelled out to landless peasants.

Right after tea and cakes, Lukiewicz said he had had a long day and excused himself. Woolley and Lily had barely spoken to him, resentfully using a few Polish phrases when they had to. They were ready to go up to bed as well, but Adamonis asked them to wait. Lukiewicz had left the three of them at the table with a bottle of the local blackcurrant wine. The maid brought in more tea after he left, and Adamonis told her she would not be required any more that evening.

"Well," Adamonis said. "Maybe before we go to bed we should make some plans for tomorrow."

"I just want to get out of here," said Lily. "Take me back to Kaunas in the morning."

"I'm afraid I have other plans," Adamonis said.

Woolley and Lily sat warily at the table. She swirled the blackcurrant wine in her glass. She was still but poised. Adamonis had taken care to make sure his own briefcase was not beside Woolley and he doubted Woolley carried any weapons with him.

"The reason I brought you back here," Adamonis said, "was to have Lukiewicz confirm that you had both been part of card parties held in this estate."

"Why didn't you just ask me?" Lily asked. "I could have told you that."

"I might have asked you except you were both so alarmed when we met him by accident at the Versailles Restaurant that I didn't dare to bring the matter up. I wondered why you hadn't told me you spoke Polish. It seemed like such an oversight on your part. After all, more people in Kaunas speak Polish than German. It was the language of the old ruling class."

Lily and Woolley looked at each other, but exchanged no message that Adamonis could discern.

"The more I thought about it," Adamonis continued, "the more curious it seemed. I couldn't satisfy my curiosity then because I was busy with preparations for our move on Klaipeda. But ever since the United States recognized us officially, we've had our own people in the American embassy in Washington, and some of them did a little research for me there. As well, I had some of our people do a little research into your activities here. I know everything now. The only thing I don't know is whether you came here as spies for the Polish government or whether you only began working for them later."

"I'm not a Polish spy," Woolley said quickly. He said it decisively, like a man accustomed to having his declarations taken as gospel.

"Indeed you are a Polish spy," Adamonis said. "Once I suspected you, I had my agents cover you and we have two of the many letters you sent to the Poles through your intermediary at the French embassy."

"You've been reading my letters?" Woolley asked.

"In those letters, you seemed particularly interested in my guarantee of the barge ports and you guessed about our move to take Klaipeda. You expected me to give you something in writing and you promised to press me for it. You suggested that the Polish army act quickly, before we took Klaipeda, but luckily for us, the Poles make their own decisions."

Lily said nothing, but she lifted her glass and sipped from it. She was watching Adamonis carefully.

"This is all a misunderstanding," said Woolley. "I can't deny I had contact with the Poles, but I had only the best interests of the population at heart. Listen, you upstarts, you Lithuanians think of nothing but yourselves. We're farther away in America and have a clearer geopolitical view. America was drawn into the war and lost over a hundred thousand men. It has no intention of letting that happen again, and the best way to make sure of that is to weaken Germany and hem it in. On this side of Europe, a strong Poland will be a counterweight to the Germans and the best way to make a strong Poland is to make sure the little nations are a part of it."

"You're speaking as if you represent the Americans, but as far as I can tell, you don't. Are you a freelance diplomat?"

"I was a diplomat once and it put me into a habit of mind. My only allegiance is to peace and the best way to assure peace is to build strong states and strong business. That's what I've been about here. I only have the interests of the local people at heart. After all, my wife is from here."

"You would attach us to Poland as a minority? Put us on a reservation, like your Indians? Is that the idea?"

"A federation with Poland wouldn't make you into Indians."

"Maybe not, but it doesn't really take local interests to heart, does it?"

"Take the longer view. What can you possibly achieve in a puny state like this? It's a joke state. It won't last. Sooner or later someone will swallow you up, and it might as well be Poland."

"Just a moment. Wasn't it your president who talked so much about self-determination? If we want to be a country, let us be."

"A country of what, of farmers? You can't even do business. Jews have run most of the business in this country for generations. People like me will help you open the doors to greater business. Just imagine what a waterway the Nemunas is, but a lot of it lies outside Lithuania. The Nemunas could be to this country what the Nile was to the ancient Egyptians. It could bring prosperity along its banks all the way up to Byelorussia."

"This is all very moving, Mr. Woolley, but it doesn't take the human heart into account. Our hearts long to be free and to beat in a free country. We have one now, and we intend to keep it. In any case, I'm not here to discuss politics. You are both spies and the fate of spies is very dark."

"We're American citizens. What could you do to us?"

"I'm not sure the Americans would stick up for you, given the proof we have. Foreign spies aren't usually executed, but their prison sentences can be long. As for nationals, execution is not out of the question."

"You can't be serious," said Lily.

"I happen to know that you took out Lithuanian citizenship, Lily. You were born here and it made your husband's business dealings that much easier. You're in very great danger."

"Do you mean to say," asked Woolley, "that you'd have your own cousin shot?"

"I wouldn't have her harmed in any way. That's why I brought you two here. To get you out of Kaunas before the storm breaks. I can't keep all of this secret. Even if you were granted bail after your arrest, which I imagine might come very soon, some hothead might beat you up on the street, or worse. You have to go. Tomorrow morning, just after dawn, I'll have a couple of my men take you to the demarcation line with Poland. Your masters will take care of you there, I assume."

"I can't leave just like that," said Woolley. "I have business interests. I have documents and valuables in my apartment. I have a project underway."

"All finished, I'm afraid. We'll send along your things when we get a forwarding address. For now, you have changes of clothes and your passports. That should be enough. You expected a walk in the woods and you'll have one, but it will be a bit longer than you expected."

"This is outrageous. I want to speak to my embassy."

"Sadly, we have no phone here and there is no time. I'm doing you a favour. Once you sleep on it, you'll realize what a good outcome I'm offering to you, the best of all possible outcomes, really. There's no future for you here. And don't think of leaving during the night. I'll have a man outside your door and another outside your window."

"And will your stuffed-animal collector, Lukiewicz, be expelled along with us?"

"Poor man. He's hospitable to a fault. Those card games he hosted here sheltered a few other spies and conspiracies. And to think he fed all those conspirators out of his good heart! No, he's innocent. He stays here, but you go."

44

AS ADAMONIS EXPECTED, in the middle of the night, a soft knock came at his door and one of his men said that Lily wanted to speak to him. The night had grown cool, so Adamonis had a fire burning in the ceramic stove and he'd been sitting near it in an armchair with a lamp at his side. He also kept a glass of Lukiewicz's own mead, produced on the estate. Unlike *krupnikas*, it was not distilled but fermented and therefore not much stronger than wine. The local variation included herbs, which gave it a slightly bitter aftertaste.

Adamonis did not stand when his man brought in Lily, wearing a nightgown and a housecoat, but Adamonis thanked him and waved her over to the chair across from him and gestured for her to sit down.

He had played this scene over again and again in his mind ever since he had discovered the truth. He had imagined he'd have sharp words for her, stinging words, but his sense of loss trumped his sense of outrage. He lit a cigarette and waited for her to speak.

Her hair showed no sign of having been slept on and she still wore makeup. She looked lovely.

"Do you think I could have one of those?" she asked.

"Of course."

Adamonis rose from his chair and offered a cigarette from his case. She took it and when he lit it with a match, she put her hand on his and held it until the match was almost burning his fingertips. He finally pulled away and shook out the flame.

"I don't think you should have come," he said after he sat down again.

"I just want you to know one thing and understand another."

"All right."

"Robert is not the sort to be a spy, but he was forced into a corner. He did this because he has no serious money anymore. Do you understand what that means to a man like him? His family has been important in Worcester for three generations. He's gentry, do you understand? But he didn't fit in with his father and brother. Robert is sensitive. He believes in culture and he believes in doing good. Before the war, he worked as a diplomat because he turned his back on business. His brother ran the family finances and while everyone else in industry was growing rich during the war, his brother drove the business into the ground. They lost almost everything. There was poor Robert, so high-minded and uninvolved. He was above business while the monthly cheques were coming in, but he could never get used to living without them once they stopped."

"Lily, you're not doing a very good job of defending him."

"But what you don't understand is that he didn't do any of this for himself. He did it for me and the irony is the miserable sums the Poles paid were barely enough to live on. He really needed the income the barges would bring. Do you understand what kind of weight that puts on me? He brought me up from the gutter like some kind of little match girl, and then he was mortified to have to lower me back again."

"You're telling me he became a spy because he wanted to keep his wife in style?"

"I'm making it sound wrong. Maybe that's so, but maybe it helps you to understand why I couldn't leave him. I wanted to be with you, only with you. I was in love with you from the first time we talked in the car on the way to Birstonas that night. I'm still in love with you. But my conscience made me stick to Robert because of all he'd done for me. To lose me would have broken him, and I couldn't do that to the man who'd saved me."

"Saved you from what? Ordinary life? Your parents had normal American jobs and you must have had a normal American childhood. But I suppose you wanted more. All sorts of illusions were lost during the war," he said. "Others are being lost after it. He'll mend in some way and so will you."

"But he'll lose everything he has if you go through with this. What little capital he had, he sank into those barges and it doesn't seem likely to me that anyone intends to pay him back. What will become of his money?"

"That's not my concern. You can write to Arturas Martynas," he said.

"Can't you see that I'm trying to save him?"

"It's admirable, really, but it's no use. He can't be saved."

"And what about me?"

"What about you?"

"Do you still love me a little for all we had?"

This was becoming too much. "What did we have, really? You led me on, Lily. I don't know if it was all part of the plan the two of you had from the beginning, or if he put you up to it later. If you'd agreed to leave him when it all began, I would have taken you with me. But then it was too late."

"I was too afraid then. I felt loyal to him. Isn't that what it means to be husband and wife? I was willing to do anything for him to set him up on his feet. But that has nothing to do with the way I felt about you. I'm telling you that I loved you then and I love you now, in spite of everything. I can't help him anymore. I'm free to go with you now. Unless you say there's nothing left in your heart for me. But there's still something, isn't there? I can still see a certain something in your eyes when you look at me. A woman recognizes that look. Don't deny it. You love me even now, don't you?"

"What does all this talk of love have to do with our situation? You're only making things harder for yourself and for me."

"This talk of love is the most important talk there is. Nothing else matters as much as love. If you still love me, then at least tell me. It will be some consolation in this terrible mess I'm in."

"Your situation could be much worse. Why do you think I chose this way of doing things? I'm saving you from scandal and prison."

"Why won't you say it?"

"Because it would do no good."

"But it would do me good. Just to hear it."

Adamonis hadn't expected it to be as difficult as this. He thought her betrayal had hardened his heart. But there she was, his lovely distant cousin, distant enough to love, the woman for whose sake he'd led the uprising in Klaipeda.

"I loved you then. It's true."

But that wasn't enough for her. "And now?" she asked.

"I still do."

She took satisfaction in that, paused as if to gather her strength, and then went on.

"I can't stop Robert from being ruined. I understand that's all over now. But what about me? Take me with you to Klaipeda. You can find a way. I understand they're going to make you governor permanently. I could help you. I'd stand at your side."

"I've stood alone most of my life. I can do it for a while longer."

"What's your secretary's name?" she asked.

"Where are you going with this?"

"Just tell me."

"Miss Pinigelis."

"Listen, Justas, you have eyes for her, I know. Don't deny it. Listen, I respect that. I know you have feelings. You've lived alone so long that you need a woman and she was there with you during all your adventures. But ask yourself, is she really suitable to be the wife of a man in your position? She's practically fresh off the farm. I've seen society. I know how the Germans behave. They'll snicker at her behind your back, but they wouldn't dare do that to me."

"It's too late, Lily. There's nothing to be done now. We had a chance once, a slim chance, but the world changes so fast and I have to change with it or I'll be swept away. Find your way in Poland or make your way back to America. There's nothing more I can do for you."

"Is there no other way?"

"No."

"Then I hold you responsible for whatever becomes of us. If you don't love me enough as a woman, I expected you to love me enough as a cousin to watch over me. Is there nothing else I can say?"

"Nothing."

Her mood shifted then. She leaned forward in her chair.

"You sound so high and mighty now, so much a master of my fate. But a time will come for you when you'll have to make difficult decisions. The world will close in on you sooner or later. And I hope you'll remember my appeal for mercy. And then I hope someone else turns you down as cruelly as you're turning me down."

"Lily, stop talking now. I'm being as kind as I can. I don't want to remember you like this. Go to bed now, Lily. Tomorrow you'll walk into a new life. Who knows? It might even turn out to be a better one."

45

ADAMONIS sat in the chair for the rest of the night, once dozing off and then awaking and stoking the fire. He walked around the room and went to the window, opening first the glass and then the creaking wooden shutters that had been closed for the night. There was no sign of illumination at all, and the light of the stars had gone out, but already a bluethroat was sounding its tweet and chirp. As he stood there in the cool morning air and the light started to come up, other birds joined in the chorus, but brought him no joy.

A soft knock came at the door, and when Adamonis's man came in, he told him to wake the couple, and then take them down to the kitchen where there would be tea and bread for them before they left. Adamonis did not want to see them again, at least not up close. Perhaps he would watch them from the window as they walked out to the waiting car.

But in the end, he had no choice. His man came hurrying back and asked Adamonis to come along to the Woolleys' bedroom. When Adamonis went in, he saw husband and wife lying fully dressed on top of the sheets, still and unmoving. For a moment he thought they needed to be roused, but the thought passed quickly. He had seen so many people in this condition—soldiers and friends, civilians and enemies. But none of those others lay so well because they had not chosen their manner of death.

"Get out of here," said Adamonis to his man.

"Should I call someone?"

"Not yet."

He glanced at the desk and the night table, but there was no note. Lily's message to him was clear enough already.

Adamonis looked to the window out of reflex, visible through partially drawn linen curtains, but of course there was no one who could have crept in, no more than Lily and Woolley could have escaped. The light was pouring in through this aperture, and a beam of sunlight fell on Lily's brooch, a silver salamander she had taken the trouble to put on. When she had come to him in the night, she'd been in a housecoat, but that would not have done for the lying in state of a lord and lady of Worcester, Massachusetts. They lay in stocking feet, their pairs of shoes set carefully on their respective sides of the bed. Woolley's shoes were freshly polished and the straps on Lily's shoes were done up. Of course they were. She would have no need to slip into them.

They lay decorously side by side and Woolley's hand was touching Lily's thigh. Her own hands were held across her breast. She must have composed this final position as a last act of pride, knowing he would see her.

There was no decorous death outside of paintings and films, however, so their eyes were half-open and their lips twisted in grimaces, likely the effect of some pain at the end. Adamonis pulled a sheet over Woolley's face and looked down on Lily.

This was the girl he had saved from a well in her childhood, but what good was that if this was what he had brought her to at the end?

He had been in the business of deceit for a long time, and he had known many deceivers. He also knew that most deceivers believed part of what they said, part of what they claimed. He wondered what had made them do it. The Poles were not cruel masters, and they wouldn't have harmed Woolley or Lily once their cover was blown. Neither would the Germans. But the Soviets had no scruples at all. Were Lily and Woolley even more deeply compromised than he had imagined?

Had they carried poison with them at all times, or had they brought it along on this journey because they suspected more than Adamonis knew? Or had the poison been intended for someone else and used only on themselves out of desperation?

He didn't know.

After Adamonis had looked at Lily long enough, he covered her too. He had Lukiewicz call for a country doctor to certify their deaths, and as Adamonis waited, he walked through the rooms of the house, and entered the specimen room.

The morning light barely penetrated this side of the house, and there in the shadows a small brown bear sat on its haunches, as if waiting, seeming as alive as alive could be, if not for the slight smell of camphor that came from its fur and that of the other mammals, all frozen as if waiting for something. But there was nothing to wait for.

Out in the hall Adamonis heard the passing *click* of a dog's nails on the floor. The animal stopped outside the door without coming in. Was it fear or training that kept the dog out and made it then tap away down the hall?

Adamonis walked along the butterfly case, looking at the great variety, from dull *Carcharodus floccifera* to its bright yellow cousin, *Carterocephalus silvicola*. Along past the beetles in their multitude and then to the small lizards under glass, and among them a salamander. Through some enigmatic refraction, the eye of the creature glinted, but the light that came out of the dead eye was devoid of meaning.

Adamonis straightened his back, stepped away, and looked around. Everything was so still and organized in the room, so much less chaotic than in nature. What would a collection of human specimens contain if he had a room such as this for people?

Afterword

SOME of my best inspiration has come from an unlikely parish library where the Lithuanian books of my parents' and grandparents' generations lie mouldering and mostly unread. Used bookstores in Vilnius, Kaunas, and Chicago also hold the stories of a small place that lay between the hammer of Germany and the anvil of the Soviet Union. No wonder a lot of sparks flew there.

Again and again I am asked why I choose to write about Lithuania when I live in Canada. The answer is that in that small country acts of great drama took place under the relentless pressures of politics and history. And if all the world is a stage, then all of humanity's character types stepped into that tiny theatre and many of them left their traces among the used books I riffle through.

One of those persons was Jonas Budrys, originally known as Jonas Polovinskas, the chief of Lithuanian counterintelligence between 1921 and 1923. He was one of those outsized characters who appear when history changes dramatically, when nobodies like Josef Pilsudski and Vladimir Lenin become somebodies in the new circumstances, or in modern times, when a playwright like Vaclav Havel becomes the leader of his country or an electrician named

Lech Walesa climbs over a fence to take Poland out of the Soviet orbit. Jonas Budrys was the James Bond of a backward former Russian province; he inspired my Justas Adamonis and as a nod toward that lineage, I named Adamonis's secretary Miss Pinigelis, which is an approximate translation of the name "Miss Moneypennny" from the James Bond novels.

Jonas Budrys is probably worthy of a full biography because the trajectory of his life is so emblematic of certain Eastern European lives—from soldier in the czar's army to head of Lithuanian military counterintelligence to governor of the Klaipeda region to Lithuanian consul in prewar USA to chicken farmer in New York State. His son is worthy of a biography too, because the late Algis Budrys went on to become an important writer in the golden era of postwar American science fiction.

But I am a novelist, not a biographer, so those historical lives serve primarily as inspiration to me. Many of the events in this novel are historical, but they must be considered fiction because wherever my storyteller's intuition told me to take the narrative, there I took it. The seizure of Klaipeda, the saccharine scandal, and the execution of a Russian hero of Lithuania's war of independence are all true, but they did not occur exactly as depicted here.

Once I get interested in a certain period, luck seems to bring many books my way. Robert W. Heingartner was an American diplomat in Lithuania in the 1920s, and his diary provided a great deal of colour to the period as well as revealing a man whose primary concern seemed to be with his nose and sinuses. Tadas Ivanauskas was the father of modern naturalists in Lithuania, and the memoir of his childhood on a country estate now found in Belarus must rank very close to the writing of Czeslaw Milosz in his description of the manor life that was swept away by WW1. Lieutenant General Konstantinas Zukas was a youthful telegraph operator in Siberia who rose to fight for the czar and to lead Lithuania's military for a while. He was a rival, perhaps even an enemy of Budrys, but some of his biographical details were too good not to incorporate into the life of my fictional Justas Adamonis. Other sources included the memoir of the MI6 station head in Riga between the wars, whose pen name was John Whitwell but whose real name was Leslie Nicholson, as well as the memoir of the first Polish diplomat in Lithuania, Leon Mitkiewicz.

Over half a dozen years ago I sat down to write a light novel set in a little-known place, something I hoped to be an entertainment in the manner of Graham Greene. It took ten full drafts and the help of many others to make it happen. Thorough commentaries came from David Bergen, Joe Kertes, Madeleine Matte, Anne McDermid, Nathan Whitlock, Chandra Wohleber, my wife, Snaige of the eagle eye and sharp pencil, and others. But it was John Metcalf who took me through three major rewrites and helped me to shape the novel into what it is. Governess, drill sergeant, coach, personal trainer, relentless perfectionist—these are all terms one could use to describe John. I prefer to describe the experience of working with him as wrestling with an angel, a grumpy one.

Many others helped me along the way. Monica Pacheco. Historian Bernardas Gailius, who wrote a monograph on the Budrys family, the late Leonidas Donskis and his wife, Jolanta, as well as his colleagues Vilma Akmenyt-Ruzgien and Arunas Antanaitis, who walked me through historical Kaunas; in Lithuania, *in loco parentis*, Silvija and the late Saulius Sondeckis; also Antanas and Danule Sipaila, Ausra Marija Sluckaite Jurasas and Jonas Jurasas, Laimonas Briedis, and Audrius Siaurusevicius, and the whole crew of the Santara organization, a lovely set of intellectuals who are curious about all things Lithuanian, and willing to help in all pursuits scientific, literary, social, and political—their annual conference in Alanta is like summer camp for me, an event I try to attend whenever I can.

Lithuania has many rich seams of narratives I have been mining for years. This mine is far from exhausted and I keep coming back to prospect for more and more discoveries about that dramatic place, and for what the events that have happened there reveal about the universal human character in all its variety and complexity.